Confessions of a Black Caucasian

Joe R. McClain Jr.

DEDICATION

Dedicated to the memory of Kobe "The Black Mamba" Bryant, Gianna "Mambacita" Bryant, Payton Chester, Sarah Chester, Alyssa Altobelli, Keri Altobelli, John Altobelli, Christina Mauser and Ara Zobayan, who all lost their lives on January 26th, 2020. Also, to the memory of the great Nipsey Hussle, who we lost on March 31, 2019, who also showed us that our circumstances do not define us. The Marathon Continues...

Contents

ACKNOWLEDGMENTS

As you looked at the dedication section of this book, it is impossible not to think about the mentality that Kobe Bryant lived by. The Mamba mentality is made up of five key pillars. Resilience, Obsessiveness, Relentlessness, Passion and Fearlessness. As you read this story, you will see each pillar thrive in different ways. **RESILIENCE** As Kobe used his mental to handle on and off the court issues, I used the dealings of the state of the world that we are currently in to deliver a great product and unfiltered story. **OBSESSIVENESS** In writing this story, I spent over a year dwelling on everything that occurred around me, tapping into the emotions of not only myself, but many others around the world. With that, I sometimes lost myself in writing, all so truth could be exposed in the most uncut way possible. **RELENTLESSNESS** I knew this book would take the universe by storm and force everyone to tap into their own emotions. It took 10 tries to get this right, but I was determined until I created a product that I knew would have the world on edge. Seven years later, and here is the result of being relentless and never quitting. **PASSION** I've been writing since I was seven years old. This has been my go-to when I needed to release to the world without causing harm to myself, or others. This passion has allowed me to bask in the presence of some of the greatest people on earth, whether they were A list celebrities, or regular nine to five people. Each, however, has allowed me to grow in ways I could not have imagined as a seven-year-old kid from East Chicago, Indiana. **FEARLESSNESS** My first book sold 33 copies. I've bombed on stage with poetry. However, that fear of failure, or coming up short, is what drives me to continue pressing on, because I know my gift is needed to inspire someone else in this world. Kobe, you never knew me. You did, however, put a drive in me to be nothing less than great. Rest up, as we allow your inspiration to move us into the next phases of our lives.

BURIED ALIVE

Plane rides weren't always cool with me. The first one I had ever experienced, I was 16. I went with my mama and grandma to Las Vegas to see my aunt, her sister, my grandma's daughter. I'll never forget how I was so damn nervous on that flight.

"Flight attendants prepare the cabin for departure."

I truly didn't get the gist of that phrase, but I knew what departure meant. We were about to take off. I don't think I was made for all this up in the air shit. Hell, it was already a damn battle being on the roads everyday with crazy drivers, especially with how crazy my dad drove. Now, you mean to tell me that someone was going to put me in the air for a few hours and say trust me, I got you. What if the shit went down? At least in a car, I stood a small chance. I remembered us rolling up to the runway, slowly. I was squished in between the two women that I loved the most in life, looking out of the window. Then, it seemed like life stopped, along with the plane. The next thing I knew, we were rolling down the runway, building up speed. Yes, I know that I was just a teen, but I had three strokes, four heart attacks and my bladder dropped all in that moment. I played it off as cool as I could because I didn't want my mama seeing me scared shitless. Then, we went airborne. After about five minutes, the tension inside of my body started to go away. The plane ride started to feel good. I leaned my head back, and just enjoyed the ride.

"A drink and some snacks sir?"

"Orange juice and pretzels please."

I mean, I really didn't have much of a choice. On Southwest, there were only so many options that you could choose from. Peanuts, pretzels or cheese crackers. The drinks were orange juice, water, pop and maybe some cranberry juice. Southwest tended to be the unofficial airline of Black folks everywhere. Nah, you didn't have assigned seating. Nah, you weren't going to get the option of having a decent meal on your flight. Shit, you bet not even imagine having a television that you could watch. Despite all of that, you would damn sure get to your destination on time, or maybe even before it. I remember once I flew out to Portland to handle some business. The pilot said two hours and 15 minutes. We got there like 40 minutes early. I wish I was making this shit up, but I'm not. Even the rental car lady was shocked at how fast we arrived there. This flight here, however, it could take its sweet time. For once in my life, I hoped that I could fly forever and never land, seeing that my daddy had now taken flight in the sky. It was the news that every child knew had to come one day, but you never expected it to come when you thought your parents had so much life left. My OG was only 65 when he took his last breath. Why? Because, like many Black men, he felt that doctors and his skin color didn't go together. And, if they did go together, it was like a sale at a store. For a limited time only. One of my folks had e-mailed me the news while I was enjoying myself on the second to last day of an Alaskan cruise, completely free from the world and all its bullshit. Crazy, isn't it? One minute you were in heaven, surrounded by booty cheeks and drunk as fuck. The next, you were slow dancing with the devil, as he tried to ease you into the hell you were about to face. Truthfully, I was already over going home. I hadn't been back in years. I had no reason to head back to the Pacific Northwest. My grannies were both dead, and now my daddy. Me and the old man didn't see eye to eye on a lot of things, but he was always there, so I had no animosity towards him at all. I made it to Seattle early in the evening. Like four o'clock early. That didn't pan out well for me, as I knew traffic was going to be a bitch, seeing how it was rush hour. Friday's were normally my favorite day of the week. Today, it was a burden that I wish I could get rid of. The most somber day would be tomorrow, when I had to lay my old man in the ground. I exited the plane and headed straight to the rental car joint. I waited in line, patiently, behind a woman with two kids. One was clinched onto her leg, being quiet as ever. The other badass, who couldn't have been more than five, was pretending to fire guns made with his hands at everything around him. He was dressed up as a cowboy, with a flannel, cowboy hat and some boots. Most people would say aww, and think it was the cutest thing ever. Today, I just wasn't in the mood for any of it. As I continued to wait, the young man turned around and shot his imaginary guns at me. I continued looking at him through my shades, as in his mind, he had probably shot me 40 to 50 times. My asshole mode was 75 on a 10 scale, and this young boy was about to get two six shooters fired at him. I bent down and stretched out my arms, giving the young boy my own version of two guns. They just happened to be my two middle fingers. I did it with a mean ass grin on my face as

3

well. The look on his face was priceless as he turned around and grabbed his mom's other leg. She looked down at him, then turned to glance at me. She didn't know what happened, but inside my head, I was laughing my ass off. As she received her keys and papers, and turned to head off towards the garage, her kid flipped me off with two middle fingers instead of two pistols.

"JOHNNY!!!"

My hand covered my mouth as I laughed but didn't want the lady behind the desk noticing. I got little man in trouble and I thoroughly enjoyed it.

"Isn't that just sickening?"

"It is ma'am. It is," I said, holding the leftover laughter I had in.

"Gosh. I mean. Who teaches kids such a thing?"

At that point, I just put my head down and grinned because I knew how much of an asshole I really was. I handled my business at the counter, with a good flirt session that I initiated. She was eating the shit up. Truthfully, she had a face that only a mother could love. Her body was decent, even though I had experienced better. I got Ebony's number, along with the keys to my whip and moved it along. I didn't plan on hitting her up, but in case I had to let off some steam before I bounced back out of town for California, she was number one on the list. I rolled out to the garage and searched out my whip. I hit that alarm signal and let the sound of irritating noise lead me to it. That shit was loud as fuck. I mean, louder than usual. It was like they put a concert speaker in the trunk. I tossed my bag in the back seat. They put the kid in one of those new style Chevy Impala's. I fucked with it. I got in, and the asshole inside of me immediately went away. I sat there for a good minute, frozen, pondering what would be the worst drive to the church in my young

4

33 years of life. I didn't know if the whip had satellite radio or not. Instead of searching for it, I pulled out my go to rider music. In a world full of downloads, iTunes this, digital that, you sometimes had to genuinely support good artists. For me, that was Big K.R.I.T. CD's were almost extinct as a Dallas Cowboys Super Bowl victory. But I inserted his and cranked up my favorite song. I sat there, and just let him take my ears on a journey through the second verse of *"Get Up 2 Come Down."*

This for those playas in those gator belts getting cheese like patty melts
Serving up game like help yo' self
Refereeing, calling plays on the sidelines
Super the bowl, diamonds and gold
Won a ring like five times
I remember wanting to be that cuz I seen it
Don't ever tell a hoe you love a hoe if you don't mean it
Unless it's bout that paper paper, got that from a playa pimp
They say it's work to p-i, easier to be a simp
Put it in motion, rollercoasting, peep the focus of a go-getter
If you flip it once and get it, it's fasho figgas
If you ain't eating with you squad, you's a hoe nigga
That's from the heart
Never pump Kool-Aid when we on a mission
That 24/7 like a waffle cook in a waffle house kitchen
Man, I'm just trying to get paid
And make it where these muthafuckas hate
I got up to come down

As I drove off, totally losing all conscious of my mental functions, Cee Lo's verse dropped right on time. I literally sung his verse like I was in the shower, getting ready for a night out in Downtown Seattle. Just as I hit my highest note, the tears started to flow. I was singing from my soul, more so for my daddy. I finally came back down to earth and headed out of the plaza towards the highway. Right before I merged, I got smart and turned back on the street, almost hitting a car. I decided to take the back streets. Yea, it would take me an additional 20 minutes than my original route, but I wasn't about that rush hour life, even after living in L.A. for a good minute. I let K.R.I.T. take me through the South Seattle streets where I grew up. Naw, it wasn't Chicago, New York or Baltimore, but we struggled here too. The struggle now was even more prevalent, as our neighborhoods had been wiped out, our land bought up and a mad gentrification effort was in the works. Hell, what am I saying? It wasn't in the works. It was well in place. There were remnants of what once was, but they were also slowly fading away. It was almost a half hour past five, and my pops wake started at six. I knew fam bam was already at the church. I stopped my tour of the neighborhood and did a B line straight to the church. As I pulled up, exactly at a quarter until six, I sat in my car, parked across the street from the church. I saw cousins, my sisters and other relatives all congregated outside. I sat back, removing my shades and placing them in the glove box. I pulled out my phone and looked at the last picture that me and my daddy had taken together. It was at an Italian joint a few years back when he came to visit me in L.A. We saw some old, dusty haired bitty walking towards our table, so we asked her old ass would she mind snapping a pic. She obliged, and crazy as it may sound, he cracked a smile. I analyzed this pic in depth. I truly realized that I was this dude's twin. The only difference was that I had my mama's lighter skin tone. Besides that, you really couldn't tell us apart. I started swiping, looking at all the pics in my phone now. Everyone seemed to be on borrowed time. Later in life, it would be them. Today, however, it was the man that made me. I got out the car and stretched. The month of June had just jumped off and the weather was gravy to say the least. As I walked up, fam bam started to scream my name. Boog this, Boog that. I don't know why in the good hell my Granny gave me that nickname. I didn't know what in the good hell a Boogalo was. I was Mac Baker Jr. Boogalo? I never met that nigga. In my head, I was thinking, damn. Can a nigga get across the street before y'all start hollering my name? I shook it off quickly, as I had no choice but to hold my head up high on this one. My daddy was tough, so I had to be like him. Who the hell was I kidding? I was the opposite of him in this regard. While he had an outer exterior that concealed the emotions he held inside, I showed mines off with no qualms. If I had to cry, I cried. If I wanted to yell, I yelled. Showing emotion didn't make you less of a man. It made you more of one.

"Boy, where you been? Gimme a hug."

That was one of my aunties. Nothing against her, as I loved her to death, but I really didn't wanna talk to anybody until I saw my daddy lying in the casket. I entered the church to much of the same fare. Family saying hi and shit, hugging the shit out of me. I know they weren't making it about me, but I was taking it that way. In all honesty, I just simply wanted to tell them to concentrate on my fucking daddy, with the F bomb included.

"Jr."

I turned my head to the side, but my reaction wasn't the same as with the others. It was my cousin Troy. Troy had always looked out for me, seeing how my daddy looked out for him when he was a shorty.

"Sup cuz," I told him, as we dapped up and hugged.

"You good?"

"Yeah I'm good cuz. Just, you know."

"Gone handle your business."

That interaction with him put me at ease. I walked through the doors of the church and headed down the aisle.

"Ma."

She turned around and cracked her version of a smile.

"Hey baby."

We hugged for what seemed like forever.

"Let me see him."

We made our way through the small crowd gathered some feet away from the casket. Ahh shit were the first words that came out of my mouth. I got up close to the casket, laying my hand on my daddy's chest. I wasn't crying. Like, seriously, I wasn't. I don't know what it was, but the shit just hadn't hit me yet. Pops was a mortician for 30 plus years. I was used to seeing dead bodies on a regular. Trust me, I had seen it all. From pallbearers dropping a casket in the cemetery, to people jumping on the casket of their loved ones, whether opened or closed. Yes, that shit really happens. It's not just some made up shit that Black folks created. I looked down at him, analyzing every aspect of his body from the clothes to his face. I knew my cousin ran the funeral home and would have him looking dapper. Still, I wanted to make sure he was on point.

"He looks good, don't he?"

"Yea ma. He do."

He was clad out in a chocolate and taupe checkerboard suit. The ivory shirt was encompassed by an ivory vest, with ivory tie. There was some ivory in the checkerboard design, so it hit right. That's exactly how he was. He wanted to match and stand apart from everyone else. I still wasn't crying. It was still hard to believe that my old man was lying here in front of me. I looked over my right shoulder because I felt someone behind me. I saw my uncle and fully turned around to face him. That's when I lost it. This was ROOSTER, my daddy's only brother. The one who had been there for me through it all.

"Listen to me boy. This yo' family now. You were born for this and he raised you for this. You gone be alright. It's yo time."

His repeated finger in my chest let me know he was dead ass serious with his words. Unc always had a way to tell me exactly what I needed to hear. He didn't mind me crying, being sad, none of that. However, what he didn't want me doing was lingering on shit. He knew it was my time to step up and that's what I had to do. It was a hard pill to swallow. The wake continued, but it was more like a small family gathering. I heard a mix of laughter and normal chatter. Me, I calmly sat on the front pew, glancing at the casket. For the life of me, I swore it was all a bad dream. I would soon wake up and this would be the worst nightmare that I ever had while sleeping. If only some wishes could come true. Eight o'clock came and I watched my cousin shut the casket lid on my pops. Everyone was going back to my mama house for dinner. Truthfully, I ain't wanna see none of them. I just wanted to be alone by my damn self. After a few convos on my way out, I walked outside and got in my car. I sat there for a good minute. It was still light out, and everything seemed so calm for this summer day. It was like peace was trying to enter me, but the shield that I had up bounced it right off. I started my whip and made the quick four block drive to my childhood home. I hadn't been there since last year this time, when I snuck into town for Mother's Day. Truthfully, it wasn't for Mother's Day. It was too beg and plead with my daddy to go to the hospital and quit being so damn stubborn, because I didn't want that pneumonia to kill him. Years ago, I had to have a heart operation, and all I remember him doing was constantly asking me did I go to the doctor. He beat that shit into my head. The advice he gave me, however, he never applied that shit to himself. That May day, I even asked him, do you love me pops? Of course, he couldn't answer that shit, and he wasn't gonna say it. I knew the old dude loved me, but the shit would've been nice to hear more than three times in my life. I got out the car. By some divine intervention, I was able to park in front of the house, seeing how the whole clan was over here. I walked in with my bag and saw my mama. She told me what was there to eat, and I said cool. I walked back to my childhood room. Gone were the posters, the jerseys and everything else I had in here as a young buck. However, the aura was still active. I looked around and soaked everything in. I opened my closet door. I just stared for a good minute. In it, were a plethora of the NFL jerseys that my daddy had collected of his favorite players. Behind them, a stack of custom hats that his man's Ponytail in neighboring Auburn made for him. I shuffled through the closet and pulled out one. I sat on the bed and just caressed it. This was one of his favorites. An authentic beaver fur joint. I ran my fingers across that thang, then threw it on my head. Damn, this nigga had a small ass head. This thing wasn't even close to fitting my big ass dome. I placed it back in the box and plopped down on my bed, staring at the ceiling. I had no intent of heading back out into the house. I didn't wanna be bothered with anyone cracking jokes or being happy because their bellies were being stuffed with food. My daddy just passed, and I had no place for any comedy at all. 15 minutes passed and I started to have a change of heart. It wasn't for everyone else in the house. It was for my mama. Losing her husband of over 30 years, getting all the food, and putting a funeral together, the least I could do was be out there with her. I put my ego to the side and went back out into the kitchen, asking her did she need help with anything. She was good, so I got me a plate and just sat on the inside porch, because it provided me with a little peace.

"A cuz. I think Shorty out here to see you."

One of my fam bam told me that from the front door. I put my plate down and walked outside.

"Nigga you gone be good?," cuz asked.

"It's Shorty nigga. It's gone be about as good as an unoiled engine doing 80 on the freeway."

Now, I love my family, but some niggas you just didn't wanna see at this moment in time. Shorty was one of those people. I love the nigga. I really do. I just hoped that the convo hurried the hell up. I walked out to the middle of the street where his car was.

"Cuz what's good?"

I watched the gold from his teeth give off a rustic shine. To be a West Coast nigga, he exemplified more than enough Southern tendencies. If you didn't know him, you would swear this nigga was from Southside H-Town and not South Seattle.

"Nothing much cuz. Just cooling. You know."

"Yea yea I know. Shit, how that L.A. life treating you?"

And this was the exact reason I didn't wanna come out here. Cuz wasn't gone be talking about shit that pertained to the situation. SoCal wasn't even on my mind. I sucked it up and gave him conversation for a good 20 minutes before he sped off into the night. Truth be told, I felt like I lost a trillion brain cells that I couldn't get back. I just knew that I was now mentally handicapped. I went back in the house and just cooled out until slowly, but surely, everyone started to leave. Around 10:30, it was just me and my mama. She was sitting at the computer, exhausted from dealing with all these folks. She hadn't cleaned up yet, and I really couldn't blame her. Me, I was sitting on the couch, looking at the TV.

"How'd it happen ma?"

"How what happen?"

"Just tell me how he died. I think I'd be more at peace knowing."

She took a deep breath.

"Well, he was sitting right there where you sitting right now."

At that moment, I was instantly fucked up. The term shock and awe was an understatement.

"He reached for a bottle of water that was on the living room table and fell over. I said Mac, get yo ass up. He yelled back. I'm aight woman. I looked back at the computer. About five seconds later, I looked back at him. He was still bent over on the floor, ass sticking in the air. Mac, I yelled. I called him again. He didn't give me any response. I went over to him, rolled him over and he was foaming at the mouth."

By that time, her words were becoming imaginary images in front of me. I was seeing it all. Moms shaking my dad vigorously, trying to get him to come too. However, it was to no avail. She called the paramedics, they arrived within seven minutes and they pumped his chest all the way out the house. Unfortunately, pops didn't have a chance to take a last sip of water.

"To be honest with you Jr. I think ya daddy was dead as soon as he hit the floor."

As crazy as it sounded, I believed her. Some people have a chance when life throws the gauntlet at them. I honestly believed that my pops didn't wanna fight anymore. His last swing was at a bottle of water, and he missed by a heavenly mile. The next morning, I got up as usual around five o'clock. I was an early riser, and it didn't have anything to do with me being depressed and not able to sleep. The funeral was at 11, so I got a head start on everything before everyone else got up. Shit, shower, eat, all in that order. I got my clothes out that I was wearing to the funeral and headed downstairs to the basement. As I hit the bottom step, everything started to come full circle. I walked to the area where the washer and dryer was. This doubled as pops barbershop. Fam Bam was nice with the clippers. I sat in the chair for a good minute. I laughed as I thought about the first time he charged me for a cut when I came back home to visit after moving to Cali.

"That's 10 dollars."

"10 DOLLARS!!!"

"Nigga did I stutter?"

"Pops. How you gone charge me? I'm ya son. You cut my hair for free for 18 years."

"And guess what? You over 18, so 10 dollars."

"I gotta go to the ATM."

"I don't care where you go. You can go to a horse's ass for all I care. Just get me my 10 dollars nigga."

I laughed and dropped a few tears thinking about that moment. Pops was indeed a hustler. He worked at the funeral home for over 30 years, worked in a production mill, cut hair, and did a few more illegal things to bring bread in. If it's one thing my pops did, it was keep some money in his pocket. 10:30 rolled around and I was fully dressed, prepping to leave the house for the church. All black everything was my attire. I truthfully didn't wanna wear all black, but the damn suit was so fly that I said fuck it. I know if pops were here, he'd say some shit like, you wish you looked as good as me. If it was one thing that nigga was good for, it was bragging on his dress game. The limo was outside. I threw on a fedora and walked out Godfather style. I took my uncle's words to heart. I was the man of the family now. I had to take my rightful place on the throne and take my family to a whole new level. Me, moms, and my aunties packed into the first limo, while everyone else set up shop in the second. It was literally a one-minute drive to the church. Once we got there, it would be time to line up and enter. We arrived, and I was locked arm and arm with my mama. She was nervous as I had ever seen her.

"It's okay mama. I got you."

Indeed, I did have her, and whispering that to her reassured her that her baby boy was here. We began to walk up to the casket. As I took about my fifth or sixth step into the sanctuary, I heard someone whisper to me, no hats in the sanctuary. If it wasn't for this occasion, I would've told them to fuck off. This my daddy hat. Shit wasn't coming off today. For one, it was my daddy. Two, do y'all know how happy I was to find one of his hats that fit my big ass head? That shit was a miracle. We got to the casket and the waterworks started to flow. This would be the last time that I saw my pops in the physical. Once that casket lid dropped, that was it. One by one, my aunts let out hollas as they got up there. Their baby brother was gone. Hell, we were all crying. I looked back to see my nephews, his grandsons, balling tears. My mama, her eyes were going to. As my cousin began to prep the lid for closing, I told her wait. I got up one last time. I kissed him on the forehead.

"Love you pops," I whispered.

I know he never said it too me, but I knew deep down, in that moment, he apologized for never saying it back. The lid was then shut, and Mac Baker Sr. was no more.

I sat at home, watching Hallmark movies, which was my usual. I know it wasn't your first thought when you thought about strong Black men, but they had more than enough good ass movies on this channel. Honestly, it would be better if they got a few more movies with Black leads in their rotation. It was the night before the one-year anniversary of my father's death. It was crazy how many things could change within a year's time frame. For starters, I didn't talk to my mother anymore. I God honestly asked for no tension between us because she was the only parent I had left. However, when me and my sister had a spat, because she pulled some fuck shit and spoke on some shit she had no business speaking on, mama flipped. It went from that situation, to what did me and your daddy do to you? Why do you think you are better than us? You swear you think because you've made it in your field that you too good. I took it all in stride. Eventually, however, enough would be enough. I calmly told her that I was at peace in my life, and if she couldn't provide the motherly support that I needed, and be peaceful with me, then we didn't need to talk. I love my mother. I really do. A few weeks later, I thought both of us had cooled down enough to be on talking terms. When I called her, she gave off a vibe that she didn't want anything else to do with me. I tried three times, and each time, she shunned me. Just like baseball, with me, it was three strikes and you were out. It was what it was. I could live with the fact that I tried to make amends. It was no longer my problem because the animosity was off my chest. If she died without ever making amends, that wouldn't be my problem. I would simply say my goodbyes, remember the good times and continue with life. Despite all of this, I was maintaining myself well. I had once again got back to being myself. I would swing up to Portland every now and then as a little getaway. Then, I shot up to the adult's playground in Las Vegas towards the end of 2018. December 23rd was the date to be exact. I stayed over at the Westgate, which was off the strip. While everyone wanted to do Rio, Harrah's, Caesars Palace, The Palms, or some of the other, more popular joints, I kept it kosher in high quality that was under the radar to say the least. I knocked out a poetry show and stood 'em up. The most interesting trip I took that next year in 2019 by far was Jacksonville. Truthfully, I was just down there for a day to do a show, but I can tell you that Duval is a wild place. I got in around midnight on a Wednesday night, in April. One of my partners scooped me up and got me to his crib with the quickness, as it seemed that he was doing 100 on the highway. I slept comfortably that night. I woke up the next morning and went over some pieces while he was at work. As I started to ramp up my rehearsal a few hours before the show, I saw the news. A kid ran his principal over in the school parking lot. I don't think y'all heard me. The kid ran his principal over in the school parking lot. I know this generation of kids was unpredictable, but those Florida kids took it to a whole new level. I mean shit, Florida was another level. I planned on doing a lot more traveling as the year progressed, but as far as Memorial Day weekend went, I was unsure of going anywhere. The soon to be here date of my pops one-year anniversary was weighing on me and I truly contemplated on being left alone. The time ticked down on this day, hitting nine o'clock. I was damn close to cutting the television off, then my phone rang. I really didn't feel like talking to anyone, but maybe, just maybe, it could take my mind to a better place.

"Sup fool."

"Boy it's over."

"Man, what the hell is you talking about?"

"I'm divorced fool. Fuck that bitch."

Man, my boy Rain had been waiting for this one for a long while. We called that fool Rain because when he was a kid, his crazy ass used to run out in that shit like it was the greatest thing ever. As y'all know, or if you didn't know, it rained in Seattle like James Harden traveled on his step back. Often. Rain was weird, but he was cool as the other side of the pillow.

"You bout to turn into a hoe again aren't you?"

He started to crack up on the phone.

"Man, I'm chilling for a while. I'm glad I'm divorced from that gap mouth bitch and ain't gotta deal with her beetlejuice built ass mama anymore either."

"Man, c'mon bruh. Leave the mama out of this."

"Nah, fuck that old ass bitch too. Bitch always stuck her nose in some business, even though her funky ass daughter was the one constantly running to her."

"Well, in all honesty, you married her. I told you from jump, and I won't call her a bitch, but she wasn't screwed right up top."

"I feel you my dude."

"I mean you said it yourself. She couldn't suck dick. Pussy was garbage eight out of 10 times. She focused more on other people more than you. Three strikes and they out my nigga."

"Hey man. Even players fuck up. But it's all good, cause guess what I did?"

I knew some wild shit was about to be said. This nigga was the king of wild shit.

"What's that man?"

"Look, before we got married, you remember I told you that she stopped giving it up for no reason?"

"Yea," I said, as I sat up on the couch, because I just knew he was about to say he was fucking another broad.

"Man, I started fucking with one of her family members. And, the bitch still hangs with her and don't even know what happened. And, her homegirl, who knew about it, she told me to have fun doing the shit. So, that just goes to show you that no one really fucked with that bitch."

"A man. No more bitches. We done had enough bitches for the night."

"Nah fuck that bitch. I hope she find out I fucked with her family. I hope she find out how many of her friends told me how they didn't know how I married her cause she was stupid as shit. And on my mama nigga, even one of her folks told me dead to my face. If you divorce my folk, nigga I understand. And I slap that on e'thang I love my nigga."

All I could do was laugh at my boy. I mean, I watched it and a lot of us know she wasn't the brightest bulb in the ceiling. But hey, his problems were over, and life could somewhat go back to normal for him. I just had one last question for him.

"Bruh. You ain't fucking with no more of her people, are you?"

"Nah. Just one and that was it. Any bitch that cosign that bitch gotta be bout dumb as her."

"Man I just said no more bitches bruh."

"Fuck that bitch"

I just laughed as we wrapped up the conversation and I got back to watching my movies. I was going to bed, but my guy gave me a second life. I stayed up for another three hours watching movies ranging from Hallmark to joints on HBO. Finally, it was 12:30 a.m. and a brother was tired. I waltzed into my room. It was officially the one-year anniversary of the day that my daddy transitioned. I was lying in the bed, staring at the ceiling, just knowing some paranormal type shit was going down tonight. I was into that type of stuff, but I damn sure didn't want it popping up on me. I loved my family, but I had a heart condition, and the last thing I needed was a full-blown cardiac arrest episode because my pops wanted to come by and say what's up. I stared into the darkness until I drifted off into dreamland. No crazy dreams were occurring, and I was sleeping peacefully. The fan was blowing, and I was sleep on top of the clouds, until that middle of the night piss crept up. You know how Black folks do. No lights get cut on. No shoes. No nothing on our feet. We literally navigated the darkness to the bathroom. As I headed out of my bedroom, oblivious to anything except getting to my toilet, I know I wasn't tripping when I saw a shadow figure come out of my bathroom. Its height was about 5'7, and it had a distinct walk to it. Crazy that in darkness, I could make out a shadow figure. It was my dad. I didn't say anything, nor was I scared. He didn't say anything either. He walked straight into the living room and disappeared into the darkness, not to be seen again. I stared into the living room for about seven seconds before I went into the bathroom and handled my business. As I walked out, back to my bed, I glanced in the living room.

"DON'T DRINK MY CROWN NIGGA!!!"

Of all the things I could've said. I love you. I miss you. Hey dad, how does heaven look? How is granny and them doing? Of all the great questions or things I could've said to him. I told this dude to not drink my Crown Royal. Yea, it was obvious that I was truly his son. I woke up the next morning at five and did my usual, which was L.A. Fitness. It was leg day, and Lord knows that there were a lot of prime legs in there to look at while a brother was on the leg press. My two hours went by quickly, and it was off to work. My desk job provided me little comfort, as I was a maintenance manager. I always had people walking in my office, wanting something, needing something, all that shit. Usually, I had three screens open. One to the book, one on work and the other one on YouTube, cause a brother needed his music. Usually, it was some trill shit, like some old UGK, Jeezy, Outkast, or Ball and G. Today, however, if only for a day, I had to soothe my soul. Barry White was my brother of choice, as his deep voice kept me calm and allowed me to avoid any unnecessary distractions. Work went normal as usual, until lunch time came around. I shut my office door, making everyone think that I was gone for the next hour and a half. Or, that I was knocked out dead to the world. In this downtime, however, I reached into my own guilty pleasure, and that was reading. It was a shame that I had to bring my books in a bag and pull them out in secrecy instead of leaving them on the ledge of my computer desk. We were a diverse workforce, and I didn't want to make any of my coworkers uncomfortable. Fuck it, let me keep it a buck 50. Most of my coworkers are white, and some of these titles might rub them the wrong way. Now, I personally didn't care for how they took something, because that was a personal issue that they had to solve themselves. However, if any of them ever popped off at me, then my entire Blackness would come out, and that's what I was afraid of. Plus, the last thing that I needed was a complaint. A brother had too much too lose to let the opinions of someone who didn't understand the struggle phase me. Plus, this shit funded my spoken word travels, which was my true passion. Today's literature of choice was simple, yet efficient. The Autobiography of Malcolm X was a clear-cut favorite, and a book that everyone knew, even if they hadn't read it before. I cracked open the book and started at page one. I had read this joint several times before and had never grown tired of reading it. Then, as I made it through the first three pages, I suddenly stopped. My urge was no longer to re-educate myself through the word of a transitioned hero. I wanted to analyze something else. I got up and walked to the vending machine. I was more so moving as if I were a thief in the night, trying to avoid detection from motion sensors. I didn't wanna be bothered while simply going to get me some Peanut Butter M&M's. I snatched up two of 'em, seeing how the vending machine had one hanging loose already. That was a sign that my day would get only better. I made it back to my office, shutting the door behind me. I pulled up Google, which was the modern-day dictionary, encyclopedia and everything else research related. Two words were born in the search bar from my fingertips. NIPSEY HUSSLE. I wasn't one of those conspiracist who swore every death was related to some all world secret society. I was just a realist. Yea, I knew some shit had secret ties to it. If you ask me, this didn't. It was a case of hood politics. It was how the hood dealt with shit. Was it right? Not at all. It was a part of the environment, and some shit would never change. It was two months ago when I was sitting on my couch, on a Sunday afternoon, when the news broke of the shooting. Like many, I was like nah, not Neighborhood Nip. Not Mr. Victory Lap. Mr. Mailbox Money. Mr. Crenshaw. Not him. It couldn't be. Unfortunately, it was. About 30 minutes after the initial report, news broke that those gunshots had turned fatal, and a legend was gone. Now, think what you want, and say what you want, but I knew what was coming of this. Temporary relief on a permanent wound. It seemed like every time a dramatic death in the Black community happened, the same old shit occurred. A gang truce, social media justice warriors came out, speeches about peace, the whole nine yards. It happened all the time. And, two weeks later, we would be back to the same old shit. I loved my Black people, but the story was the same from South Seattle to Watts. I looked up so many stories and watched the footage so many times. That shit was personal. To kick a brother in the head, you had to be on some vindictive shit. It made me wanna go hunt the nigga down and blast him in his jail cell. But I started to move past that. I left the bickering men in the comments of several articles alone. I left all the conspiracy theories alone. I started to delve into the man. Sure, there were several interviews about the stores, the building projects, L.A. culture, all that shit. That was fine and dandy. But as I read and read each story on him, it eventually led me to a song of his that I heard but hadn't necessarily listened too. *"Rap Niggas"* had a booming ass beat and he murked that song with simple, yet efficient word play. However, a few lines stuck out to me that made the hair on my skin stand up:

Open trust accounts deposit racks, nigga
Million-dollar life insurance on my flesh, nigga
Beamer's, Benz, Bentley's or a Lex, nigga
Ferrari's and them Lambo's that's what's next, nigga

People didn't comprehend that shit. So many times, we as Black folks get knocked on for having good shit. Our own had this notion that we automatically are consumed by material instead of what's important. But, when you hear this, it summed up a lot of us. Trust accounts and life insurance came first. Then, the material shit. It was okay to live in both worlds if you had everything prioritized. People killed me man. In one breath, they were worshipping what this man stood for, and it should be commended. In the next, they were knocking the next Black man who embraced this same concept. If you raise your kids up in better surroundings, put some money in their accounts before they turn 18 and ensure they are well off in case something happens to you, all of a sudden, you sold out and your kids are privileged. It's like too many of us embrace the aspect of staying in the struggle. Many of us would rather stay in the same projects or dilapidated surroundings just so our kids can say they made it from the bottom. That's if they do make it. I never have and never will understand that mindset of many of my own folks. It was like being offered free ice cream for life, but a muthafucka would rather churn it out the hard way. I know my goal was to pass down prosperity, not poverty. In the same breath, I wasn't naïve either. I knew white folks would hate us whether we lived in the 20-story project building, or the $20 million dollar mansion in Brentwood. The next 45 minutes consisted of me going back and forth through YouTube, listening to many of his classics from Blue Laces, to Killa, to my all-time favorite, Dedication with K. Dot. It was in the middle of that song that I decided to pause the joint and open my Google docs. I was a poet by nature, and the thoughts and words were flowing in my head. It was time to put them to paper and bring it to life.

C.R.E.N.S.H.A.W.

They say you don't have to explain what's already understood, but when you screamed out neighborhood I know it wasn't for a Crip set, cause throughout time the neighbor aspect was left out, that's why we simply called that shit the hood, but you made some of us go and check on our neighbor, no need to be a hater against the next man cause we all classified as twins through this black skin, and much like you, my body is inked with stories of our generation, I look at him and think he may be Vice Lord nation, I look at another and think he bang six point stars, he wear blue, he wears red, but the government want us all dead, so the least we can do is go out this bitch swinging, see you were literally a community revolution in progress handing out community reparations in pockets, I liked how you hired ya own, took care of ya own, literally had em collecting mailbox money cause the checks from the government is nothing more than blood money printed on the backs of our great grandparents who built this country in slave fields bought on slave deals, so I got to the middle of the intersection and had to yield, I looked both ways before I crossed the street, but couldn't decide which path I wanted to take, and then I remember what my grandma used to say, never let the right side know what the left side doing, but for once granny, I gotta admit you was wrong, so I let my right arm become Crenshaw and my left became Slauson, I crossed them bitches cause you made that shit

24

like Wakanda, and you was like T'challa, but it's always a Killmonger
lurking in the shadows, more like a colonizer painted in black face,
cause the biggest enemies is the niggas from ya own race, so that's why I
stay doing victory laps cause the minute I stop running is the minute
they start gunning, see life is literally a marathon, so I tied up my blue
laces, walked out the house praying to God I don't get shot down by those
blue faces, while trying to steer my city away from the blues we used too,
cause that's the music we play at the funeral homes, so I turn up the
sounds of that dedication, **this the remedy, the separation, Tupac of**
my generation, blue pill in the fuckin Matrix, red rose in the gray
pavement, young Black nigga trapped and he can't change it, know
he a genius, he just can't claim it, cause they left him no platforms
to explain it, *but since they left you no platforms I decided to build one*
myself, stand on top and speak to God, how is it your son could survive
40 days and 40 nights and we can't survive 40 glocks and 40 ounces,
we supposed to be your chosen people, why we gotta deal with this shit,
cause now when I look at Crenshaw Imma think damn, first Rick, now
Nip, then God got quiet and said this, Crenshaw is for Communities
Repairing Everyone N Sickness and Health Always Win, meaning
when you good you good, when you down, you bounce your people back,
you are Black, you beat slavery and damnation, shot Jim Crow and
turned that nigga into bird shit, but peep this, turn to your neighbor,
and tell em, Black man, no more hatred, I love you

I had no choice but to throw a line from the dedication in there. That was my shit and by this time, I had it on repeat for about the fifth time. I was so in my zone that I ain't even hear the banging on my office door.

"Ahh shit," I said out loud.

I knew it was just my narrow head ass boss about to come in

here and say some stupid shit. I clicked pause on the screen and rolled over to the door in my chair. I opened it expecting a stern look.

"Boy you having a party in this muthafucka?"

"Man look. You can't be scaring a brother like that, beating like you the damn police."

"Well shit those baby knocks wasn't doing nothing, seeing how you was hoping the whole West Coats heard yo ass."

"Man bring yo skinny, narrow ass in here. Looking like you weigh one pound."

"Shit I weigh about the same size as that rock you got on top of ya damn shoulders."

This why I fucked with my boy G. He originally was from VA, and we went back and forth like this every day. He probably was the only one who could come in this office and I wouldn't be secretly hoping that they'd get hit by a bus or some shit.

"What's up with you and that baby nigga?"

"Man, you all in my business ain't you?"

"Just saying fool. I ain't gone take her man. You ain't gotta worry about that. Nervous. I understand."

I leaned back in my seat giving him that negro please look.

"Man, the day I let you, or any East Coast dude take my prize is the day a pig's pussy ain't pork."

"Well you about to see a pig with a beef vagina real soon."

We both sat in there cracking up. This was every day before we had to go back to the hustle and bustle of what America called the American Dream. In truth, 40 hours, five days a week was a fucking nightmare. We just had to survive it on a daily. 2:30 p.m. came around and I was back on my BS as usual. Back in the ride, I tuned into Shade45, and I was off. For the next few hours, I could feel like myself again. The gym wasn't an option, seeing how I already beasted that. However, what was an option was that I needed to clear my mind in a way to where nothing distracted me. Only problem was that the normal shit just wouldn't cut it at this point. The beach? This state was full of them. After a while, it didn't get boring, but it did get stale. I didn't wanna rip and run to the same spot. So, being the man that I am, I just drove. I didn't know where I was gonna end up, but I was sure to end up somewhere and be gravy by the time I parked.

"Yea lemme get 12 wings hot, plus four, with the breadsticks."

"Ranch, or blue cheese?"

"Just vegetables."

It didn't matter how much thinking you had to do, or to what level. Everything, and I mean everything was better when food was involved. I pulled up to Epic Wings in Mission Viejo, which was in Orange County, a good 45 minutes south of my crib, without traffic. Solo, and one of only three people in here at the time, it was a perfect wind down. I didn't have to deal with a lot of chatter, and me and this baseball game could enjoy each other's company. The Angels were on the tube tonight and that was fine with me. Personally, I was a Seattle Mariners fan, but this was the LA turf, and I ain't see my boys unless they had a series on ESPN, usually against the bum fuck Yankees. I sat there fixed on the game, but then started to drift my eyes around the restaurant. Shit always seemed to come into focus at the oddest of times. I looked at the only other people in here besides me. It was a young couple. I wouldn't put them over the age of 20. They were all cuddled up and shit, like young folks do when they madly in love. That was never me, and I didn't plan on it being me. That's why I dug my lady. All that cuddle up in a restaurant shit wasn't for neither one of us. When it was time to eat, it was time to eat. I remember our first date like it was yesterday. When she first told me that she was a chef, I swore she was on a high horse. You know in today's world everyone exaggerates what they are. You work the deep fryer at Popeye's and folks wanna call themselves a chef. Naw playa. You don't do shit but dip the chicken in the grease. Get your money because I will never knock a nigga for that. However, don't be speaking up on more than what you are. I met her through a friend, and I found out shorty really did graduate from culinary school and had held some high positions in some high profiled restaurants. We ended up at this semi vegan joint. Now, I for damn sure didn't knock anyone on their food choices. I knew this generation was in a craze about vegan everything, much like low fat foods were all the craze in the 90s. She didn't exaggerate it. They still had meat in this muthafucaka, because as hungry as I was, a brother wasn't trying to eat on a crushed bell pepper burger. She ordered some chili cheese fries and I got me a chicken sandwich with fries. Nothing impressive, I know, but here's where shit changed.

"Taste this?," she told me.

In my head, that was strike number one. I didn't share food, so I damn sure was hoping that she wasn't gone turn around and ask for any of mines. I obliged to her request and ate the joints off the fork. In that moment, she started to go into detail about the type of beans that were used to make the dish. How in the good hell could anyone on this earth make chili cheese fries sound nutritious? I really didn't know, but she did, and that shit turned me on. We made it official later that day. If she were this smart with the contents of food, I could only imagine what more she knew. Hell, these new age women couldn't even tell you the difference between corn starch and corn meal. Thank goodness for a very picky selective process with who I choose to roll with. I took my focus off the couple and started to look at the artwork on the walls. It was unique to say the least for a chicken joint. I never noticed any artwork in a chicken joint ever. The multicolored chicken on the wall being chased by a seasoning salt container with legs was amusing to say the least. I was hoping none of those PETA idiots would come in and say some shit on it. Next to that and continuing along the wall, a few L.A. sports photos from some iconic moments. From Kurt Gibson's swing in the 1988 World Series, to Kobe's pull of his jersey after he hit the game winner in the 06 playoffs against the Suns, you literally felt like you could jump in the photo and watch it live firsthand. There wasn't anything on the back walls, seeing how three flat screens occupied that. As I made my way around the rest of the walls, I happened to look directly above me, and I instantly paused. It was out of the ordinary and didn't go with the flow at all. In this frame, it was low riding green plains. Now Cali had some flatlands out in the country parts but wasn't shit accurate about this photo. Green rolling fields with antelope? Naw. We ain't have no damn antelope out here. Maybe some mountain lions and some angry ass city pigeons, but no antelope. It also had an oil drilling machine in the pic. Were we sitting on oil? I truthfully couldn't tell you. The only thing that I did know is that we were sitting on a huge ass fault that they say could go any day. When that bitch went, we were gonna break off from the rest of the map. I just hoped my Black ass would be gone when that finally went down.

"16 wings and 4 breadsticks."

I whipped my head around as the voice bellowed my order out.

"Yup."

She sat my plate down and it was on. I got up real quick to fill my cup up with some of that fire ass sweet tea that they had up in here. I was smart to fill up after my food came. Lord knows that if I started drinking tea before my grub came, it was gonna fill me up and a brother wouldn't be able to smash. I dug into my first wing, which was a flat. After that first bite, I dropped it back on the plate and counted how many flats I had compared to drums. Four to 12. That was a great damn ratio, as drums were just outright sexy. I don't know why, but that's just how it was. People who preferred flats over drums were like those who put sugar in their grits. They were spawns of the underworld and should be jailed for a minimum of 10 years and fined $250,000. I went through those four mediocre parts of the bird and mashed one of those buttery breadsticks. As I wiped my mouth, my eyes caught the photo again. I don't know why I was so intrigued with this photo, but it was starting to perplex me. I kept on eating, getting up twice more to fill my cup with some more tea. Between the food, the game and this bomb ass tea, my mind was everywhere. Finally, after sitting in there for over an hour, with about 30 minutes of that just sitting down and letting my food settle, I finally got up. The place had now gotten crowded from when I first came in, and I was leaving at the perfect time. As I hit that world-famous Black man stretch, the pic caught my eye one more time.

"What the hell are you saying to me?," I asked it.

I know it was weird talking to a damn photo, but it seemed art was trying to tell me about life. I headed back to my truck and made the drive back up the 5. As I expected, the traffic was fucked beyond belief. I didn't trip on it, seeing how I was the one who randomly drove down to clear my head. However, being full of chicken wings, bread, and tea, that itis was seriously kicking my ass right now, especially considering that I was moving at probably five miles per hour when I did move. I did every type of lean I could to stay up. After 20 minutes, I probably moved about a mile and a half. Getting out of Orange County was a pain in the ass. At this point, it was only one thing that I knew could cure my woes, and that was music. As usual, K.R.I.T. was my go-to. Just as I was about to crank that up, I flipped. I switched my music selection to Wale's third joint, The Curse of The Gifted. That intro track was a beast. Like every rap verse I knocked in my speakers, I did more than hear it. I listened. That first verse did something to my soul, I swear on my life:

WALE: THE CURSE OF THE GIFTED
(FIRST VERSE)

Life's better when your niggas good, and your mama straight
though honestly still looking for some type of balance
Cuz the status got me jah tripping
Cuz I like my bitch, but I love these bitches on my dick
When spitting tell me what you feeling different knowing you's the breadwinner
And it's rare you hear niggas say he can't feel you
But in your ears like he dope, just not dope enough
And ya closest ho be probing you to open up
And to do so you must roll one up
And it's lonely at the top
They tell me that they feeling me

31

I eat this game and shit this out
My dirty draws got winning streaks
I'm in too deep, this industry is saying to a nigga
Got change like them niggas, but ain't changed like them niggas
They only fuck with my old shit cuz I'm on shit
But I was potent in '06, niggas slow as shit
Now my dreams is nothing more than minimal thoughts
And my cheese gone fluctuate though sleep is the cause
And I'm tired though
And I'm high too
But it's like my music made these niggas turn they pride to fool
Yea, ye ain't even gotta love us
But you will respect this motherfucking hustle, real nigga shit

I broke this whole verse down, but the first two lines got me. Life was better when your people, including your mama, was straight. Unfortunately for me, I didn't know if either were good. I wasn't gonna make any more attempts to talk to my mom or anyone who I deemed toxic to my spirit. Sometimes, you gotta love people from far away, and that was perfectly fine.

"HEY ASSHOLE!!! MOVE IT!!!"

I turned to the side, looking at a driver who was telling me that I was number one in his eyes. I snapped out of my trance to hear horns blowing at my Black ass profoundly. Yea, I had got caught up in this music, as I saw traffic had moved, but I stayed stagnant in one spot. I hit the gas and continued with traffic that was highly pissed off at me. After another five seconds, my fucks given went back down to zero. They'd be alright, and so would I. I made it home around 6:45 in the evening. I plopped down on my sectional and let out the loudest woo ever. I would've made Ric Flair jealous. I cut on the television and it really started watching me. That meal might have been a while ago, but that itis was still hitting. As I drifted in and out, that damn picture popped up in my head. This shit was starting to irk me. Fuck it. I went to Google and just started searching country shit, literally and figuratively. After five minutes of searching through random images, I crossed one that caught my eye. Yellowstone. Man wasn't any brothers that I know fucking around in Yellowstone. I had watched enough National Geographic in my day to know that Black people and mother nature were best acquainted when they were far apart from each other. That was white people shit, going out into the woods and messing with mother nature. Bison, bears and beavers. The only B's we messed with as Black people was Bacardi, Bloods and Black-Eyed Peas. Anything else besides that, you could cancel that shit. Plus, this shit was in Wyoming. Why in the good hell would anyone with a hint of tint in their skin even get the nerve to fly up and stay anywhere in Wyoming? I googled the population of the state. It was a mere 577,000. Out of those 577,000, we were 6,000 strong, which equaled out to a tad bit over 1%. I closed my computer and just laughed. Memorial Day weekend started for us on the 24th, but we got a half day on the 23rd. A half day where I worked was nine o'clock, even though I stayed a littler later to collect some extra money. So technically, ours was a five-day weekend. I needed somewhere to go. I was tired of spending Memorial Day out here. Booty and beaches were nice, but I had to expand my horizons. My job and passion had taken me to places across America. It hadn't once taken me somewhere that challenged me. This Wyoming shit started to really fuck with my mind. I ain't know anyone up there, but it was starting to intrigue me. Possibly, wherever I went, I would be the token Black guy in a majority white world. I could already imagine the stares, the snickering between people when they saw me walk down the street. Naw, it wasn't the south and I had never heard any tales from that state as nasty as the south. However, I didn't put it past them. I mean, they did have the Black 14. In today's day and age, the Black man was public enemy number one. Whether that enemy came from the cops, or everybody trying to feminize us, turn us into women so we couldn't reproduce, the targets on our back were large, with a lot of white and red. Being Black was lit. The shit was kind of dangerous, but it was lit. Our culture was world culture. In the same breath, our culture was what scared folks. The older I got, the more I realized that shit. I tried not to beef with my fellow brother. I had my moments where I had just lost my fucking mind on some shit, or I got sucked into an argument. At all cost, however, if I could avoid arguing with my brethren, I did. We had enough going against us, and I didn't need to add to the beef. That was unless a brother owed me money, and purposely didn't pay me back. Then, they were just a bitch ass nigga. Just then, my phone rang. It was a number that I didn't recognize. I did what Black folks do best when an unrecognized number comes through the phone. I ignored that joint. I went back to scrolling through my computer and my phone rang again. Who the fuck is this calling from some 307 shit?

"Hello?"

"Mac."

The voice sounded familiar, but I still didn't know who the hell it was. "Man who this?"

"Lemme give you a hint man. Remember when you met me in California? My first year in the Navy? I sung karaoke with the wife

34

one night and you said I sounded terrible. I responded with yea, I'm a white guy with no rhythm."

"Man get the fuck outta here. Johnny?"

"How's it going brother?"

This was my dude Johnny. I had completely forgot that he was the only person that I knew from Wyoming. He was born and raised in that joint, in a small town somewhere out there.

"Man what you up too?"

"Well, I'm back here in the country, good job and living off some VA benefits."

"What's wrong?"

"Oh nothing. Couple of tweaks and cracks of my knees from time to time, but nothing too bad in general. The VA don't know that though. I got 100% workable disability. And up here, along with my job, man I'm living like a king."

"What's like a king?"

"Well I got a nice house in town. Got a few chickens. Huge garage with a weld shop in it. Two girls and a beautiful wife. To me, that's a castle.

"Hold on man. Hold on. You no shit got some chickens?"

"Yea. Got a good gang of them. Used to have some sheep and turkeys when I was living out on the farm. But it got a bit much after a while. So, chickens it is. They are much easier to maintain."

"Man, that's crazy."

We rapped for like an hour on the phone, catching up on old times and shit. He was in the service and I was on a summer internship down in San Diego. We crossed paths at a bar out there, and that was all she wrote. We were doing good for ourselves, so it was lovely seeing that shit. Furthermore, I couldn't remember the last time I seemed to have a normal conversation on the phone. I was so used to talking with Rain about his problems with his then wife, that I got accustomed to hearing bitch, bitch, bitch the entire conversation. Then, he hit me with it.

"So, what are you doing for Memorial Day?"

"Man shit. I'm tryna figure some shit out. Trying get away from here. If all else fails, I'll end up at the beach, looking at some women, hitting up a barbecue. You know. The usual holiday shenanigans."

"Why don't you get a ticket and come out here for a few days? Let your hair down. See something different for a few days."

Everything at that point had started to replay in my head. The drive down to Mission Viejo. The chicken wings that I had ate. The country ass picture that was on the wall of the chicken joint. I didn't tell him what had occurred, but somehow, I knew that The Good Lord was indeed talking to me subliminally.

"Hello?"

"Yea man sorry. I got stuck daydreaming. Where you stay at exactly out there?"

"Riverton."

"Riverton. Where the hell is that at?"

"In the middle of nowhere. We're about 10,000. Almost two hours outside of Casper."

I then had to ask him the most important question of all.

"Look man. If I come out there, it ain't gone be no mess is it? I mean, I know you're good, but this country is in another mindset right now."

"Well Mac. You know I wouldn't be out here if it was that type of stuff. You gotta remember I'm not like everyone. I get it. A lot are, but I believe in love. Come on out man. To be honest. You're family to me. I didn't understand city life a lot, but our talks way back yonder really helped me and Brenda out. It'll be cool. Matter fact, I'll pay your way if you come out tomorrow. If that makes it easier."

"Naw man. Naw. You ain't gotta do all that."

"Well one of my in laws works for the airline. I could just call her and she can credit it on her account."

"So, what time would I need to be at the airport? And is it possible to fly out of Long Beach, because LAX is a fucking nightmare?"

"Well I'm looking on my computer right now. There's an 11:00 flight flying out of Ontario to Denver tomorrow. You'll have to connect over there. And from there, you'll hit Casper. I'll be there to pick you up at five. Is that okay?"

I thought about it quick in my head. Ontario, even though a little bit farther than Long Beach, I could manage that. It's much more relaxed with less hassle. But, Wyoming for Memorial Day? I mean, all the signs I had received up to that point kind of told me that this was the best choice.

"Man, you sure you cool with your family to use their credits for me?" "You're family Mac. That's the way I see it. Now, are you coming tomorrow or not?"

"Yea."

"Alrighty then. Make sure you bring some hoodies and a coat, or something warm. Wyoming can be bipolar, even in May."

"Man hold on. Its May. Y'all still cold?"

"I mean it's okay right now. It gets like in the 60s around this time. But I think it's supposed to rain, so it may be in the 40s."

"WHAT???!!!"

"Yup. I said 40s. I didn't stutter"

"Man, how the fuck are y'all that cold in May? It's May."

"It's Wyoming. Look, can you text me your email so I can call my in law and let her know to book your ticket?"

"Got you man."

"See you tomorrow."

"Later bro."

He hung up and I let out a chuckle. I was really going to Wyoming and the shit was funny in a way. It was getting late, but damn, I had really agreed to this shit. I texted Johnny my email and waited for a reply. Until I got one, I wasn't packing shit. He was my dawg, but I lowkey wanted him to say no, because something didn't seem right about this shit. We'd say one thing one minute. The next minute all the plans went to shit. I had no personal vendetta against him, as he was always open to different perspectives and wanted to understand me as a person. However, I couldn't speak for everyone else in the state. 10 minutes later, my phone began to buzz. I saw my text messages indicator was lit up. I read the words *Everything is good to go.* An email came through, and a ticket confirmation for a flight out of Ontario at 11:00 was solidified. How many brothers would I see up there? That was the million-dollar question. I was hoping to see a brother and have that nigga experience. You know, when two brothers talk in code. I would see him. He would see me. I'd be like what's up fam. He'd be like shit, I'm tryna be like you. That's when I would come back with the response of man if I had yo hands, I'd cut my shits off. Someone who ain't hip on game would probably call 911 saying that a Black man threatened another Black man by saying he would cut his hands off. It was funny, but at the same time, it wasn't. It seemed like white folks had this knack of calling the police on us for no fucking reason at all. There was the little girl who was selling lemonade, and someone called the cops on her. Let's not forget about the crazy ass troll who called the police on Black folks having a barbecue in Oakland. The brother who got killed for selling loose cigarettes. One of our brothers who was shot down for selling CDs outside of a store. Then, came the time that outraged us all as Black people. How an officer in Dallas blatantly kicked in the door of a brother that she was seeing, shot him to death, but then say she mistook it for her apartment, or whatever idiotic shit she said. It was shit like that which kept us in an outrage. To be a Black man, is to almost be in a rage all the damn time. The actual words from James Baldwin were:

"To be a negro in this country and to be relatively conscious is to be in a rage almost all the time."

He wasn't lying either. As I glanced back at my phone, my blood boiled at the realization of his words. I did what I usually did when fits of rage started to envelope inside of me. I went to my computer. The words began to flow off the tips of my fingers.

BULLSHIT

Bullshit, noun, definition as stated by Webster's Dictionary, stupid or untrue talk or writing; nonsense, example: Black shooters, thugs, Muslim shooters, terrorists, Asian shooters, communists, White shooters...mental health, see I don't know if they think I was born last night, but I'm not immune to the fact that Black men and prison go hand and hand like a Crip who only eats seafood, we are replaced with numbers as if they pulled a ticket at the DMV, now serving C35 at gate number four, we are stripped down of more than our clothes, because our manhood is also bagged up, these are your privatized dispensaries where petty narcotics can get you a minimum life sentence and there is no maximum on the tenants, you call this the department of corrections, but it's really filled with all the wrong answers on how to make me human again, your chain fence and metal is meant to sing my sad song, but just like mumble rap, there is nothing meaningful about your bars, don't tell me to live in silence behind this iron, because remember, even the caged bird sang and beat his wings cause he was tired of being stuck in the prison he was in, and I sleep on his feathers, because they are much more comfortable than the mattress you provide, my tears leak from tier C down to ground level, in here, my fears have fears, and I now understand what Kendrick meant when he said if these walls could talk, because if yours could, those bricks would be Kawhi Leonard, dead silent, mourning the loss of the humans that you have reduced back to three fifths from the plantation, because 40% of us make up this population, then I add em up, at least I am a whole person now, so maybe that's my consolation prize, for being a three time loser...

I began packing my clothes up. It was gonna be hoodies galore because I didn't have any thick ass coats. Three pairs of jeans, a few beaters, some t-shirts and my house shoes for around the crib, and everything was good to go. I would get all my toiletries in the a.m., seeing how a brother still had to get up and brush his teeth, and do all that other shit. Bedtime was here. I plopped down on the bed. The next time I opened my joints, it was five the next morning. I

40

swear that I had only taken one breath. I arrived at the airport a full two hours before my flight. If nothing else, Pre TSA is the shit. A brother didn't have to take his shoes, belt, or anything off. Usually, you had to get damn near naked to even go through the airport. $85 for five years was a lovely deal. I made it through and got to my gate, plugging in my phone, and doing what half the world does for 12 hours a day. Social Media. As usual, I scrolled my Facebook timeline, seeing who was mad at what, who baby daddy pissed them off, or whatever else entertainment was being provided. Then, I thought about something. I went into my search bar and typed a name. Lord oh lord, the comments from this thread was something straight out of a comedy show. Some people understood the position, while others didn't.

"She's catching heat on both sides when at the end of the day, we all want to feel desired. We all like to feel like we still got it from time to time. You can be confident, but sometimes it still feels good to hear it from someone else. It doesn't mean she wants out of her marriage, that she lacks self-confidence, or suffers from low self-esteem. It means she's a human being, just like the rest of us. We get so consumed and divided by the wrong shit."

"It's crazy how one can say it's not about men, but she clearly said she wants attention from men. "She doesn't want it, but it would be good to know someone is looking." GTFOH. It's clearly about wanting attention from other men so she can feel good about herself. Women out here calling her a Queen for her statement. Man, princesses talk like that not Queens."

"Any man arguing about women's issues must be a woman too we supposed to be in this together sis."

"I never knew it was /is a crime to express a personal thought. Clearly, she shared it because she wanted ppl to know her struggle she deals with in her marriage including self-esteem issues. I don't see anything wrong with her expressing her Personal Thoughts. If she was acting on it then it would be different. But basically, she finds herself unattractive at times and it bothers her because her husband is getting all the action, and nobody seems to see her. Her for who she is. Nor nobody other than women give her compliments and she just still wanna know/feel like she's beautiful. She only been with him her whole life so it's natural for her to have those feelings. If his mama didn't say shit, they why are You?? IJS"

I laughed my ass off and shook my damn head at the same time. All this because a woman was honestly expressing how she felt. It just goes to show you that this world is never satisfied. We ask people to keep it 100. Then, when they do, they are still vilified for it. All this from expressing a feeling. It made for good entertainment, but it showed the sad state of the world that we lived in. Time flew as I continued to read through a barrage of nothings from people. I found it amazing that folks can type 50,000 words on a social media site in a matter of days but found it hard to sit down and write a book. If you're gonna give your two cents, you might as well allow it to make yourself some dollars. Everyone had opinions, true. However, not everyone was banking off those opinions.

"Ladies and gentlemen, we are now boarding for Flight 4711 into Denver. All passengers with pre board privileges, people with disabilities, active duty military, you may now board."

Ahh pre board. It was my favorite time of the flight. It was the time that I looked at all the peasants boarding after me to let them know what's up. It didn't hurt that Johnny's sister hooked me up with first class. This wasn't Southwest at all. Nothing wrong with them, but Southwest ain't have no first class. I stretched my legs as I hit my first-class seat. It was bigger than most, and I really didn't have to stretch. I was just showing my ass at this point. I ain't pay for it, but they didn't know that.

"Excuse me sir. I believe you are in the wrong seat."

"The fuck if I am," I said, looking up at this privilege with pale skin.

"This is first class sir."

"And this is fuck you sir," I told him, followed by a middle finger.

"Excuse me gentlemen, is there a problem?"

He took a deep breath and looked at the flight attendant who asked him the question. Me, I kept my eyes locked on this Klansman in a cheap suit.

"Ma'am. I am simply trying to sit down, and this young man has decided to sit in someone's seat."

As I jumped up, the flight attendant put her hand in my chest.

"Sir, this man has a ticket and you are disrupting people boarding this plane. Now sit down please, or you will be directed to leave the flight."

"I'LL LEAVE MY DAMN SELF!!!"

She kept her hand on my chest as my fists balled up, and I watched this racist piece of shit move through the few people who were stuck near the cabin.

"AMAZING HOW TIMES HAVE CHANGED!!! THEY'RE SUPPOSED TO BE IN THE BACK!!!"

The nigga in me took over as I attempted to leave my seating area, but old girl put both hands on my chest.

43

"Don't. He's not worth it. Enjoy yourself and don't stoop to his level. **FOLKS, COME ON AND CONTINUE TO BOARD!!"**

You could tell that the people who saw this transpire were now uneasy. She sat down in the plush aisle seat of my row as I was fuming in my window seat. People dared not even look my way because I was likely to throw someone off the plane at this point.

"I'll take care of you all flight and past this. Don't worry. Be calm for me. There are some idiots still living in 1950."

People continued to board. Now, the crowd was completely oblivious to what happened. A brother with a Lakers jersey came on. Shorty was still sitting next to me.

"Sir," she said, stopping ol boy.

"Whoa whoa. Is there a problem?"

"No problem. Are you flying coach?"

"Umm. Yea."

"Congratulations. You've just been upgraded to first class. Here's your seat," she said, pointing to where that old, racist cracker would've been sitting.

She took his bag and placed it in the overhead. Homey looked at me, then back at her.

"HELL YEA!!!," he let out.

She walked off towards the back of the plane.

As the last bit of people got on, I looked to see that there were only four of us in first class. As the last few passed out of our section, the brother who got blessed leaned over.

"A bruh. Something happen?"

"Yea. Ol cracker ass nigga was about to get cracked. He thinks our kind ain't worthy of first class. But homegirl straightened him out."

"Nigga for real?"

"Nigga," I said, emphatically.

I glanced up to see the white lady up here with us turned her head quick. Yea, I said nigga. I'll say the shit again too. The flight attendant came back through and went into the cabin with the Captain.

"A playa. Did anyone see it?"

"Yea man. The attendant who just walked in the cabin."

"Excuse me gentlemen," she said, coming back out. "I talked to the Captain. All drinks are free. Food is free. You will also be credited two free flights, round trip, from the airlines, anywhere in the continental U.S. By the way, I'm Sarah. Is there anything you all need?"

"You got Henny?," homeboy asked.

"No sir. We have Crown."

"I'll take a glass."

I wasn't mad at homeboy. We took off, with the situation still heavy on my mind. Once we reached 10,000 feet, shit was smooth. I learned homeboy name was Ron. We talked the whole damn two hours almost. Judging from the slow speech we had with each other over an hour in, it was safe to say that the drinks were hitting. The sausage pizza that we both had couldn't absorb shit. We may not have been fucked up, but we were on the road to it. I kind of wish that racist piece of shit was still here. I'd thank him. His ignorance allowed me to connect with another brother and get some free shit in the process. As we began our descent,

I started secretly praying to God. The approach into Denver was no hoe. These Rocky Mountains had the plane shaking harder than the ass in Nelly's Tip Drill video. I mean, you would've thought another plane connected to her in midair, hit her with a good stroke and had her climaxing to the T. For about 15 minutes of my life, I literally thought I was about to meet Jesus Christ himself. I could just see Him above the clouds getting the book ready, because he knew a brother was coming. Luckily, I was wrong, and we landed smoothly. Once in the airport, I was pissed off even more. I landed at B43. My connecting gate to Casper was all the way at A75. I wanted to smack whoever the CEO of this airport was. I had an hour to get to my connecting joint. Luckily, the train terminal was right there, so I jumped on and swung it over to A. When I arrived at A terminal, it literally dropped me off at A20. My Black ass had to walk over 50 fucking terminals just to catch a flight. I was highly pissed. This air was already crispy and thin. Now, my legs were going to be crispy and well done. After what seemed like forever, I finally got there. I was now hungry, and they had a barbecue joint right here at the gate. I ain't know if Johnny had cooked or what not, but a brother needed some grub now. I looked up at the menu and saw a hot link.

"$15.95!!!"

The workers looked up at me, and I looked back, shaking my damn head. They must have thought I was Billy the plum fucking fool if they thought I was paying damn near $16 for a fucking hot link. That bitch had better cure cancer if I got it. Still, I stood there, scanning the menu. Why did we as Black people do this? I had no clue. We would look at shit three or four times, like some magical shit that wasn't there before was supposed to pop up. It was the same way with the refrigerator. We opened that bitch and wasn't nothing to eat. Then, we go back 15 minutes later as if the Fairy Godmother was supposed to stock it up.

"A lemme get that hot link?"

The sister behind the register looked at me, laughing. The other two sisters started doing the same shit.

"Well I ain't gotta tell you the price."

"I'm sorry. It's just I ain't expect a hot link to cost 15 something dollars."

I inserted my card into the reader.

"What you doing down here at this terminal anyway?"

"I'm going to Wyoming."

"What the hell in Wyoming?," the other sister asked, bringing the hot link up to the counter.

"Gotta homeboy out there. Going to visit. You know. Check it out."

"White or Black?"

"Excuse me?"

"Is he white or Black?"

"He white."

"Well, all I gotta say is stay home. Don't go up there diving in the snow."

The other two girls started hollering. She was dead ass though.

"Trust me. I ain't leaving mine. I like chocolate."

"Mmmhmmm. Kanye said that shit too," the girl said in the back.

I shook my head, laughing, and walked the few steps to the gate. Time passed as I observed the 10 or so passengers that were waiting with me. We were gonna be in one of these small joints for the 40-minute flight. I was excited, yet nervous at the same time. This hot link was vicious. The bitch was hot than a muthafucka. After downing the Sahara Desert ass swine, and three Orange Vanilla

Cokes to quench the fire in my mouth, it was time to take flight. As they announced boarding call, I looked back at the barbecue joint. All three of them were staring at me. I waived at em.

"GOOD LUCK!!!," the heavy set, chocolate one yelled.

I laughed, they laughed, and everything was a go. It was time to become a speck in a world that I have never ventured into before. Wyoming, here a brother come. What you got for me pimpin?

— 2 —

WY-O-ME

After 40 minutes of rolling green flatlands and snowcapped mountains, which were mouth dropping in beauty to say the least, I landed at Casper International Airport. Casper was one of Wyoming's bigger cities, with almost 60,000 folks. I knew their airport wouldn't be a monster like Denver's, so that was a big sigh of relief. We exited off the plane and I saw this small ass building. I couldn't see to the other side, but I knew damn well this wasn't the airport. Then, I walked in, and saw that it was. The shit was a mini Lego set. I saw my big ass luggage sitting on the carousel. That shit wasn't a carousel either. It looked like a small spinning circle, that wasn't even spinning. Then, I looked again. My shit wasn't even on the carousel. That shit was on the floor next to it, chilling. Casper International should've been called ghost airport because the only thing international about this place was missing. As I grabbed my bag, I saw Johnny Boy through the windows in the doors. In country fashion, he had on his hunting cap. Everyone knows white boys and their hunting caps. I walked through.

"Sup man," he said.

"Ain't nothing much man"

I let my bag go, dapped him up and hugged my guy.

"Man, I thought this was an international airport. This shit ain't even a sectional airport."

"Well, I mean. You got here didn't you?"

"Yea, but that ain't the point. I'm thinking I'm coming into some glorious shit. How the hell the main airport the size of a one-bedroom apartment?"

"Well, we don't have large numbers coming in and out of this place like L.A. They built it just big enough to make people happy."

"Yea I see."

"Come on man. Let's get outta here. I'm pretty hungry and the wife is cooking tonight."

We walked out the main entrance of the airport and into the parking lot, looking like total opposites of each other. Me in a hoodie and loose jeans. Him in a bent ball cap, tight pants, and flannel shirt.

"Oops, I almost forgot to ask you. You gotta use the pisser before we leave?"

"Naw, I'm good."

"Are you sure, because it's a pretty long drive."

"Yea man. Positive."

"Positive?"

"Do you want me to pee?," I asked him, opening the passenger side door. "I'm just asking man. It's a long drive into Riverton."

"How long Johnny, cause you itching to tell me."

"Two hours."

"TWO HOURS!!!"

"Yea man. I told you it's gonna take a while. This is the country. We drive everywhere out here. This isn't the city where everything is close. Everything is spread out over here."

"Since you put it like that man. I'll be back."

I ran back into the airport, turning around to see him putting my luggage into the trunk. I waltzed into the bathroom, whipping my shit out and hovering it above the toilet. I knew if I concentrated hard enough, I could get something out. As the water began to flow, and the fish thanked me worldwide, I looked above the toilet at a picture. *"Welcome to Casper. Oil City."* Even with the nickname, it still sounded like something bland and blah. Not knocking them at all, but in my culture, you know our cities nicknames are everything. Houston is called H-Town. Dallas, Triple D. Atlanta is ATL, or Hotlanta. Chicago is Chi Town. Indianapolis is Naptown. Miami is M-I-Yayo. All those nicknames just sucked you in. I couldn't tell my boys yea man, I'm about to head to Oil City. They'd look at me like I was crazy as hell. I finished up and made my way back to the car. My bladder was empty, and I was ready to get on this road. As we got to the booth to give the clerk our ticket to get out the gate, I looked up and saw a brother. At first, he ain't notice me. When he got a good look, he let out an AAAAA. I pointed at him, nodded my head and we took off through the open gate.

"Do you know him Mac?"

"Nah man. Just how bruhs greet each other sometimes."

"Oh okay. I thought he maybe had to clear his throat out or that someone was behind us."

I started cracking the fuck up. Yea, this was gonna be one interesting trip. The conversation was going steady, and I know this car ride would be an intriguing one indeed. Five minutes in, and my whole demeanor changed.

"Damn man. You weren't lying."

"I told you there's not much out here. Look to the left, look to

51

the right. There is nothing but green pastures, mountains, a few oil rigs, and some antelope. It's good for me, but I know you're a city boy. It's definitely different."

"Bruh. I seriously thought you were bullshitting."

"I told you man. This is it. This is Wyoming. You won't see much until we hit the town. And even then, it's gonna be country. Just how it is man." We continued to ride, making conversation throughout the trip. Catching up and shit.

"Yo, where the music at? We been rolling about 30 minutes and I haven't heard anything."

"I mean look around. What radio station is gonna get some signal out here?"

"You got an aux hook up?"

He pointed to it and I hooked up my phone. The beat dropped.

"Man, c'mon now," Johnny said. "I can't take hearing this darn song again."

"Man look. I figured if anyone loves this song, it would be you. This is literally country with a twist to it. You should be vibin' out to this."

"You just don't know how many times I have heard this song. I have two teenagers. I gotta hear this all day long. This is all the kids sing. Well, I'm gonna get some gold or a big pole, or whatever the hell he says."

The laughter that echoed out of my stomach at that moment was legendary.

"You for real man?"

"I'm serious Mac. I don't know the words, even with hearing it so many times."

"Man, it's take my horse to the old town road."

"Old town road, yellow brick road, road to redemption, I rode a horse. It doesn't matter. I'm about sick of this song."

"Yo, do you know this kid's back story?"

"No not really"

"I gotta cheer for this kid to win man. I mean, I don't get down with his lifestyle, but not liking something a person does, does not mean you hate the person. I think people today need to realize that. I mean I'm happy for the kid. He's 19, got some money in his pocket, ain't sleeping on the couch at his sister house anymore. I applaud it. Don't necessarily like the song, but it's catchy as all hell."

"You said his lifestyle. Is he gay?"

"Out there like the moon in the night sky. Can't cosign how he dresses or any of that. But I'm rooting for the kid. Lord knows I wish more kids would make money the right way and not looking for a buck with robbing people."

"I definitely understand that. My wife keeps the girls in art and music. Plus, they both know how to shoot well. My daughter Kyla, she's still getting her down range practice. My daughter Ella, well she can shoot a fly off a deer behind at 500 yards."

"Damn, you got 'em bucking like that?"

"Gotta teach my daughters everything, you know. I don't want them to ever have to depend on a man to do anything for them. We work on the cars together. I had them helping me tend the farm when we lived on it. They can operate weapons properly. I'm just trying to prepare them for a world they need prepping for."

I could respect it. Johnny was spot on man. It was important to teach our kids the ins and outs of life. If us as adults didn't prepare them, then all we were doing were breeding a bunch of spineless zombies.

"Look man. Listen to what I'm about to say, and don't take this the wrong way. Have you prepared them to interact with people of different skin tones?"

"Well I teach them to treat everyone with respect and dignity, regardless of skin color."

"I understand that, but it's a whole different ball game when you have to interact with people of different backgrounds on a daily. Peep this. Y'all nearly all white right?"

"With a few of the Natives, yea."

"Ok cool. So, imagine them going to college. Now, I get it. Most colleges are majority white. But there are Black, Mexican, Asian, whatever other race. They gone go to parties. They gone hear shit like the N word. They gone see things that may make them stereotype everyone of one race. It happens. I ain't saying it's right, but it's the way of the world. You can't prepare them for that by saying treat everyone with respect, because I've treated plenty of people I didn't like with dignity and respect, even when I didn't want to."

"Yea. I never thought about that in that way."

"Yea man. Just something else to think on."

"You know me Mac. I'm always receptive to learning. Can I ask you something though?"

"Man, you know you can ask me anything."

"Ok, and I'll answer the same question about mines. What do you see as the biggest problem with Black people, in your eyes? Cause I have a whole novel as to what's wrong with mines."

Had this been any other white boy, I may have felt a certain type of way. But this was my brother. The guy who I groomed on a regular when he was out in Cali, so he could understand a different way of life. We weren't in our 20's anymore. We were grown and saw the world different than when we were 25.

"Aight, so you watch basketball right?"

"Yea I follow it every blue moon. You know."

"Yea. Aight. So, take a situation that happened with one of mines for instance. Now, he attempted a business venture. Were there some brothers genuinely rooting for him to fail? Hell yea. You ignore them though. You can't do shit about a crab except cook him and eat him. And that's it. Now, what a lot of us were upset at was the way fam went about his business. One, you can't live through your kids. That shit ain't, and never has been cool. Two, you gotta let ya folks control their own narrative at some point. Three, in business, and I know this for a fact. Its methods to the madness. You can't always be yourself. When you go to a business meeting, you are one way. When you go to an event, you are another way. When you go home, you are another way. You not changing who you are. You are simply adapting to the environment of which you are in. Everyone has to do it. I can't talk like I'm talking with you to students. Don't mean I'm selling out or selling myself short. I'm in a different environment. That's all man. Basically, crabs in a barrel, or you a sell out when you do better. Because regardless of the mistakes he made, even if he had been perfect, a good number of brothers would've still been secretly wanting his downfall, and that's the shit I can't fuck with. If you Black, and ain't selling drugs, I'm rooting for you. Even if I don't think you moving like you should be, I'm still rooting for you."

Johnny nodded his head and stayed quiet for the next 10 seconds, as we passed a group of antelope.

"So, here's my problem with my people. As a majority, white

55

people expect minorities. Excuse me. People who aren't white, and I'm sorry to say minorities because I think it's disrespectful to label someone a title for the sole purpose to make yourself feel better. They expect others to bow down to white people. We already have the world in a hold, and we get upset with anyone outside of us trying to make an honest dollar. Why can't Lebron James start his own shoe company? Why can't Jay Z start up schools in Brooklyn? That's our problem man. We tell others what blueprint they need to follow, all the while we haven't constructed a thing. We've only stolen everything from other cultures. From dance, to music, to land, to this whole country. Oh yea, we stole it. You see how we are talking? All calm. If this was on social media or in some random group, someone would've been a name, a racist slur, whatever else. We have two ears and one mouth for a reason. You listen twice as much as you talk. Anyone who does the opposite, they are a plum fool. It's not that some white people don't want to see others succeed. It's that a lot of white people want you to go about the world in their way, and that's not right. It's a time and place for everything, but if you go into a bar guns blazing, shooting when no one is in the room, then what are you going to do when all the cowboys come out the back room and you don't have any more bullets? That's what I hate man. Our history is so messed up, that none of us can be genuine. The sad thing is that it is most of my people, and it irritates me, because the majority will always outnumber the minority. And lastly, you notice a heck of a lot of white people are always silent on matters that don't affect them and their privilege."

Just then, I looked back up towards the windshield.

"My dude is this rain and snow?"

"Oh yea. It's still May. This is common."

"But we just drove and it was all clear."

Johnny shrugged his shoulders.

"Welcome to Wyoming."

As soon as the sleet came, it seemed to disappear, not lasting more than four to five minutes. Judging from the time, we still had a good hour and some change to go.

"Man bruh. My bladder movements feel like they're kicking in again."

"You used the bathroom before we left right?"

"Yea, but those three pops I had at the airport ready to release some more."

"You had three sodas?"

"Yea. Three pops."

"You back east folks with this pop mess."

"That's what it is."

"Well screw the drinks. The next closest town is Shoshoni. Can you hold it for about 20 minutes?"

"Yea, I'll be good."

We rolled on and on as the music from my phone kept playing and convo kept being had. Finally, we hit this small town in the middle of nowhere. I was skeptical as ever when we pulled up at the gas station. It looked normal enough, but I just knew the minute I got out, there would be a noose that dropped down as soon as I walked through the door. To my surprise, as we walked in, there wasn't a stare, snicker, or anything. It was like these white folks were literally minding their own business. I fucked with it. I went into the bathroom.

"Evening."

"Evening," I responded, as I stood at the urinal two down from him.

You know the rules. You never piss next to another man. That was a violation of man code.

"Visiting?"

"Yea with a friend. He stays in Riverton."

"Welp," he said as he flushed. "Better than this shit of a town. Hell our fucking library is in a trailer."

He washed his hands.

"Enjoy Wyoming."

"Thank you."

Well, that went good. I exited the bathroom to see Johnny in line already. I went and grabbed a sweet tea, pork skins and Peanut Butter M&M's. Once copped, I took it back to the car and we were back on our way.

"A man. Why you driving so slow?"

"It's two cops in this town and he doesn't have anything better to do than pull someone over. So, everyone who comes through here literally does 29. You go 30, and the cops get dirty."

"Damn."

Once we got out of Smallville, U.S.A., we were back up to normal speed. I passed by some shit that just blew my mind. Poison creek. Yea, I guess they really named shit for what it was out here. Much of the drive was back to the same old same old that I had experienced in the first hour, apart from a whole lot more antelope and cows.

"Damn man. Is everybody farmers here?"

"Naw man. It's a big part of the lifestyle, but we have normal nine to fives like everyone else. Doctors, lawyers, scam insurance salesman. The one good thing about being a small town is going to the DMV. It's like waiting in line for an order at McDonald's. Four or five people is crowded. I'll take that any day over LA, San Diego or any other big city."

We kept rolling. It was damn near seven o'clock and the sun was bright as ever. This was some other world shit. I had seen skies all my life, but something about this Wyoming sky was different. I couldn't put my finger on it quite yet, but it just was different. The entering Riverton sign was now upon us.

"This it man?"

"Almost. We're just passing through the beginning of it. Yes, it's still farms and run-down houses in some areas."

"This ain't gone be like no GET OUT type shit is it?"

"Yea Mac. I'm working for the secret society to steal organs. I'm gonna settle you in for two days and then hit you with some hot tea, a cup, spoon and a basement."

"I didn't know you had a sarcastic gene in you man."

"The only thing in me is good food and some beer."

"I'm just saying bruh. Ever since that movie, you know how shit is." "Man, I'm married. I don't swing that way. I'm trapped everyday with three women and three times of the month. So, if anyone is gonna trap you, it damn sure wouldn't be me."

I looked to the right as we passed into the prime part of the town.

"Ahh shit. Y'all got a Hampton Inn."

"Is that supposed to be impressive? I mean, it's a hotel."

"Naw man. Not saying it like that. I'm just saying I expected some shit like The Cowboy Inn, or The Ranchers Motel."

He just stared at me.

"Man what," I said laughing.

"You gone get enough talking about my country folk. I'm going to drop you off in the lake at Boysen."

"The heck is Boysen?"

"You'll see."

Great. A surprise involving some water is all I needed.

"Hey man. I have to stop at Walmart real fast."

I looked to the left and sure enough, they had a damn Walmart.

"Damn. I guess the mom and pop joints don't even stand a chance out here."

"Naw. It ain't that bad. We still have a solid 10,000 country folk, so the other stores are still lasting, because they have loyal customers. Now, if this was Shoshoni, or Thermopolis, then yea. Everything else would be out of business."

We pulled up into the lot, parked and began to walk inside. The first thing I noticed before anything were Mexicans. And they say brothers are everywhere. Naw, Mexicans were everywhere. I mean truthfully, this was all of their shit before anything. Also, I saw a few Natives. That was crazy in a sense. I remember Chris Rock had a comedy special years ago, talking about when was the last time you saw two Indians chilling on a bench. As I walked in, there were two Native tribesmen sitting on a bench, chopping it up with each other. It was crazy how sometimes art reflected the life we thought we would never see.

"Hey man. Get what you want."

"Naw man. You brought me in the crib for a few days. That's enough." Fam stopped that cart with the quickness.

"Alright. I'm about to be as nice as I can possibly be without raising my voice. I'm gonna tell you one more time. Get what you want. Because after this offer, there won't be any more offers. You will have to pay for it."

That's all I needed to hear. I was respectful and didn't want him spending crazy amounts of dough on me. However, since he made it clear, I was gonna rack up, at a limit. I grabbed me a few bags of pork skins, Reese's and cashews. Basically, some fat boy status foods. I was on vacation, and the words eat healthy were not in my vocabulary until I returned Tuesday to California.

"What you grab?," I asked, as we waited in line at the register.

"Man, my girls are like night and day. Ice cream man. Ice cream. There is nothing else in the world that matters to them. Ice cream. Oh, and feed. Gotta have feed man."

"The hell is feed?"

"Grub for the chickens."

"You got chickens man?"

"Boy you are getting old. Yes man. Got a gang of 'em. You don't remember us talking about it on the phone?"

"You damn sure did. Damn, maybe I am losing it."

Johnny paid for the food and we dipped out the store, headed towards the house. After two hours and some change on the road, and a bunch of cool and unusual sights, we were finally at his crib. To my surprise, it was a house, next to other houses. To keep it plain and simple, a city block with a country feel.

"Man, I expected you to be on a ranch or some shit."

"Used to man. Had a few turkeys, sheep, all that. Had to come back towards the city."

"Did you say sheep?," I asked, shutting the car door, and heading back to the trunk.

"Yea, you are getting old as dirt."

61

I let out a loud ass laugh as we headed towards the door. He opened it and the smell of good food saturated my nose.

"BRENDA!!!," Johnny shouted.

I saw a woman with a red scarf on her head come around the corner.

"Well hey. Mac, Mac, Mac."

"Yes indeed miss lady."

"Well come here and give me a hug. He has ranted and raved about you."

I walked up to the kitchen to hug her.

"Brenda, you can call me whatever you want as long as I get to taste whatever that smell good is."

She let go and laughed.

"I never knew you were a junior?"

"Yea. Well, it almost didn't happen. My mama said that my daddy said I had some chunky legs when I came out. So right then and there, he thought of a big hambone. That's how Hamilton came about. And my mama said hell no. So, I became a junior instead of a Hamilton."

She laughed hysterically, walking back towards the crockpot.

"Well look Mac. You just gone head and relax. Take your things downstairs and walk straight back. You'll be in my daughter Ella's room."

"Yea because everyone gets my room when they visit. Hey Uncle Mac." This young, energetic lady came up and hugged me.

"Well hey to you too. I done heard a lot about you. And your boyfriend."

"Yea you're gonna meet him tomorrow night," Brenda said from the kitchen.

"Umm. Yea. I'll take your bags down to the room uncle."

Johnny was just standing in the living room laughing at all of this.

"You all are crazy. What are you cooking love?"

"Bison chili."

My eyebrows raised. I thought I was tripping with what she said.

"Oh, y'all country for real," I said, taking a seat on the couch.

"Yup. Just how it is round here. Brenda came down and greeted Johnny with a kiss before taking a seat on the adjacent chair.

"So, you're originally from here to Brenda?"

"Yup. Born and raised."

"May I ask. How did you go from here, to the city with Johnny, to back here? I mean, wasn't there really an adjustment through it all?"

They both looked at each other and smiled.

"Hey Uncle."

I turned around to see his other daughter.

"Oh Mac. That's my daughter Kyla. Are you gonna give your uncle a hug. This is dad's good friend from a long time ago."

"I will in a minute mom. I'm thirsty."

"DON'T DRINK MY APPLE JUICE!!!," Ella shouted coming up the stairs.

"NO ONE IS DRINKING YOUR STANKY APPLE JUICE TURD!!!"

"BOTH OF YOU BE QUIET!!!," Brenda yelled out.

"Now, back to your question Mac. We were both raised out here. And, you're right. We were a speck of dust on a carpet floor in

63

San Diego. But, you can either make the best of it, or the worst of it. That's how we saw it."

"What about the girls?"

"Oh, these two, they're good. They don't have any problems. With how busy they stay in sports, music and reading books, they have no worries. Plus, they have left the last two summers on projects involving colleges. That gets them out of Wyoming and out of our hair for a while. So, they're okay."

"Yea uncle, and Ella just be yelling at girls in school. They're scared of her."

"I don't yell. I just tell them that I'm going to mix their face with the concrete."

"That's being mean."

"You need to be mean."

"These hands will be mean to your face."

"GIRLS!!!," both of their parents said.

"Go to your rooms. Grown people in here," Johnny told 'em.

They both walked back to the room they were sleeping in, bickering away. I was laughing. I thought the shit was funny.

"Mac, I hope you get boys. I thought girls were gonna be easy. Those two give me three strokes a day. And then one of them are dating. It's a constant terror."

"Oh, John stop. He's a good kid."

"Never good enough for my baby girl. I'll bury him in the Grand Teton Mountain Range."

"Whatever. Mac, are you ready to eat?"

"Yea but hold on. I can call him John?"

"I've never called him Johnny and never will. That's for his friends."

"Babe you know why I like to be called Johnny."

"Oh, yea sure. Because the girls called you Johnny Boy when you won the town pumpkin fest our junior year of high school. And I almost called them dead meat."

I couldn't do anything but laugh. I could tell it was a running joke in the house, but as with all jokes, there was some truth to it, and she was dead serious. She got up and fixed our food, as Johnny kept rambling on about how a man would have to jump out of a plane at 30,000 feet without a parachute and break no bones to marry any of his girls. She brought the bowls on down and we just began to indulge.

"You're not gonna call the girls," I said to Johnny, with a mouthful of tender bison chili in my mouth.

"They'll be okay," Johnny said. "Their eating habits are that of a rabbit having sex."

"Excuse me."

"Constant Mac. Constant."

"Well excuse me for not knowing how rabbits screw."

His wife spit her food out in the bowl, laughing her ass off.

"You two are going to be entertaining for these next few days I see."

We sat there, mashing this deliciousness of food, talking and bull jiving for a good while. Once done, we kind of just sat there as the night winded down.

"Man, what time is it bro?"

"8:30."

I was shocked, seeing how the sun was still shining through the blinds. "Man naw. I gotta go outside to see this."

65

I got up off the couch and walked out the front door. It was no shit still bright as hell out here at 8:30 at night. I mean, you could see the sun was about to begin its descent, but this was some beautiful shit. At 8:30 in California, the stars would already be out. I stood in front of the house for a good minute and just soaked it in. I took a deep breath. I still couldn't believe that I was breathing good air. Even crazier, a bit of the layout reminded me of some parts of Seattle. I walked out onto the street and continued down the block. I couldn't recall the last time that I simply just walked down the block. Where this street and the next street merged, I saw a little kid shooting hoops in his front yard. That was an odd sight to say the least. Then, I looked down even further, and there were kids out riding bikes. The shit was meaningful to say the least. Riding bikes with my friends was the social media of the world when I was growing up. We weren't bogged down with technology or any mess like that. It was like humans had become computers and computers had started acting more human than people. I was now standing in the middle of this intersection in awe. Watching the sun going down and having a reminder that there were humans that were still human, it was a beautiful sight to see. I concluded the night sitting with the fam in the living room, all of us, watching Major Payne. For some strange and odd reason, this was Ella's favorite movie. It was great being in a family atmosphere, seeing how I didn't have much of that. One day, I hoped to get married. However, after listening to the homey, I knew I had to be cautious. The last thing I wanted to end up with is a not knowing, nothing ass woman that lived off everyone else. Most importantly, I needed a strong woman. Not a run to mama or daddy, sensitive ass, I'm gonna kill myself every time something goes wrong woman. One of the homeys I knew experienced that. At some point, every man more than likely dealt with a shitty woman. A woman who didn't fix her shit before a relationship, that was something that I wasn't willing to deal with. His old lady, as he told me, made two attempts to kill herself. Once, he said, she grabbed a butcher knife, and if he didn't grab it from her, she was gone. The second time, she went to the patio of their condo, ready to jump. In that moment, he called her best friend, and knowing that she was on the phone, she stopped. I didn't have patience for that shit. It was one thing to go through problems. It was another to be all fucked up in the head. The movie ended and I retired to my room for the night. Ella had some interesting stuff in here. The first thing that popped out was the Green Bay Packers bedspread and sheets. Seeing how I was a Seahawks fan, due to the beast they called Marshawn Lynch, I lowkey wanted to burn these shits. However, my niece got a pass. Next, I saw what seemed to be like a hundred Lego statues of all sorts of stuff. She had a serious obsession with these things, as I saw figures and constructs of all kinds. She had books, just like her mama had said. I mean, tons of books. Having a downstairs room as well, I could just sense that she delved at least a good five hours a week into educating herself. She had two signs posted up on her makeshift library. One stated *"My other card is a library card."* The other said, *"You can have my book when you pry it from my cold dead fingers."* Seeing this, I wasn't gonna touch her books. I mean, I wasn't scared of a 14-year-old. But, as smart as she seemed, I assumed she was the type who could kill you in your sleep and leave no types of evidence. This was true to form for a basement room, as I went over to one of the small windows that looked out directly to the backyard. In the hood, this would be a boom boom room for a nasty ass teenager. Here, it was just a room. I thoroughly enjoyed my less than half day here. Tomorrow, I already knew it would be on and poppin' with whatever the fam had planned. I cut out the lights and started playing a movie on my phone. Then, I got back to thinking about how I saw those kids riding their bikes together outside. How a kid was shooting hoops in his driveway. Immediately, I cut the movie off. I swiped it over to my notepad. I stared at it for a hot minute, figuring out what to write:

Cellular

I remember when we were human, riding bikes down streets, playing hide go seek, memorizing addresses without dot com added to the end, see I remember when we were human, when 69 wasn't a sex position but a way to call someone back, when tape decks had to be rewound, when you actually talked to chicks and delivered a message that wasn't signaled in their inbox, I remember when we were human, but what we are now are just technologically sound with microchips for brains, and fingers that serve as cars traveling long distances over keyboards, these are our new versions of family trips as skype has taken the place of walking two blocks to grandma's house, see as time passed we became bored with one on one interaction and replaced it with AOL telling us we got mail, and we eventually combined 5 instruments in one to become our cell phones, cause now our life is our cell phone, we die for our cell phones, we can't exist without our cell phones, I mean we will turn the car all the way around to head back to the house for our cell phones, men, when we can't find our phones we scramble like quarterbacks cause if your woman calls a few of those numbers back all hell will break loose, women, you don't feel beautiful anymore on the inside, so you take 500 selfies, post em on the web and hope those on those outside hit like, this cell phone is something in the shape of a small box that reminds me of the box technology has encased us in, see I used write complaints to governors with a pen, but now I hit send on sex tapes and hood fights from world star and YouTube, all this from my cellular, I even have the choice to pick from different carriers, the same way humans choose to carry different diseases, so I guess when our phones catch a virus we are so close to it that it makes us sick as well, I won't be surprised if the abnormal chips in my pocket phone cause me to get sickle cell, so that's why I refuse the ESPN app, cause I may catch HIV like Magic or Cancer like Walter, all because I am this close with my cell phone, and the funny thing about phones is that they told us more about us thru their designs, we had brick phones round the same time we had hardened minds, we had flip phones when we were unsure about our mindsets, now we have I phones to show we are only concerned about I, it's easier to send that rant thru text or simply Wi-Fi, and I hate Wi-Fi, so I'll drop the W and the last I and go back to if, what if we never had these cell phones, what if conversation with a person was still face to face, what if humans didn't become computers and computers didn't start acting more human than people, cause 20 years ago I memorized all my contacts, now I lose my phone, I know no one's number by heart, so that shows you that our heart beats with a barcode, a battery and serial number attached to it, I'm just waiting for my surgery to get a charger slot embedded in my spine to be plugged up when I am low on life, because a cell phone has taken over all of our lives, so just imagine the destruction that will occur, when we all go out of service

— 3 —

THE PITS

I woke up the next day, light shining through the curtain less windows. My eyes squinted as I rolled back over and threw my head under the covers. I swear on everything, that morning light hitting you was damn near like someone lighting fire to your soul. I kept my eyes closed and continued with my sleep. When I arose, only five additional minutes had passed by. I swear I had slept for at least a whole additional hour. Shit was crazy. I got up and went to the bathroom. Pops always taught me that you could tell a lot about a person by how clean their bathroom and kitchen was. Yea, the living room could be a little junky. In the dining room, there might be some clutter on the table. But, the place where I gotta shit and eat at, oh that muthafucka better be spot on immaculate. From the looks of it, as I gave the fish additional water, with a rough shake, everything was kosher. I finished up, washed my hands, and brushed my teeth, with my own toothpaste. That was another thing that I always did when I went out of town. I kept toothpaste on deck. I only fucked with AIM and Colgate. My mouthpiece always had to be minty fresh. And, floss. A brother kept floss on him like a drug dealer kept crack. The cleanliness in between the teeth was the key to truly preventing bad breath. More so, it prevented gum disease. I had enough people I knew with black ass gums and stained teeth. I refused to be the next one. I walked upstairs to the smell of magnificence. The aroma was making my nasal passages sing old R&B tunes from the 90's.

"Morning," said Brenda. "I got antelope steaks and fresh eggs cooking up this morning. Some potatoes over here too. How'd you sleep?"

"Hold on. Did you say antelope?"

"I surely did. Don't knock it until you try it. Now, you can cook these several ways. You can deep fry 'em. John, he likes his a little seared on each side, with a nice red center. Either way, it's good and not tough at all. Try one."

She handed me one of these small steaks on a fork, which wasn't more than the size of a chicken nugget. I took a bite.

"Damn, these joints are the business."

"I told you. Wait until you throw some sauce on 'em."

I poured up some A&W that they had in the fridge. I had stopped drinking pop a long time ago. But this was my vacation and I could go back to shit that wasn't full of sugar when I got home. As I drifted down to the side door, I noticed the chickens all hovering around it outside. It was five of them.

"Look like your chickens hungry."

"Go feed 'em."

"For real?"

"Yea. The feed is in that big garbage pail in the pen. The scooper is in their as well."

I was stunned man. Like, these fools were country to the core. I never knew anybody who kept chickens in their back yard. The only shit I ever saw like this was on the movie Friday, and it was Deebo with his own bird coop, except they were pigeons. I opened the door with caution, as I didn't know if these birds were gonna attack me. These had to be some Black men reincarnated into birds, because they weren't playing no games with their feeding time. I walked out the door and the sea parted. I headed into this monster yard that had a huge ass trampoline in it. I opened the gate to the coop, and there meeting me was the rest of the clan, including a duck. Why the fuck was there a duck in here with all the chickens? That shit boggled my mind. I went over to the giant garbage pail and they had literally congregated in one spot. They were waiting on this food. Whatever it was, the shit had to be good. Finally, after some struggles, I got the lid off. It was a big ass scooper too.

"WAIT!!!"

I turned around to see Ella running towards me.

"Go ahead Uncle Mac. I just don't see Dolly. But, drop it off."

I didn't know who Dolly was, but I flipped that scooper over and the chickens went to town. It was like a free for all. I had saw people go ham at a buffet. They ain't have shit on these chickens.

"Uncle Mac, that's Thomas the Duck."

I'll be damned. The damn duck had a name. I continued watching the chickens with Ella and recording on my phone at the same time. This had to have been some of the most extraordinary shit that I had ever done. I mean, there aren't too many of us Black folks that can say we got up and fed chickens first thing in the morning.

Ella was hollering Dolly's name while walking over to the huge enclosed pen. She opened the door and I followed her inside. In here was even more amazing shit. Each chicken had their own hole, which was like their house.

"She's sitting on the eggs. She's not supposed to."

Ella reached in and grabbed Dolly. Dolly got to squawking. I can't blame her. It was early and she probably was sleep. I don't like people fucking with me either when I'm getting me some shuteye. I looked around and saw that there were several eggs, just waiting to hatch. This was some cool shit. Ella brought Dolly outside and put her down. She immediately darted for the food pile. Seemed like Dolly was just hungry as hell.

"Oh. Uncle. That spotted one is Muchacho."

"Y'all got a Mexican chicken?"

Ella laughed, but I was dead serious. All he had to do was break out into a suavemente dance and the shit would be official. I sat here for another two to three minutes with my niece, watching the birds feed. I don't know what it was doing to me, but I could feel a change occurring inside me. Once back inside the house, I washed my hands as I saw that the table was prepped for breakfast. Johnny was up, so was Kyla.

"Morning niece."

She gave me that hand wave, with her eyes half squinted. I could tell she was the one who wasn't a morning person. I don't think Ella was either. She just knew that she had to be up to feed the chickens. We joined hands and prayed before passing the bowls around.

"Take as many as you want Mac. We got steaks for days," Brenda said.

I put six of them hoes on my plate, along with the fresh eggs and some hash browns.

"Now Brenda. I noticed the eggs were sitting on the counter, in containers. You ain't gotta throw them in the fridge?"

"Not fresh ones. You can leave fresh ones out for weeks at room temperature and they'll be good to go."

That was interesting to say the least and I learned something new. I bit into my first mouthful and oh my fucking goodness, it was the best damn eggs that I had ever tasted in my life. I knew they would be different when I saw that they were a darker yellow than normal store-bought eggs.

"Put some of that green sauce on those steaks man. I'm telling you Mac. You'll be in heaven."

Johnny said all that with his mouth full, much to the chagrin of his wife. Trust me, I thought it was nasty for folks to talk with their mouth full as well, even though I did that shit all the time when I ate burritos. I put some of that green sauce on one of the steaks and bit into it. I really wanted to get up from the table and do the Bobby Shmurda dance.

"Brenda. So exactly what part of the antelope is this?"

"Well," as she said chewing her damn self, contradicting her own words. "This cut of meat is from along the spine of the antelope. That's where the best cuts of meat are at."

That was wild. You wanted prime chicken; you ate the breasts. You wanted prime pork; you had some bacon. Antelope. Cut that bitch right along his backside. We ate up, as I had a total of 11 antelope steaks and two platefuls of eggs. They told me to finish everything off, so I did just that. We had so much, however, that we had enough food to last us for the next two days, even if she didn't cook anything else. An hour passed by. I washed up and threw my clothes on. Johnny was taking me to his job today. I guess the folks at his job couldn't believe that a dude he hadn't seen in nearly 15 years would just randomly come here to see him. But hey, when you are bonded by brotherhood, no distance, whether time wise or physical, is ever too much. We linked right back up as if we had never stopped in the first place.

"Man, y'all ain't got no radio stations for real."

Johnny looked at me, laughed and shook his head.

"You thought I was lying? Man, we in the middle of nowhere. I'm happy with deer sounds."

The boy was bonafide backwoods to say the least. The drive through town wasn't anything spectacular. We drove off the main road that passed through the middle of town and into a residential. It honestly looked like any other residential I had saw, except they had much more grass. The land space out here was nuts. The prices were bomb dot com. You even think about getting something in California with a decent amount of land, and you were gonna fork over some millions. We pulled up to a building off a side street and got out. Walking around the corner, two gentlemen were talking to each other. Shockingly enough, one of them was Black. Mission number one was accomplished. See another brother in the city. You couldn't tell me shit now. I knew GET OUT wasn't going down because he still had an afro and wasn't attached to a big white woman who was using him as a sex slave. We walked in with Johnny introducing me around to all his coworkers. Not shockingly enough, most of the guys and girls here were either retired military or had served in some capacity. I thought it was some cool shit to see vets running a business to help other vets. Job placement was important, but more so to those who had come back from wars and needed a fresh start. Regardless of how you felt about a conflict or whoever is sitting in the big chair inside of The White House, you had to give it to these guys man. They put up with a lot of shit in the military.

Not saying that I put them on a pedestal, because I would never ask for that treatment, regardless of what I did. However, if you serve your country, the least this country could do was make sure that you had a job, where you had the ability to make a decent living, with a roof over your head. The crisis of homeless vets was appalling in this country. As much money that the government spent on the dumbest shit you could imagine, the least you would think is that they could set aside some funds for those that really needed it. As a famous poet named R.J. Wright said in his classic spoken word piece *Soldier's Creed*.

"What does America call the veterans that they love so much? Homeless."

We left Johnny's job, heading back to the house.

"Hey Mac. It's almost Memorial Day. Let me show you what we raised funds for."

We stopped behind the Riverton Police Department. Naturally, I was on pins and needles. I know Johnny had been here all his life, but as a Black man, you couldn't be too cautious when it came to the police. In most cases, two or more of us gathered in one place was a gang. In this part of the country, where Black was rare, you were a one-man gang. It didn't help that I had on some black sweats, a black shirt from my tattoo parlor back home and a black du-rag. I'm quite sure that I was the prime suspect in the state for any crime that occurred. We exited the car and walked out to a makeshift monument of a rifle and helmet, which was known as the battle cross. Surrounding it on the concrete, were bricks, with the names of veterans who had made the ultimate sacrifice. It was indeed intriguing to see.

"When did they put this here man?"

"We got it completed about two years ago. Just something to give us some pride you know."

It was amazing to say the least. These bricks seemed like they spoke to me. I could hear them saying hi, don't trip on us. We knew what we were getting into when we signed up for it. They indeed were the greatest generation. It reminded me of 2008, when I had visited the USS Arizona Memorial in Hawaii. Standing on the ship, where over 300 men were still buried, gave me an emotional rush. I didn't care if you were the hardest thug on the planet. You were dropping tears while there. We got back in the car and made our way back to the house. It was early so I decided to just lounge around. I plopped on the bed, expecting to just chill for a good minute.

"We'll be ready in about 10 minutes Mac."

I looked up and it was Brenda.

"Oh, we going somewhere else?"

"Remember last night we said we were going to the hot springs in Thermopolis?"

"Aww damn. You right. That chili that you cooked gave a brother the itis and I lost track of everything I was thinking about."

She laughed and walked back out. I was lowkey going nuts trying to figure what the hell I was gonna wear. Then, I remembered. We were going to jump in some water. What the hell did I need to throw on a full fit for? What I had on was perfectly fine. I headed upstairs to see Brenda in the kitchen making sandwiches.

"You want mayonnaise on yours?"

"Nah. Just whatever meat you got with some cheese."

"Mom, I want mayo?," Ella said.

"You look like Mayo," said Kyla, coming into the kitchen.

"Shut up turd."

"You're a turd."

"BOTH OF YOU TURDS SHUT UP!!!," Brenda yelled.

They rolled their eyes at each other and went their separate ways. I looked at Brenda and she just started laughing.

"Is it like that every day between those two?"

"Everyday. They go for the jugular with each other."

"Man, and I thought me and my siblings were bad."

"Y'all probably were, but y'all don't have anything on these two."

As she finished saying that, we both could hear them behind the closed door in Kyla's room yelling at each other, calling each other turds. Brenda shook her head again as she started to pack the cooler.

"Ok, this is done. You got a towel?"

"I got 'em baby."

We turned around to see Johnny. He tossed me a pink towel.

"Pink man. Really?"

"Be happy I'm giving you one of my good towels. **GIRLS!!!**"

They both came out of the room, highly irritated with each other. The shit was hilarious to me.

"Do you two have everything?"

"Yes dad," they said in unison.

Those attitudes. Wow. We got into the whip and headed down the desolate road past Walmart, and out of Riverton.

"Uncle Mac. Ella's boyfriend is coming over tonight."

"Turd," Ella responded to Kyla's out of nowhere ass statement.

"So, yea Ella, what's his name?"

"Sheesh. Its Tyler."

"What mama name they son Tyler?"

"It's not a bad name Uncle Mac."

"Mac," Johnny said. "You're not the only one who wonders. I asked the same question when she first told me. Like when you see him, the first thing you will think of is Shaggy from Scooby Doo. I couldn't believe it. I was looking for the mystery machine outside of the house and a Great Dane."

"He's that ugly huh?"

"HE'S NOT UGLY UNCLE MAC!!!"

I couldn't help but laugh my ass off with that one. Ella got no shit pissed off. However, I quickly snapped back into uncle mode, because a young man was still dating my niece.

"I gotta check young homey temperature."

"I don't think the kid is sick or anything."

"Nah man. Nah. It's a figure of speech around the way. Basically, I must chastise him. Make sure he has a good head on his shoulders, except I have to do it very aggressively."

"Okay. I get it now. I've tried to find something wrong with the kid, and I swear I can't. He's respectful, good in school, goes to church, stays in sports. He picks her flowers from the family farm."

I turned around with the quickness. Brenda was sitting in the back cracking up.

"What you mean he be bringing you flowers?"

"I mean, he's sweet Uncle Mac."

"Yea, a sweet turd," Kyla whispered.

"Be quiet turd."

"You're a turd, and Uncle Mac is gonna kill him."

"I surely will baby."

This was the funniest shit I had ever experienced. Ella was pissed right now. She didn't know that I was fucking with her. Kyla didn't make it any better. We continued with conversation flowing, with a few antelope roaming the plains. We got to a point and slowed down dramatically.

"Why you slowing down bruh?"

"Man, we in Shoshoni."

"Oh, this that small one light town. I remember."

"Yea," Brenda interrupted. "Their two-man police department doesn't have shit better to do but to pull people over."

"Mom."

"Sorry baby."

Ella sure knew when to call something out I tell you. We stopped at the gas station to fill up. It was crazy that I had already been up here with no problems, yet I was feeling nervous again. This time, I was with three white women. I didn't tell Johnny, but the last woman he introduced me to at his job, her energy spoke volumes. She didn't want me in that office. I felt it, but I smiled, because I didn't want to draw attention to it. If my skin made you uncomfortable, then I wasn't the one who needed to grow up. They say that 90% of all human communication is nonverbal. Trust, people sometimes said the loudest statements in sheer silence. I walked in and everything was normal like before. Everyone here was minding their business. I copped me my usual. Pork skins and a Reese's. When I got up to the cashier, I saw the thickest white girl I could imagine. She was so nice and polite, but just the fact that I saw that ass from the front was crazy. I don't know if she was on the Kanye West workout plan, but whatever she was on, she could damn sure keep it up. I walked back out to the car right as Johnny had finished filling up. We took off and hit a left at the light. Next thing I know, I didn't see shit but mountains, sky and cliffs. I mean, like jagged cliffs. One good shake of the earth and one of those sharp ass boulders were coming down.

"That's the lake where there are a lot of good fish at?," Johnny said.

I looked to my left and saw what he was talking about.

"That's what's up man. How many times you been out there?"

"Oh, every blue moon or so. It's a peaceful feeling. Have you ever fished on the open water?"

"Nah man. I mean, played with a few fishing joints off a pier when I was a kid, but never way out there."

"Yea my father in law has some boats. It's almost a religion to him. We'll see if we can head out there and see if we can catch a few."

"Cool man."

I enjoyed the ride with all the beautiful scenery. This wasn't anything like anywhere that I had ever been before. Hell, just breathing the clean, crisp mountain air was something to marvel in.

"Alright girls. Show uncle what we do."

"What you talking about Brenda?"

"Ahh," Johnny said. "It's this tradition when you go through the mountain tunnels out here that everyone in the car screams and I honk the horn like crazy."

I just looked at 'em. This was white people shit indeed. We came up on the first tunnel. The car let out a huge roar. Johnny was blasting his horn like he had lost his damn mind. I had all this madness on video and I was falling over in the front seat cracking the fuck up. Why did something so out of the ordinary feel like a once in a lifetime experience? The noise stopped, and then continued when we got through the second tunnel. Again, it stopped once we got out, and started again once we entered the third and final tunnel. We drove for what seemed like forever. This place was truly out in the boondocks. Hell, all of Wyoming was the boonies. I couldn't even imagine living here when it came to some things. Man, if some shit happened, like your car broke down on the side of the road, I was wondering how would you report that? Telling the deputies that you're on the side of a freeway, on interstate whatever, by a big ass red cliff. It was crazy just to think about it. We got within the town city limits after about an hour and some change.

"Look man. You got your own liquor store."

I looked over to my right after Johnny said that. The sign literally said Mac's Bar and Package Liquor.

"Oh snaps. Yo, I gotta get a pic under that sign when we leave."

This was Thermopolis. Now, here's the crazy shit. When you thought about Wyoming, a few things came to mind. Stretches of uninhabited land. Elk. Lots of damn elk. Mountains, Yellowstone National Park, nature, all that. You never thought about violence. I mean, if you go back to Butch Cassidy and the Sundance Kid, then I guess you could say that for their robberies they committed throughout Wyoming, Montana, and parts of Utah. Well, here, in this town, a heinous murder was committed years ago that I once saw while watching Forensic Files. It was a kid; I believe he was 16 or something like that. He was charged, tried, and sentenced to life for a quadruple murder of his entire family. He killed his mom and three younger brothers. That ain't some shit that you would expect in Wyoming. Reading up on the story, of course it was the typical narrative. He was a good kid, good athlete and people couldn't fathom how he could've done that. Of course, that was part of the privilege of being white in America. A perceived resume would always trump the real problem. Had it been a Black kid, he would've been an animal, thug, unworthy of the skin he was in. Most of all, he would've been executed at the quickest moment possible. Knowing this country, they would've probably gone full slave days and hung him in the middle of town, with a crowd gathered, and hailed it as a celebration of preserving white existence. It was indeed a sad situation all around. Driving through town, it honestly looked like the country regurgitated its little brother. At least Riverton had a Walmart. It wasn't shit here but the simple mom and pop joints. We passed the high school. I balled my face up. Shit looked more like an administration building than a high school. We drove down probably another 30 seconds and we were here.

"This the hot springs?"

"Yea man. It has a smell to it. It's the sulfur," Johnny said.

"Sulfur?"

"Yea man. Trust me. You ain't gone die."

The family exited the car and I followed suit.

"Bruh. Didn't you deal with this shit enough in your military days? You were a plumber correct?"

"Yea, but unlike on the ship, the sulfur isn't coming from human turds." He raised his eyebrows and walked off. I shook my head and followed them in. We changed in the locker room, meeting Brenda and the girls in the lobby. We walked out to the pool. The smell of the sulfur and whatever other minerals they said were in here were strong as fuck now. I ain't gone lie. I was highly skeptical.

"Man, this stank."

"Just get in," Brenda said.

Everyone else was already in, but I was still hesitant. I grabbed my phone and decided to record myself just in case I walked in this pool and died. I hit record and spent time giving a final message. When I stepped in with that first step, something changed. The warmth of the water was one thing. The smell, it didn't even bother me anymore. Once I brought my other foot in, the shit felt like something was stripping negativity off my body. I immediately got out, put my phone on the chair and with the quickness, got my Black ass back in that water. The fam was at the basketball rim in the pool goofing around, but I was on some other shit. Your spirit literally felt like it left your body. I was more amazed that I felt like I was watching myself for some other dimension. If you really wanna know what death felt like, you found it here. I saw why my grandma said she was tired and ready to go years ago. Knowing this feeling, I wasn't rushing death by no means. However, when that time came, I would indeed be happy that my time was arriving. I got into the activities with the family. The adults, we decided that we were going to play horse and just enjoy this. As always, I started to observe my surroundings. For the most part, there were a bunch of old people in the pool, trying to get their youth back. As I took a shot, I saw a group of youth come in. One boy looked like he hadn't missed a meal in all his life. His titties were bigger than some strippers that I had seen in my day. A gothic girl was in the group, looking like she was gonna drop a voodoo curse on someone. Then, there was the rainbow haired kid, who was obviously gay by his mannerisms. Deep down, it was different, but some cool shit to see. These kids today, they had a whole other battle than we had growing up. If you were gay, you didn't say that shit. You kept that on the low. If you were goth, with whom I had quite a few interactions with during grade school, you didn't fuck with them. You were too scared that they were gonna burn a house down or some shit. Being different in my day was considered some weird shit, but we let everyone do them. Now, with the internet and all the social media shit that was going on, it was a totally different ball game. Bullying was different in my day. You got bullied, and you fought back to let that muthafucka know not to fuck with you. Now, kids are bred different. Either they are committing suicide, shooting up schools, stabbing classmates, or worse, taking it out on a family who has a hard time accepting them, or doesn't want to. I looked at my nieces Ella and Kyla as they were wrestling with each other and calling each other turds. God forbid that one of them would choose to be different in any way that normal people couldn't accept. I wouldn't even think about not accepting them for who they are, even if it wasn't too my liking. Times was different, and whether we liked it or not, that's just how the cookie crumbled. Trust, I would never cosign the feminization of the Black man, wearing female clothes or any of that shit. However, I did realize we were in different times. I just hoped people knew that when I did spoken word, my feelings were gonna be my feelings, and I wasn't gonna dumb down my words to satisfy them. I had more than enough run ins with the LGBT community and people who proclaimed I was promoting division. Just because I don't preach the expansion of your lifestyle, didn't mean I hated you. And just because I told you directly how it was to be a Black man in this country, didn't mean I was anti-white. For those who couldn't comprehend that, it was fuck 'em, and I continued with my life. I was kicking Brenda and Johnny ass in horse. This shit was fun to say the least.

"What in the hell," I said, as I felt something tugging at my leg. It was Ella, as she came up laughing. That's when I proceeded to grab her and hit her with a rock bottom in the pool. This continued for the next half hour. Kyla wasn't about that wrestling life, but Ella was. These two were so night and day. Ella literally had the energy of 50 people. My old ass was tired after five minutes. Her motor ran on premium fuel and got 70 miles to the gallon. I hit her with a few Brock Lesnar F5's, some John Cena attitude adjustments, an RKO out of nowhere and a plethora of other wrestling moves. By the time we were getting out of the pool, two hours had elapsed. It truly was two hours of family madness that I wouldn't trade for all the riches in the world. We showered up and met back at the car.

"We gone make a stop at the actual heated pools. Wanna see them?" "Yea. Heck yea."

The drive was two minutes, if that. We stopped and got out the car. One cliff side road had the gate down, as its access to traffic was restricted on this day. Brenda was upset, because whatever was up there, she really wanted me to see.

"Well, it's some more over here," she said.

We walked over to the natural hot springs in the other direction that were sizzling out of the earth. I mean, the site of this was amazing. Johnny and the girls walked down further, as I stayed at the sign, reading it.

"*Long before the arrival of fur trappers in the West, Native Americans discovered the hot mineral springs, found in the park. The Shoshoni Indians called the springs BAH GUEWANA -meaning smoking water, and the Crow Indians called them MEDICINE WATERS.*"

I stood at the sign in amazement, just in awe of the history lessons I was receiving from some dead ancestors. I say ancestors because the Natives were us.

"WHAT YOU SAY BRENDA???!!!," I shouted, not hearing what she had told me.

"127 DEGREES!!!."

"Wow."

That was crazy. 127-degree water with medicinal purposes. I didn't question that Native Americans at all. They thrived so much without European influence and sustained everything they had, much like the Ancient civilizations of Kemet. But, again, whenever Euro influence put their hands on something, they fucked it all up. I went down to the base of the hot springs where the family was. My phone was recording this because I wanted to remember this moment for the rest of my life. The girls were dipping their hands in and out. Me, I got on both knees and bent down. The smell was still terrible, but it was nuts watching the smoke come off the water. I lowered my hand and skimmed it across the water. Yea, that shit was hot. I did it two more times, hoping that whatever I had in me, that wasn't pure, was out of me. I got up and looked around at my surroundings. The cliffs, mountains and open terrain looked very much different now. I was feeling different. I don't know if it was the water, or just the realization that I was out here in Wyoming. Either way, the shit was life changing. We left for the car and started heading back into town. The girls were in the back complaining over what to eat. The adults, we wanted solid food. However, the spawns of evil wanted milkshakes. In all of this, I later realized we all totally forgot we had a cooler of sandwiches. We hit Main Street in Thermopolis, which was their downtown. As I looked up, anger came over my face.

"So, I see they're real open with it here huh Brenda?"

"What do you mean Mac?"

"Right there. That building," I said, pointing to it.

She looked out the window and saw what I was referring to. There was a building at the end of the block, with about six swastikas near its rooftop.

"I'm sorry you had to see that, but hopefully I can explain the actual history behind it. We'll talk when it's just us and not the girls.

"Why can't we hear it mom?"

"Cause you're not grown Kyla."

I hadn't heard Brenda with a stern voice this whole time. Kyla froze up. The questioning was over. It was like she knew she struck a nerve, and that the next question might result in a backhand. Regardless of what was to be said, I was no shit pissed to see it. It was something else that they stole from us and turned into evil. We hit a U turn at the end of the street and came back towards the light, stopping in front of a nutrition store. I got my phone out, recording all my experiences once again. We walked in and the smell itself had good oxygen written all over it. I lifted weights, and if I had this joint at the crib, I would marry her. It was organic everything. The girls got their milkshakes and I ordered mines. Peanut butter and chocolate.

"Wow Mac. Same old stuff huh?"

"You know me man. Nothing is better than the PB. Where the girls go?"

"They ran across the street to the arts store," Brenda said. "Ella loves beads. She makes a bunch of stuff out of beads. She is an art fanatic." Brenda's milkshake came and we headed back out, walking across the street to the art store. Once inside, I noticed Kyla was off in her own world, looking at whatever. Ella, on the other hand was rummaging through the beads as if she were looking for a needle in a haystack. If writing and spoken word was my savior, then art was hers. I started to look around myself. These Wyoming shirts were hitting something serious. I was a fitted cap guru, but if I couldn't find a good fitted cap, then a good shirt would do. We stayed in here about 15 minutes. The swastikas had me a little on edge. I made sure that as I looked, I kept an eye on the guy behind the register. Odd, I know. It was usually the other way around. I wasn't about to be caught slipping and catch five in the back from an owner who suspected me of stealing, or some other shit. The girls were now at the cashier, and I made my way to join 'em. He was surprisingly polite in welcoming me to his state and didn't give me a side eye for my complexion. I knew it was genuine due to the feeling in my spirit. Nazi shit on one end of the street, and humble white man at the end. The irony was mind boggling. We bounced out and started the drive back home.

"Hey man. You wanna stop and get a picture under that sign right?"

"Hell yeah man. Oops. Sorry Brenda. Didn't mean to curse in front of the girls."

"It's okay. They here the pastor say hell so much in church that it doesn't bother them."

"Hell isn't a curse word," Ella said.

"When you say hell it is," Kyla responded.

"Can both of you shut the hell up?"

Once mama said that, the games were over with. Johnny pulled up to the liquor store which had my name.

"I NEED A FEW GOOD ONES MAN!!!"

Johnny was just laughing as I hit different poses under the sign. MAC'S BAR AND PACKAGE LIQUORS. It was amazing indeed. Now, if only they were open so that a brother could get some Henn Dog. Being out here had me missing Undisputed, and Uncle Shannon was my motivation to keep the henny flowing through my system on occasion. We got back to the house around five in the evening. Gary, one of their Mexican friends around here was coming over to make burritos. Homey had the only Mexican food truck out here and was killing the game. I loved burritos, but I would be the final authority on the say so of him having some good shit. Outside of that, Ella's boyfriend was coming over and today was judgment day. I showered up extra nice. I had to be clean for the guests. Aight, fuck the bullshit. I want to get clean, gloss up these tattoos, so when he walked his ass in the house, he'd know who he was dealing with. I don't know why we were like this as men. Actually, yea I do. We remembered all the shit that we use to try and pull with someone's daughter. We weren't gonna let that fly with the girls in our life, especially our nieces. Daddy's are crazy, but uncles are plum nuts. I got dressed in some sweats, a wife beater, tied up the du-rag and went upstairs to the kitchen to fix me a drink. Brenda was in there, washing dishes and getting everything together. I heard the doorbell ring. Johnny opened the door and you could hear the conversation going on. There were several people over, so this was gonna be an eventful night. I heard Ella come out of the room and one of the parents greeting her. Then, I heard his name. Tyler. I took a sip of the A&W I poured up and walked out the kitchen to see him.

"Oh Tyler. This is my Uncle Mac."

The first thing I noticed is that this boy really did look like Shaggy from Scooby Doo. An ugly joker he was, but I guess person-ality really matters. His parents were looking over at us like oh shit, the angry Black man is in the building.

"How you doing young man?"

I walked down the three steps and extended my hand. He ex-tended his and I gave him a strong ass grip. I squeezed his shit with the most malicious intent, as I inadvertently told him through my

91

handshake that I will fuck you up if you hurt my niece and bury you under Yellowstone. I then introduced myself to his folks and the night continued. Everything was chill to say the least. We sat around the dining room table making jokes and getting to know each other on a deeper level. Gary was in the kitchen finishing up the burritos he was making, while his kids were in the living room doing what bad ass little kids do. Johnny was a bit more laid back throughout all of this. This was the Wyoming in him. Had he been from Compton or some shit, he may have lost his marbles with all these damn kids. You know old, Black grandmas and how there was no playing in the house at all. Luckily, they weren't tall enough to reach one of the moose heads that hung on the wall. Their bad asses would've probably taken it and ran down the street with it.

"So, Tyler. How long you been dating my niece?"

The whole table got quiet, aside from Brenda letting out a chuckle. I had to hold my laughter in.

"Umm. A while sir."

"You treat her right?"

"Yes sir."

"You spoil her?"

"Yes sir."

"Ok. Cause that's my baby. Kyla my baby too, but you know Ella is my crazy, psycho, yet sweet niece. You know I'm good with a shovel." "Okay," Brenda interrupted. "Food smells delicious. Lemme go check on the burritos."

Ella kicked me under the table and looked at me with her eyes all big. A smirk came across my face and I raised my eyebrows up at her. She knew I was fucking with him. I don't know if he knew it, nor his parents. They may have only seen chill Black folks if they

92

had even seen any. I had to show my ass when it came to my babies. Gary came in the dining room and started to pass around plates of this burrito goodness. You know me. I had to analyze it. It wasn't as phat as the ones that I was accustomed to, but for a home cooked joint, it was a decent size. The smell coming off it started a party inside of my nasal cavity. The kiddos got down, as they didn't wait for a prayer or none of that bow your head shit. All the adults were steady chit chatting, and here I was still staring at it. I looked over and saw Gary's toddler daughter, standing next to me, pacifier in her mouth, looking like she wanted to kill me.

"You wanna come up little mama?"

I reached my hands out, but she ain't budge. She was giving me that look saying I don't know you like that homey, and you on my turf. What set you from? Kids were amazing. I went back to looking at my plate. I grabbed it and took my first bite. Immediately, I went back to the day that I lost my virginity. That's how good this shit was. I don't know if he was originally from Wyoming, but this Mexican here definitely could compete in Cali with these joints.

"Gary, man, what's in here?"

"Shredded chicken. As in freshly killed, cut up, non-processed chicken. Two types of beans, my special sauce, cilantro and some other secret stuff."

Man, fuck Victoria's Secret. I wanted to know the secret to how he mastered this goodness in Wyoming of all places.

"Jesus Uncle Mac. Did you breathe?"

"Kyla, baby. You'll understand one day the goodness of what they call a burrito."

"Yeah turd. He lives in California."

"I was just asking him a question."

"Well it's obvious he knows about burritos."

"You look like a burrito."

"And your burrito is stuck in your braces."

I bust into sheer laughter, because the girl did have a huge piece of chicken stuck in her braces.

"Is this everyday Brenda? I have two girls myself and they haven't been nice to each other since they were born," said Tyler's dad.

"Yea, but, if they're not arguing, then I know something is wrong."

Both girls left the table and went in the room. Tyler got up and followed, and I stared a hole through him. I knew nothing was gonna happen, but let me hear one knock against the wall, and I was determined to put his head as a mantle on the wall. In a Black household, this would never fly. They would've had their ass in the living room, and he wouldn't have been allowed to go further than that. Time passed, we slowly got full and contracted that God blessed itis. Somehow, we all managed to make it to the living room. Brenda and Johnny had a huge ass projector television.

"What are we watching guys?," Brenda asked.

"Major Payne."

I turned around to see it was Ella running towards the living room. "Mom, can we watch Major Payne?"

"Ughh. You always wanna watch Major Payne," Kyla clapped back.

"So what. I like Major Payne."

"You are a major pain."

"GIRLS!!!," every adult said in unison.

"Mac, do you want to take them back to Cali with you?"

"Nah I'm good man."

"I don't blame you Uncle Mac. She's a pain, who likes to watch Major Payne. Take me."

"Why would he take you? I'm sure he doesn't have metal cleaner for you to gargle with."

"Aight y'all hush," I told them.

"Darn it. We're watching A League of Their Own."

Brenda and the girls started moaning and complaining. I looked at Tyler and he ain't give a fuck about what was going on. He was just sitting on the stairs, playing on his phone. His parents, they were off on the couch having their own convo.

"So, wait everyone. Wait. Which are we watching? Major Payne or A League of Their Own?"

"Mom," Kyla said. "Dad always watches A League of Their Own. A League of Their Own is an old movie."

All the adults looked at her.

"You calling us old Kyla?," Tyler's father asked.

"I mean no, but."

"She's calling everyone old," I said.

"Are you crying Kyla? Really? There's no crying in baseball."

With Ella's words, the whole room literally started cracking up. Damn the movie. The events occurring in this living room was a Netflix comedy special. Finally, we settled on A League of Their Own. We sat there for the next two hours in silence, enjoying this time. Occasionally, I would glance over and look at Ella with her head on Tyler's shoulder watching the movie. Man, the kid was cool. I liked him. I just couldn't let him know that. I know what puppy love is like, as we more than likely have all been through it when we were in high school. Time went by quick and it was now nearly eleven o'clock. We all hugged each other, said our goodbyes, and I especially gave a good, firm goodbye to Tyler. As we shook hands again, I gave him that brother dap, pulled him in and combined it with one of those old granddaddy back slaps. You know when old folks asked how you were doing; they gave you the meanest back slap known to man. It was just me letting him know that I liked him, and I would haunt him forever. As the house once again got quiet and I retired to my room, I sat there looking through old YouTube clips of David Banner speeches. Thank God for this Wi-Fi because my signal here was dead to the world. The universe for that matter. I loved the gems dude would drop. To see the growth from his first album to where he is now, it was nothing short of amazing. Hell, we all should be growing daily. After watching 20 minutes worth, I wanted to read. I passionately believed that everyone should read at a minimum of 20 minutes before bedtime. I googled David Banner interviews. One popped up from Billboard Magazine, and you could tell they didn't alter his words, or none of that shit. You know some publications will get direct words from a person and twist the shit to fit their narrative. Nah, not with this one. One portion struck a chord with me. It was when he was asked what he was going through when he was recording the God Box album, which in my opinion is something that needs to be in everyone's rotation. Any who, when he was asked on that, this was how he responded.

"We rappers always say that we're keeping it a hunnid. But right now our people are struggling and are going through a social shift. And I believe Donald Trump has a lot to do with it. We're now forced to be more conscious. A lot of the things people have been talking about socially, we thought it was over! Because of the way this president acts, it put back in the face of the world.

Black people knew what was happening every day in the hood, we knew cops were beating the shit out of us. That was nothing new. But for the other people who washed their miseries of white supremacy away by moving away from the situation, it never changed for the average black person. It used to be our job to be the CNN for the hood -- to tell our side of the story to the world, because CNN and FOX isn't doing so. Now rappers are pandering to brands and labels, and not accurately telling what's going on in the streets.

And the other thing is, if you are what you listen to, and all we ever hear is nigga and bitch, how can we expect our kids to be anything more than what we put in our ear? I didn't believe it was any other rappers' responsibility, God put that on me.

We have certain experiences that we feel other people know, but maybe that's your experience. Maybe it's up to you to teach. And I'm a grown man now -- some of these rappers are young enough to be my kids. I see a lot of rappers who are my age, and some who are much older than me, still doing teenage music. How are they gone grow if they don't get knowledge from the elders? I'm not saying I don't like having fun or that I don't kick it, but there's enough of that. We as black people have to be careful to not turn into a caricature. There's more to our culture. So I just felt it was my responsibility as a man.

The thing that bothers me sometimes is that different magazines and websites always criticize rappers for not doing better. But when someone does do it, they don't put in the same effort that they put behind when our lives are in jeopardy or when we're tearing each other down. It took Charlemagne to say The God Box was one of the best albums of the year. I heard that from smaller, more white-based sites. This was a conscious, revolutionary album. But one of my elders told me it's gonna take a while for others to catch up and to just be patient.

We actually created a "god box" for the album. I took a lot of the things that helped me become conscious: the Hidden Colors 3 DVD that I did with Nas, the Black Friday DVD that was about finance, the book that introduced me to consciousness when I was in 11th grade called The Browder Files, a chopped-and-screwed version of the album, a version of the Black Liberation flag that I created. One magazine said it was one of the dopest marketing schemes that they ever seen. But I said that the reason why I think the boxes did so well was because it wasn't a marketing scheme. I wanted to help people get to where I am now just a little bit quicker.

With that read, my mind was once again concentrated on drifting to sleep. As my eyes adjusted to the darkness, I swore I heard wood creaking. I looked up and my door was cracked. I know damn well I had closed the door behind me. Ain't no fucking way this house had better be haunted. I didn't fuck with ghosts. I immediately grabbed my phone to hit the flashlight feature. However, before I could do that, I felt the bed move on the end. I jumped out of bed, not knowing what in the good fuck was going on. I ran over to the wall by the door to hit the light switch. Once on, the shock of my life occurred. It was their two cats, sitting on the bed, staring at me, as if they were saying, what the fuck is your problem dawg? Ratatouille and Daisy were their names. Rat pack for short, she was all white and looked evil as all to be damn. Daisy, she was the don't fuck with me cat, who stared a hole through you. It didn't mean necessarily that she was evil. It just meant that she wasn't to be fucked with. After getting my breathing back under control, I went and sat back on the bed. Ratatouille crawled up on me and relaxed, like she was checking my temperature before she threw them paws.

Daisy, on the other hand, she wasn't having none of that cuddle shit. She jumped back down and started investigating my shoes. My forces were mostly white and she was mostly black, so I was seeing that race shit was popping, even with the cats. I sat up on the edge of the bed, rubbing Ratatouille for a while. She looked up at me after about 30 seconds and just continued to stare. This may have been Wyoming, but these cats were from Dade County. Finally, they vamped back out the door. I went back over to the light switch, cut it off, shut the door completely this time, and got back under those covers.

"AHH DAMN!!!"

I lifted the covers from over my head.

"DAMN MAN!!! FUCK!!!"

I let out one of those deadly ass anthrax type farts. Shit was loud and smelling like old cabbage and boot soles. My asshole was about to have a long night. Once atomic fusion was out from under this thick ass Packers blanket, I put my head right back under the covers and crashed out. I hoped the kids didn't walk in here waking me up first thing in the morning. They were gonna pass out the minute they opened the door.

— 4 —

FEELING YELLOW

Growing up, the only Stones Black people rocked with were the P. Stones out of Chicago. Anything dealing with mother nature as far as mountains, cliffs, any of that, we didn't mess with. In saying that, the crazy shit is that a realization hit me as soon as I got up. I'm about to go to Yellowstone National Park. Yes, I said it right. Yellowstone National Park. Folks probably were thinking okay, ya Black ass gone get messed up, going up there, fucking with mother nature. I used to think the same way. However, you only live once, and I for damn sure was ready for this adventure. All the shit I saw on National Geographic was finally about to come to fruition. I got up and stretched. It smelled bad in this room. That burrito had really set my asshole on fire. If I lit a match right now, half of this damn state would explode, and the UN would've had to declare a worldwide emergency. I walked out the room to the sounds of conversation upstairs. It seems like for once I was the last one up. Usually, I'm the first one up. I brushed that halitosis breath of mine while letting the shower water run. I needed a good, crispy hot shower this morning to open those pores. After a Listerine swish and literally boiling the dirt off my ass, I walked back into the room.

The smell was still lingering in here. I went and cracked open the window. I had to let some air in here or else I would die by my own hand. As I looked out the window, I found myself staring out in amazement like I hadn't looked at this backyard the past two days. The giant trampoline and chicken coop still had me in awe. I wasn't used to this, but it had opened my eyes up to a wonder of the world that I know a lot of people from where I'm from could never imagine. I still had to pinch my damn self. I was really in Wyoming. I was really staying with white friends. I was the token Black guy. A Black Caucasian if you think about it, because niggas weren't known to do shit like this. Eat antelope, feed chickens, look at moose heads. That wasn't us. And the craziest shit of all is that I wasn't scared to be out here. I wasn't in fear of my life. Skeptical at times, but never fearing. That's one thing my pops taught me. You never live in fear. If shit is gone happen, then it's gone happen. Now, I am not talking about being stupid and walking down the street with your hat broke off to the left in a hood full of Gangster Disciples, or purposely red flagging in 60's turf in L.A. Naw, not that type of having no fear, because that type of fear would have you buried six feet under with niggas putting your face on an t-shirt. I'm talking about being Black and diving into unchartered waters. That was the crazy deal with a lot of us. We became so used to our surroundings, that some of us didn't wanna see anything else besides our surroundings. We were bred to embrace the hood, yet not smart enough to leave the place that took life away from us. It sucked it out of us as individuals. Sure, it's easy for people to say, why don't you help rebuild the hood and stay in it? What good would it do to rebuild a hood, when the people in the hood wouldn't rebuild their mindset? It boggled me at times. So, especially with this trip, I wasn't gonna let white America scare me into not going everywhere. My ancestors built this muthafucka. As far as I was concerned, they were living on our land rent free, and it was time to collect back pay. I threw on my royal blue hoodie, which I got made at one of the many swap meets in Cali. L.A. vs EVERYBODY is what it said. Sorry Seattle. I was feeling real SoCal today. I threw on my jeans, royal blue and white forces, and looked in the mirror. That blue had hit different since Neighborhood Nip had passed. Niggas was really fucked up behind his passing because it was typical hood shit. I don't give a fuck what you thought about the music, or his past. The fact is that he told the real, he kept it 100 and he moved as a G should move. Investments, prosperity, all of that. I still remember being on Crenshaw watching his funeral procession. The shit was beyond ill to see. It was indeed a celebration, but one that shouldn't have occurred prematurely. The most amazing thing about it all was to see all the sets coming together for unity. It was like those boys in Chicago with Hoover and Fort back in the 80's. The sets came together out there. 60's next to 20's. Hoovers next to Bounty Hunters. Denver Lanes, Playboy Crips, Crenshaw Mafia, East Coast Crips, everyone and they fucking mama was out there. Even old ass grannies who couldn't walk no more were on the blocks, paying their last respects to the great Ermias Joseph Asghedom. I walked upstairs to the smell of antelope.

"Good morning y'all."

"Morning," Brenda and John said in unison.

I went for the bagged-up antelope steaks because I was gone smash some more of these before we bounced.

"So how long is the drive to Yellowstone?"

"About three hours Mac," Brenda replied.

"Oh wow."

"Yea. Everything is far out here."

"Yea I gotta remember this is nothing to you. I was still shocked you would've picked me up in Billings if I would've flown there."

"No really. We don't mind. When you live in Wyoming, driving becomes second nature to you."

"Morning Ella," I said to her, as I saw her walk in the kitchen.

"Mom," as she said with the most irritating look on her face. "Kyla's being a turd and hogging the bathroom."

"I wasn't hogging it. You just got up to late and mad I took my time." "Shut up turd."

"You hush turd."

"Both of you turds be quiet and get the rest of your stuff on," Brenda said.

I was laughing and Josh was just shaking his head in the corner of the kitchen, eating an antelope burrito.

"Those your nieces Mac."

"Yea. Don't remind me."

I warmed up my steaks and headed outside to peep the chickens. Soon as I walked up to the gate, they rushed the cage door, knowing that feeding frenzy madness was about to occur. However, they were gonna wait, because I damn sure was gone finish these last two steaks before I gave them anything.

"Excuse me Uncle Mac?"

I turned around to see it was Kyla coming up behind me.

"I thought Ella fed the chickens."

"Yea well she's being a turd this morning. **HOW BOUT YOU FEED YOUR CHICKENS TURD!!!**"

"HEY, I'M NOT GONNA INTERRUPT YOUR FAMILY TIME WITH YOUR COUSINS TURD!!!"

That clap back Ella said from the window was savage. Oh boy, these two. If they weren't dropped on their head as babies, then they damn sure gave each other headbutts at a young age.

"Kyla, why y'all always going at each other like that?," I asked, scooping up some chicken feed.

"I don't know. We have like this weird, loving relationship. She's my sister, but she's a turd."

"So, who called who a turd first?"

"She probably did when I was born. But I'm taller than her now, so she's upset that she's older but shorter."

I just shook my head. I knew siblings had rivalries, but this one took the cake.

"Uncle Mac?"

I turned around and saw it was Ella.

"Yea baby."

"Did you fart in my room last night?"

"Umm."

"Umm yes you did. Even the window didn't take the smell out. Yuck. Smells like Kyla."

"Well someone needed to fart on that ugly Packers blanket."

"Better than a Cowboys lover."

"I don't even watch football."

"Yea well if you did, you would surely be a Cowboys fan. Loser recognizes loser."

I turned around and hollered. Ella was in my good graces now. Anyone who hated the Dallas Cowboys was a friend of mines. We went back in the house so we could grab everything and help load up the car. We had everything for a full day in the wilderness. Turkey and ham sandwiches, Gatorade's, and snack bars.

"We're leaving in 15 minutes, so girls go back and make those beds up." **"MOM!!!"**

"Mom nothing. Go."

They both made the ugliest faces and went back in the house. Brenda looked at me, shook her head and started laughing.

"Girls Mac."

"I don't want any."

As Brenda went back in, I took the time to breathe in this crisp air. I sat on the front patio and just stared into the sky. Pops was up there, granny was up there, a few more family and friends as well. However, it was one thing that plagued me more than anything. My nephew was locked up. 16 years old and already in the system. I know that every man is responsible for his own destiny, but how could you be when your surroundings raised you to be a nigga more than a king? It was like he had a third strike at birth, but he got the chance to get some extra swings in. He had struck out and it was fucking with me hard. I somehow felt responsible because I knew hadn't been around. If I had never moved, I don't believe that he would've fallen. Then, I remembered something that my daddy taught me. You gotta do what's best for you. That's exactly what I did. I couldn't save everyone, nor could I be active in everyone's life like they wished me too. At some point, individuals had to take responsibility, and Mac couldn't, nor wouldn't be bogged down with blame. I sat there and thought about that for a good five minutes. This trip was slowly but surely curing my depression, expelling my inner demons, and helping me release all the other shit that was going on within my world. I may not have been moving it out of my life, but I was damn sure learning how to live through trauma.

"Ok. Does everyone have everything? Once we leave, you know that we aren't turning around for anything."

Before Brenda pulled off, we doubled, tripled checked our pockets and anything else we thought we may have needed before taking off.

"Does anyone need to use the bathroom?"

"Hey turd do you have to drop a few turds before we leave?"

"Only on your face Kyla."

John smacked his forehead. Brenda shook hers. I just laughed. I guess Saturday was roast your sister day, because these two hadn't stopped since early this morning. She backed out of the driveway and we hit the roads of Riverton.

"Oh yea. Her boyfriend is coming with us Mac."

I turned around doing the Birdman hand rub to Ella with the evilest grin on my face.

"Uncle Mac, please don't hurt him."

"I won't baby. I'm gonna just chop his body up into 50 pieces and bury a piece in each state."

"That's worse than hurting him."

"Ok. But, if he tries to get touchy, I'm quite sure it's some hungry bears out there in Yellowstone that just woke up from an extended winter nap."

Her eyes rolled up into her skull as if she were the Undertaker. Kyla and her mom began to laugh. Johnny didn't care. He was simply happy someone who hated Ella having a boyfriend as much as him was there. The drive to his house was five minutes away.

"Oh. Uncle Mac. His brother likes Kyla."

"Does not."

"Does too."

"Who's this boy Ella?"

"You'll see him when we pull up. He's always in the field messing around with the tractor, the horses or whatever other chore his mom has him doing at the time."

"What's his name baby?"

"Ricky."

"**RICKY!!!** Pretty Ricky what they call him. Nah. Let's get here. Pretty Ricky Fontaine gotta see me."

Brenda was laughing her ass off. We pulled up to the house.

"I'll go get him," Ella said.

"Hold on Ella. Is that Ricky by the tractor?"

"Yea that's him."

I looked at Brenda. I then turned back and looked at Johnny.

"Get him Mac."

That's all I needed to hear from him. Kyla put her face in her hands as me and Ella got out the car.

"I wanna see this."

"Nah. Go get your boyfriend. I wanna talk to Pretty Ricky. Alone." "Who's Pretty Ricky?"

"I'll explain to you later," as I began to walk towards him.

As I knew everyone was watching me, I stormed up to the little punk with the last of my steps. This kid was short and skinny as a damn twig. **"RICKY!!!"**

He looked up.

"Hey. I'm Kyla's Uncle Mac. The most dangerous uncle that you have ever met."

"Oh. Hi."

He was as nervous as a pig crossing a barbecue grill with a Black family reunion going on.

"So how old are you?"

He looked around me and saw the family car, so he knew I wasn't a random guy.

"Your Kyla's uncle for real?"

I then bent over and looked at him dead in the face.

"Naw. I'm your worst nightmare. How old are you?"

He was so scared shitless that he didn't answer.

"How old are you? I ain't gone ask again."

"12 sir."

"You little pumpkin head punk you look 30. You trying to date my niece? You tryna take her for rides on tractors and stuff?"

"MAC!!!"

I heard a yell from behind me. I thought his father had caught me. However, it was Johnny walking up.

"Who is this guy?"

Immediately, I caught on to what he was doing and stayed in character. "It's Ricky Mr. John."

Johnny got up within a foot of his face.

"What do you want with Kyla?"

"H-Hi Mr. John."

"How old are you Ricky?"

"Mr. John you know I'm 12."

"You look 30. Show me some I.D."

I wish he had used the muthafucka part. I had to remember the young man was only 12, so letting the muthafucka slide was cool for this instance.

"She says you want to ask her out to the spring harvest farm dance."

He swallowed and a lump in his throat the size of Texas formed. "Yes sir."

"Well listen. You can take her. But she will be home by nine. Not 9:07, not 10:41. If she is not in the house at that time, I'm in the truck, locked, loaded, and I'm gonna hunt you down. Do you hear me Ricky?"

"And if I'm there you know what it's gone be. Chitty chitty bang bang boy."

Damn, I shouldn't have did the gun sign at him. Even more, I was mad I couldn't say chitty chitty bang bang **NIGGA!!!**

"JOHN!!!"

We both turned around.

"HEY THERE LISA!!! C'mon Mac. Let me introduce you to his mother Lisa."

We walked towards the door, but I turned around and gave the young man one last menacing stare. He looked like he wanted to shit bricks and piss rivers.

"Hey man," I whispered to John. "See you been watching Bad Boys huh."

"Yea, well, you know. I caught a few YouTube clips in my spare time. Not my style, but hey. You're here, so I figured I might as well join in on the fun."

"So, what's your style?"

"I got over 50 rifles Mac. Just shoot 'em."

I loved this dude man. I met Lisa. We talked for a good five minutes, and then we were off, back on the road. Lisa had no clue what trauma we had just caused to her younger child. After about 25 minutes on the road, it had just hit me that there were four people piled up in the back.

"Are we driving to Yellowstone like this?"

"Nope," Brenda said. "My brother's house is about another minute up the road and we're taking his truck."

Man, I know Ella's young punk and Johnny was happy. His nuts had to have been crushed by now. We pulled off the main road and onto a dirt road. Like, literally, a dirt road. It was a bright, sunny day outside, but this shit here started to look like one of those old stalker ass movies. There was a huge farm and a lonely house. Not gonna lie. Instantly, I thought that I had entered the twilight zone. We got out, and I realized that I was truly in the deep country. There wasn't shit for miles but farmland, cows, some trees, and the highway leading out of here. Her brother came out, and he yelled his dog's name repeatedly. Out of nowhere, I saw a small speck coming out of the field, growing bigger and bigger as it got closer. It took him a good 15-20 seconds to even make it back within the gate. It was a baby four-month-old German Shepard. I swear if I was that dog, I would've thought I was being raised in The Hamptons. He probably was out there chasing around squirrels, rabbits, and all kinds of other shit that the world hadn't even discovered yet. I was introduced to Brenda's brother and his wife, and all was quaint. As the conversation continued in the house between everyone, I crept back outside to record where I was at. As soon as I looked at my screen, no signal. Man, if something did happen to my Black ass out here, no one would be able to help me. At least if shit jumped off, I could have a series of videos for the world to witness when they eventually found my phone. It was like being John Kramer when Hoffman first threatened him in Saw 5. Kill me, and everything

111

would be released to the public at the right time. Google backups was a muthafucka. We finally said our goodbyes, piled into the truck and we were headed on our merry way. Now spaced out with room to stretch our legs, Johnny now had the driving duties and he seemed much more at ease. I kicked back and enjoyed what would be another few hours of passing through the wilderness. Over the first hour and some change, it was the same old shit. Cliffs, mountains, groups of antelope. Cliffs, mountains, another group of antelope. Don't get me wrong. The shit was magnificently gorgeous. However, it's only so much landscape and animals that any one person could look at. I wanted to go to sleep, but this was my vacation, and a brother wasn't gonna take the chance and miss something extraordinary. That extraordinary came when I least expected it. We entered civilization again. I saw homes, trees and deer. Matter of fact, a whole shit ton of deer were off in the distance. They looked up at the car like we were entering their hood. This shit reminded me of The Ring Two, except they weren't directly up on the side of the road.

"What's this place Brenda?"

"Dubois."

"Oh like Mr. Dubois on the Boondocks."

"Close, but its pronounced Dew boys."

That was indeed strange. It was always weird seeing words spelled one way and pronounced a whole other way. We went down their main strip and I saw a fucking giant rabbit statue with deer antlers on it in front of the gas station. I knew white people were weird sometimes, but this shit took the cake.

"Look mom. It's a giant statue of Ella."

"You're not funny turd."

"At least I'm not a turd with antlers."

112

"Can you girls go 30 seconds without going at each other's throats? I mean y'all literally just went over and hour not saying anything. Can y'all do that for your uncle. Please?"

I looked back to see them mean mugging each other.

"Only if she was never born."

With Ella's words, they went right back to arguing. Brenda just looked at me and shook her head.

"Okay Brenda. What is this giant rabbit thing that look like it cross bred with a deer?"

"Let's get out so I can show you."

We all exited out the car.

"I gotta piss. You all have fun with the damn jack," Johnny said, power walking into the gas station.

"Jack," I inquired, looking at Brenda.

"Yup. This is a jackalope. So, it's an old Wyoming story about rabbits. It's a disease they can contract called papilloma. It's like a keratin cancer."

"So, like keratin that grows our nails."

"Yea, except the keratin protrudes from their bodies, mainly on their heads, in between their eyes. So, it'll appear as if the rabbit has horns. It's crazy. The name for it is a jackalope."

Well I'll be damned. A fucking rabbit that can grow horns. This was some country shit. I had never heard of this, and the only thing I knew about rabbits up to this point is that they fucked a lot and tasted best when smothered in gravy. The children were already rotating off this thing taking pictures on their cell phones.

"You want a picture Mac?"

"Oh yea. Let's do this."

"By the way, to the Natives, it meant wellbeing."

"Huh?"

"It meant wellbeing. The swastikas."

"I'm lost Brenda."

"In Thermopolis. I apologize for it making you feel the way it did. I told you I'd tell you later. I didn't want to discuss this in front of the girls."

Immediately, it clicked back into my head.

"No need to apologize for ignorance."

"But, it's my people's ignorance. We made something beautiful into something terrible. It is what it is. May not have been me, but one actions reflects on us all unfortunately."

"You good with me though. I'm glad you acknowledge that there are a lot of white people who wanna see my people demised. You're unbiased and truthful. Trust, Black people don't hate white people. We hate racist white people."

"I get that Mac, but the minority will always be outnumbered by the majority."

It was crazy to hear a white person say that, whether I knew them or not. I handed Brenda my phone and proceeded over to the jackalope.

"Kyla fill the truck up."

"Why can't Ella do it?"

"Do you want me to gas you up? Now, come over here and get this card."

Oh shit. Brenda had some Black in her I see. I did a quick jump up and quickly came right back down.

"You okay?"

"Yea. Just these knees are a bit older than they used to be."

She laughed as I made my second attempt to jump up on this thing. I got it, but I felt like I scaled a 20-story building. It was at this moment that I wished I was 24 and not 34 again. I sat atop this thing and spread my arms out. I crossed them on one pose, threw up west side on another and took about six more pics in other random poses. You know Black folks can't just take a picture in one position. It's in our nature to pose. Some of these other folks weren't used to this shit. This elderly white lady walked pass while I was sitting on it and looked at me strangely. She was probably just mad her old ass could barely move anymore. After getting my picture fun on, I now had to take a piss. I ran to the bathroom. Before heading inside of it, I paused. Wow. First, it was a giant statue of a rabbit with deer antlers. In here, they had a full stuffed elk, and I swore he was saying what's up to a nigga. I laughed, shook it off and continued towards the bathroom. I went through about five or six genuine hellos. It was weird. No strange looks, unlike the one I encountered outside just now. What I mean by weird, is that everyone who told me hello had these creepy smiles. I don't know if they were genuinely happy to see a nigga, or if they had Tourette syndrome. I fed all the fish in the Pacific Ocean, washed my hands, and proceeded back into the store. The first thing that caught my eye was the freezer section, which was full of gracious ice cream. I opened the freezer door and anyone who knew me, knew exactly what I was looking for. I scanned and scanned until it caught my eye. Bingo, I found it. There it was. Chocolate peanut butter ice cream. This was a whole pint of it as well. In this moment, I really had to think. A brother was already lactose intolerant. If I smashed this ice cream, there was a great chance that my asshole was gonna clear out the entire forest. Oh well. Fuck it. I would be outside by the time it kicked in and started fucking with my stomach. The air would carry that shitty smell to the birds or something. I walked up to the register, looking at the other souvenirs they had. Of course, there were about a billion key chains and shot glasses to choose from, because if a city didn't have anything else available for tourists, they for damn sure had shot glasses and key chains. I decided to hold off on buying memorabilia. I was tired of the same old shit.

"$3.99 sir. Are you enjoying your trip here?"

"Yea. How'd you know I was from out of town?"

"Well your sweater says L.A., and the only L.A. around here is little antelope. So, enjoy Wyoming."

Ain't gone lie. That shit made me laugh. I took my ice cream and headed back towards the truck, where everyone was waiting. I looked off into the distant brown mountains to see that a huge white D stood out. I chuckled. It was amazing that they knew a brother was coming through. "Ready Mac?"

"Yea man. Let's roll. I got peanut butter ice cream and family. I'm gravy."

"Uncle Mac. What's I'm gravy mean?"

"It's what comes out of your butthole after you eat eggs and drink juice," Ella so ruthlessly said.

"GIRLS!!!"

I see by now that Brenda had enough of these two crazy knuckleheads. As my laughing subsided, I explained.

"It simply means everything is good. So, niece. It's like if one of my friends back home asked me how everything is, I can say I'm gravy, and they would know that everything is ok. And trust. You can use it with a lot of stuff."

116

"Ok. So, if I say hey Ella, was that kiss gravy when you kissed Tyler?"

My head snapped around quick. Brenda and Johnny couldn't help but to laugh. I wasn't down with the rainbow hair type snitch shit, but in this case, I didn't call it snitching. I called it informing. I knew they were growing up and the young punk was in the car, but I had to pretend like I didn't know what it was like to be a teenager. Ella legitimately looked scared as shit.

"You kissed my niece man?"

"Umm," he muttered, as his eyes went from side to side, knowing he fucked up.

I bust out laughing. At this point, all the adults and Kyla were laughing their asses of. Deep down, I wanted to choke his ass. We rolled back down the road, headed out of Dubois, which wasn't nothing but five additional minutes. As we hit the edge of town, two things popped out. To my right, there was an orange digital road display that stated something obvious to Black folks, but white people perhaps needed further clarification. DON'T GET OUT AND FOLLOW THE BEARS. See Black people, we kept shit simple. In the words of the great Eddie Griffin, if the shit had more legs than us, it wasn't to be fucked with. You didn't have to give Black people a lecture on leaving mother nature alone. We let her do her. You never heard about us getting ate up by sharks, mauled by Bears or tossed up by a pride of Lions. Why? We left shit alone. White folks were always adventurous. Always wanting to go mess with shit. I understood Johnny's knack to hunt. He grew up in Wyoming. It's what they do. However, he was hunting. Meaning shoot, kill, fry that muthafucka up, add some gravy and call it a day. He wasn't out there trying to pet the damn bears and tell them how pretty they are. A lot of my Caucasian people didn't understand that. To my left, I saw what Brenda had told me about Dubois on the way there. It was kind of where the semi rich stayed. They weren't Denzel Washington balling, but they were good for some B list type shit. These were some beautiful mountain homes; whose aura grew due to the surrounding snowcapped peaks and trees. It was to desolate out here for my blood, but if it worked for them, who am I to tell them they are wrong? This was one of those places where if you got murdered, it may take a week before someone discovered your body. I don't knock anyone for how they live, but civilization was a must for me, even though right now, it felt good to be away from it. The drive continued without much fanfare. Brenda and Kyla were in the middle seat watching a movie on the IPAD. Ella was in the back seat, knocked out on her boyfriend's shoulder. I looked out my window, taking in the upcoming snowcapped mountains and signs that told us that we were rising in elevation. 9,000+ feet was where we were at now.

"Well I'll be damned."

"Yup Mac. Its snow. Yea, this is common when you're up this high." "This is crazy man. Like, we literally went from somewhat chilly, to warm and decent. Now, we up here with the abominable snowman. What else in store man?"

"Well, we're going to hit over 11,000 feet before we get there."

I looked at him with my mouth dropped and turned back to see this mountain on my right side. It was the prettiest, yet most awe-inspiring experience I had ever had in my entire existence on God's beautiful earth. You grow up in Seattle, move to L.A., with every gang imaginable, smog filled skies and liquor stores at every stop, and you don't think you will ever see some shit like this. I guess this is what heaven looked like. The next hour was much of the same. Snow and trees. Then, the road lanes collapsed, and an abundance of cars were in front of us.

"We at Yellowstone man?"

"Almost. This is Grand Teton Park. It's the park before you drive into Yellowstone."

I lowered my window, and upon the first breath I took, it was like I sucked in the entire earth's atmosphere.

"Oh my God man. I can breathe."

Brenda laughed.

"Yea man. It's crisp air up here."

"I know bro. My lungs are smiling with a huge grin right now."

We got up to the gate with an older white gentleman. Johnny pulled out his VA identification card and handed it to him.

"Yea this is my buddy Mac from California."

"Mac. Welcome."

"Glad to be here sir."

He was excited, jubilant. My mental radar again pinpointed genuine hellos and smiles. I was keeping tabs. We rolled into the park. I hadn't seen this many fucking trees in my life. It was like a nightclub for foliage. I was literally stuck in a trance. I had become oblivious to what was around me. What I hadn't become oblivious to however, was the fact that I had to take a piss for all of mankind. I don't know if it was all the elevation switches, traveling through the mountains or lowkey having dreams of a big ass grizzly bear breaking loose a park fence and chasing my Black ass. I really didn't know. All I knew is that I had to refill Yellowstone Lake. We arrived at what I believe was the welcome center. Parking the car, we all got out and stretched. That was a long ass ride and my legs had to regain their proper circulation. I stretched and took everything in. There was the tour bus of Asians and they were already snapping pictures, as if the park was gonna disappear in five seconds. Others were conversing, laughing, joking, even eating sandwiches out of the back of their trucks.

"C'mon Uncle Mac," Ella said.

Kids were something else. They were always in a rush. Ella, her sister and Tyler ran inside the building. As for us adults, we slow bopped it. Our joints didn't have the lubrication they did 20 years ago. Our back and leg muscles took some time to get stretched out and warmed up. I had no plans on running in this bitch unless necessary. When I say necessary, y'all know what the hell I mean. We walked into the welcome center. The first thing I noticed was two bruhs. Either I had entered the twilight zone unknowingly, or I really wasn't tripping at all. I closed my eyes and opened them again. Nope, I wasn't tripping at all. It was two niggas working in here. The sites in here were awesome. They had a stuffed bear inside of a glass case. This was indeed some wildlife safari shit. Had this been owned by Black folks, we would've stuffed great grandma with a belt in her hand, because she would've whooped all our asses for walking on her floor with our shoes from outside. Johnny went off to get something to eat as I followed Brenda out the back of the center.

"Holy shit."

"Beautiful, isn't it Mac?"

"The only thing sexier is a bunch of surf-n-turf burritos tied together." "You really love burritos, don't you?"

"Like dumb asses love red hats."

I said that shit while not taking my eyes off this monstrosity. I had driven up a mountain and saw them in the distance driving. It was way different standing in the middle of nature, staring at them. The tops, you couldn't even see because the clouds were draped over them. I walked up to the sign and learned a few interesting facts about this mountain range. The range was made up of eight separate mountains, including one named Rolling Thunder. That had to be the mountain where the spirits turned up at. At the base of the mountain range was Jackson Lake. You could make out some of the lake, but it wasn't in full view due to the eerie fog that hovered over it. Lastly, I read the most important part of the sign. WILD ANIMALS ARE WILD. DON'T FEED OR TOUCH THEM. That's all I needed to see. It was great they were handing out warnings up here. I hadn't read any stats, but I know damn well this park had caught a few hundred bodies. Me and Brenda ended our sightseeing and walked back into the welcome center. The girls were in line for some ice cream and Brenda joined them. More than likely, it's because she probably wanted to know where the hell they got some money to get the ice cream, or she knew they were hoping she came over to pay for it. I saw Johnny walk off into the gift shop as I strolled on over to one of the restaurants they had in here. Just like that, another amazing sight caught my eye. Working in the restaurant was a sister. Then, my mind clicked. Either it was more niggas up in Wyoming than I previously expected, or the movie GET OUT was indeed true. We caught eye contact and I waved to her. She smiled and waved back. My concerns were put at ease. She looked normal, so it was obvious that no one had taken a piece of her brain out. The restaurant was kind of like a Panda Express type joint, except the food looked like actual food and not processed bullshit pulled out of a box. I walked out and headed into the gift shop. In here, I met up with Johnny and we just started going through everything.

For him, this was nothing. For me, this was like being in a foreign candy store. Replica bear teeth, rock carved statues of birds and other animals, mini beaver tail key chains that weren't made from actual beavers. This shit was tight. In it, like every gift shop, they had refreshments and snacks. I copped me some quote on quote glacier water and a bag of bison jerky. Now, did this water really come from a glacier? Maybe it did, maybe it didn't. All I know was that the PH level was 8.8, and alkaline was the shit. I wasn't an obsessive health nut, meaning I didn't get upset at people who ate meat. Some of these vegans really needed to get laid and work out, cause some of them are fatter than the carnivores that they talk about. I've been on earth long enough to know that it's the process of how food is prepared that's bad. Up here, everything was natural, from the eggs laid in Johnny's chicken coop, to the air, to the antelope I ate, to the water I drank. I was healthier than most, but that didn't mean that I wouldn't fuck some fried bacon up every now and then. Much like amusement parks, this shit was overpriced, but I knew the game. Six dollars for alkaline water and over five dollars for a bag of jerky that should've cost no more than four dollars. It was what it was though. We left and met up with the ladies in the center of the building, tearing up some ice cream out of their cups.

"You guys ready?," Brenda asked.

"Yea. We can roll hun."

We vamped out and headed towards the truck. Steps from the passenger door, with everyone else in the car, I felt a tap on my shoulder. It was a young white lady. She couldn't have been no more than 35.

"Yes ma'am?"

"Umm. I don't know how to explain this, but I just want to

commend you."

Her eyes were a little watery, so whatever place she was coming from, it was one of deep emotion.

"Umm. Can you explain?"

I heard the passenger side window lower down.

"Everything okay Mac," Johnny asked.

"Yea man. Poetry fan from California whose up here with her family. Gimme two minutes."

"Alright man."

I don't know how in the good hell I came up with that lie that fast. I just didn't want them alarmed. Me and the lady took a few more steps away from the truck. I ensured to keep my back towards the truck, as a sign that I wasn't worried about this situation.

"What are you talking about ma'am?"

"I'm sorry. You don't know me, and I know this whole situation is awkward. But, I'm from a small town in Montana, called Helena. Nearly all white, with a Black mayor. I know, it sounds like some Hallmark stuff."

My eyebrows raised up.

"Any who. What having a Black mayor over a white town has taught me is to learn the soul of a man. I can never understand what it's like to be Black, nor know what it's like to not have a privilege. But, continue being strong and I apologize for any negative stares you may have received here, any words, or anything my people have done to you. Judging from who you are here with, I see ignorance and you don't connect. Can we take a picture?"

My mind was completely blown. Take that back. I was completely mind fucked. The shit that she said had fucked me up in a way that I had never been fucked up before. One of her friends had her phone out and we posed for a pic.

"Thank you. Enjoy Yellowstone."

She walked off towards her friend and the crowd they were here with. I turned around and walked back to the truck, still trying to process everything that had happened.

"Who was that Mac?," Brenda asked, as I got back in.

"Some girl who said she saw me perform in L.A. one time, and apparently, I dated one of her friends. Small world."

"Uncle Mac, you're a singer?"

"Nah Kyla. I do poetry."

"Oh, Uncle Mac. I have a poem," Ella said.

"Lemme hear it."

"Roses are red, I eat curds. I am pretty and Kyla looks like a **TURD!!!**" **"SHUT UP ELLA!!!"**

"YOU SHUT UP!!!"

"BOTH OF YOU SHUT UP!!!"

Again, Brenda shut that shit down. We got back out to the road we came in on and drove for another 20-25 minutes. We had now officially entered Yellowstone. As we pulled up to the parking lot of whatever part of the park we were in, I was just in awe. I pulled out my phone. It was at a good 87%, so I didn't have to worry about it going dead while I was here. I could film all the videos I wanted. Besides, if I wanted to make a call, it was useless because we were in the middle of nowhere, and I ain't have signal to save my damn life. We exited the car, and the Grand Teton Mountain Range had now become a mere appetizer at a steakhouse. This was the main entrée, the bread and butter, whatever you wanted to call it. Me and

Johnny began to walk out onto the huge grassy patch of green land that enveloped this entire park.

"**DUDE!!!**," I yelled, as I stopped dead in my tracks.

"Yea you got lucky. That Bison poo man."

Had I taken another step without seeing it, I would've been ankle deep in Buffalo Bill's dinner last night. There was no atrocious smell and you could probably chalk that up to the weather conditions. However, it gave a new meaning to the term, *I didn't know that they could stack shit that high.* Even the late, great Gunnery Sergeant Emery would've let out a holy fuck with this one. I wasn't any expert, but it looked like a good 20 pounds of shit. As I moved my camera around, I saw not too far from this spot, another bison turd pile was visible. Then, my Blackness kicked in.

"Hey Johnny. Ain't no Bison over here is it?"

"Naw man. They are across the river. Look."

I looked up. Off in the distance, I saw two Bison grazing away, minding their own business. Thank the Lord they were on the other side of the water. As he walked towards the river, I followed slowly, ensuring that I didn't step in any shit along the way. There seemed to be a million piles. I was literally playing hopscotch just to move forward. Johnny was about ten steps ahead of me when I saw him stop.

"What's that?" I asked, catching up to him.

"Oh nothing. Just a mini geyser. That's a baby."

I looked down and saw the mini bubbles coming up out of the earth. "This bitch ain't gonna explode is it?"

"Nah man. Not this one. But if this park ever goes up, we're all dead." "What you mean?"

"Oh, Yellowstone is a giant volcano. If it erupts, the world is done and we all will be dead in an instant."

Aight, my Blackness kicked back in for a good minute. I had to comprehend what my man had just said. One big giant volcano. So, it was possible that my Black ass could be cooked up extra crispy with a side of collard greens at any given moment. I was all down for exploring the ends of the earth, but damn. I didn't want to be walking one minute, here a boom and then the next thing you know, I'm talking to Jesus and St. Peter over a card game, and a nigga only had three spades in his hand.

"Man, this shit crazy."

"The bison shit or the volcano?"

I stared at him and he looked back. Damn, I really couldn't pick one over the other. We left back towards the car after a good while of just admiring nature. We continued our journey into Yellowstone. I must say, it seemed like it was cracking up here. You look to one side, and there was a lake, with all kind of RVs', and people just fishing like there was no tomorrow. You had people along the banks, partially in the water, all that. You look to the other side, and you saw nothing but trees. Every damn tree you could imagine. True, the leaves were gone, but each had its own unique skeleton. Some looked like they were lonely and kicked out of the forest club for not paying their membership dues. Others looked like they overlapped each other, like their branches were shaking up GD or some shit. Amazement was an understatement. After almost another 10 minutes of driving through mother nature, we came upon our second stop. We got out the truck, all stretching as if we were in here for 10 hours and not 10 minutes.

"Anyone hungry?," Brenda asked.

We all raised our hands in unison.

"Sheesh. Bellies, bellies, bellies."

Brenda popped opened the back of the truck, opening the cooler. I swear a Gatorade and a stack of sandwiches never looked so good in my life. The kids got their fill first, as they grabbed their food and walked off, arguing as sisters do. I took out my ham and cheese joint. Two of them to be exact. I grabbed a Fruit Punch Gatorade, some Lay's Potato Chips, leaned up against the truck and stuffed my face away. There was a huge bus filling up with Asian tourists on the other side of the parking lot. Then, what sounded like the loudest squawk in the history of mankind occurred. I looked dead in front of me and spotted a raven. He took steps towards me, squawking, like he was saying, what's good homey, and what the fuck you got on my meal today? I mean dead ass, he stopped a good six human steps ahead of me, like he was an officer in the armed forces or some shit.

"Sup homey. You ain't getting none of this sandwich, and that's on my mama."

"SQUAWK!!!"

This one was louder than the first. I stopped mid bite and my face turned up. I know they say dogs and cats have human tendencies, but damn. Did homey just squawk loud when I told him that he wasn't getting any of my meal?

"Naw fam. Gone on somewhere, before it gotta be a situation and some furniture moving around these parts. I'd hate for the ranger to have to come out here and white sheet ya body. Feel me?"

"SQUAWK!!!"

Oh yea. This raven had been a human in his past life. Probably straight out of Baltimore for that matter. I tore off a piece of my

127

sandwich and tossed it behind him. He hopped his ass over and snatched the food up, gulping it down in one giant bite.

"Well I'll be damned. This flipping bird is human."

"SQUAWK!!!"

"Look man. I ain't gone be feeding you all day. You see the signs. It says don't feed the animals. Why don't you go hunt or something? You got wings don't you?"

"Mac, are you really talking to a Raven?"

"Johnny man, you see this shit. Dawg. It's like he human."

"SQUAWK!!!"

I tossed out a chip this time. Of course, it didn't make it as far. He hopped up on it, pecked it a few times.

"SQUAWK!!!"

"Haha," Johnny laughed. "Guess he doesn't eat chips."

"Yea crazy right? Guess he's a Doritos type of brother."

I tossed one more piece of my sandwich out. He devoured it with the quickness. He took two hops and turned back around to look at me. **"SQUAWK!!! SQUAWK!!!"**

With that, he took off into the forest, never to be seen by me again. For many, it may have been a funny and random moment. For me, however, it meant something much deeper than that. Naw, I wasn't one of those Hotep, take shit deeper than deep ass dudes. I couldn't stand them fuckers, especially the fact that you would see most of them with no woman, or white baby mamas. However, sometimes, mother nature can holla at you on some G shit in the weirdest of ways. I literally broke bread with a raven. I gave. Universal energy tells me that it'll be received back 100 times over just due to generosity. I finished my sandwich, only to turn around and see the rest of the fam on a bridge overlooking the falls, which you could hear a mile away, crashing against the rocks. As I began to walk in their direction, I noticed the drop off cliff, and the sign that sat right in front of me. DON'T VENTURE TOWARDS THE EDGE. HUNDREDS OF PEOPLE IN YELLOWSTONE HAVE FALLEN AND DIED. I listened, but then I didn't. I slowly paced my steps until I could still see the base of the ground. I wasn't risking walking all the way over until the dirt got loose, and the next thing you know, they were pulling my body out of a shit pile left by some grizzly bears. I looked down into the lower canyons, which were full of trees, rocks and of course, water. It was a surreal site. I was getting over one of my fears you could say. It seems like a Black man today was always living on the edge. One minute, we are driving with our significant other. Then next, we are pulled over and shot repeatedly, only for the officer to come up with some shitty excuse as to why. More amazing is that a lot of white America failed to open their eyes to this. They were too busy going with the notion of, they should have complied with orders. They were so entrenched in a racist past, that they believed in their own lies. I stood there for about 15 seconds, thinking of all the Black men who lived on the edge every day. I thought playing organized basketball against a rival school was challenging. Naw. As I got older, I realized just leaving the house as a Black man is a challenge. You really didn't know if you were gonna return at the end of the day or not. I backed back and headed towards the bridge where the rest of the fam were at.

"UNCLE MAC!!! COOL, ISN'T IT!!!???"

"Yea Kyla. Never seen something so beautiful in my life."

"Of course you have Uncle Mac. Me. But, Kyla. Well, she fell out of an antelope anus as a baby."

129

"SHUT UP ELLA!!!"

"YOU HUSH BRACEFACE!!!"

At this point, I had a headache from the bickering that these two were doing. Johnny and Brenda were off to the side, hugged up, admiring each other, and the view. Me, I was stuck in between motor mouth one and two. They didn't stop. Not for the next five minutes. I think this was God reminding me that when I have kids, buy muzzles so they can shut the hell up at times. I glanced over to see this woman staring at me, but I paid it no mind. The girls continued to bicker as I glanced over again, and she was still staring at me. I told myself Mac, don't trip. Just let it go. 10 seconds later, I caught her again, but this time, she tried to cut her eyes away.

"Is there something that I can help you with lady? I mean is there something you need?"

"Ummm yes," she said with a cracked voice. "Whose little girls are these?"

"Why the fuck does it matter to you?"

Right then, the girls got quiet, as did the few people in our vicinity who had heard me. I wasn't loud yet, but I was itching to cuss this old bitch out.

"Excuse me?"

"I said why the fuck does it matter to you?"

I had crossed that threshold. I would apologize to my babies later. I knew they were scared. I could tell by the way they now clutched each side of me. Judging from the quick glance of the people around us, they were scared shitless too.

"Well, I'm sure their parents wouldn't appreciate them hanging around a stranger. We are having too many of our precious white children disappearing and dying in this day and age, mainly due to those who look like you."

I looked up and saw Johnny and Brenda walking back towards us. I looked up at God and asked him to forgive me for what I was about to tell this old bitch. I saw a few people start to walk away, because they knew all the nigga inside of me was about to come out. For a moment, I thought about what I was about to do. Inside of my head, the Kermit the Frog meme popped up. The Black, well educated, mature man said, ignore the ignorance. However, the petty, South Seattle raised nigga inside of me said to set this old bitch straight. I was in my 30's and I had no time to be the crazy person that I was back in the day. However, in this case, it was very much warranted. Survey says, petty nigga activated.

"LADIES AND GENTLEMEN!!! CAN I HAVE YOUR ATTENTION PLEASE!!!"

Johnny and Brenda looked at me without a clue in the world as to what was going on. The girls were now behind me, scared out of their minds. Tyler hadn't talked or interacted much with anyone this whole trip, but from the look on his face, he considered giving Ella whatever she wanted in life so that he would never have to deal with me. Something told me that the evil man that they were about to see would be etched in their minds forever. Everyone was now looking.

"HERE WE HAVE AMONGST YOU, ONE LIKE YOU. A WHITE WOMAN. SEEING HOW I AM THE ONLY BLACK MAN IN THIS SETTING. OR, AS SOME OF YOU HAVE PROBABLY SAID IN YOUR HEADS. THE NIG-GER IN A BLUE HOODIE!!!" I made sure to emphasize the nigger part, just so I could make their cracker asses feel comfortable.

Crazy right? I wanted them to feel comfortable about a lashing I was giving them.

"HERE I AM. WITH MY BROTHER!!! YES THIS COUNTRY MUTHAFUCKA!!! RIGHT THERE!!!," I said, pointing to Johnny. "HERE IS HIS WIFE!!! MY BEAUTIFUL SISTER IN LAW!!!," as I pointed to her.

"AND HERE ARE MY TWO BEAUTIFUL NIECES, AGES 14 AND 12. HERE IS ONE OF THEIR BOYFRIENDS!!! HE HASN'T SAID MUCH THIS WHOLE TRIP, BUT HEY, HE'S A COOL KID!!! NOW, WHY IS A BLACK MAN SHOUTING IN THE MIDDLE OF YELLOWSTONE???!!! WELL, BECAUSE THIS FUCKTARD OF A LADY, OF MIDDLE AGE AND SOMEWHAT WRINKLED DESCENT, ASSUMED THAT I WAS A STRANGER, AND THAT I, MAC BAKER JR., BORN AND RAISED IN SEATTLE, WASHINGTON, BUT NOW LIVING IN LOS ANGELES, IN SOME WAY, SHAPE OR FORM, WERE PUTTING THESE GIRLS IN HARMS WAY!!! WHEN IN FACT, THEY ARE MY NIECES!!! YES, MY SKIN IS A LITTLE BIT DARKER THAN THE SHIT YOU ALL ARE ACCUSTOMED TO SEEING!!! THEIR EYES ARE BLUE!!! MINE ARE BROWN!!! MY HAIR IS BLACK!!! THEIRS IS BLONDE AND BRUNETTE!!! HOWEVER, WE ARE RELATED!!! NO, I NEVER SERVED THIS COUNTRY BEFORE. NO, YOU WOULDN'T GIVE A FUCK IF I DID BECAUSE STILL, I'M BLACK!!! RATHER, A NIGGER FOR SOME OF YOU!!! SO, TO THIS MIDDLE AGED, SOMEWHAT WRINKLED, DUSTY ASS BITCH, WHOSE HUSBAND IS

FUMING NEXT TO HER, BUT IS IN FEAR OF GETTING HIS ASS WHOOPED BY THE ANGRY BLACK MAN AND TOSSED INTO THE FALLS!!! I SAY FUCK YOU AND HAVE A NICE DAY!!! DOES THAT ANSWER YOUR QUESTION WHO THE FUCK I AM, BITCH!!!" I flipped her the bird, hawked a wad of spit at her husband, which hit him right between the eyes, and stood there, applauding myself for the damn speech I had just made. No dead ass, I was literally clapping like Denzel in Remember the Titans, when he introduced Gary and Ray in only a way Coach Boone could. Johnny and Brenda were now staring a hole through the lady, and the only noise you heard out here were the falls. That old bitch husband, he was walking around in circles, wiping his face, but he didn't look up at me one time. He knew what the business was.

"C'mon girls. Tyler. Let's go back to the car. See the next part of the park. You know. Cause that's what family does."

I wrapped my arms around the girls, and we walked off, Tyler trailing behind us. I stared at that old miserable bitch the entire time. I took one glance at her hubby, and he was still off fuming mad. This was one battle he didn't wanna be a part of. I didn't blame him either. The last memory you want when you go to Yellowstone is a Black man tossing your ass up and feeding you to the wolves. He was probably gonna divorce her ass the minute they got home. I walked my nieces back to the truck. Tyler stood at the door like he was in trouble. Amid this, I heard Brenda going off. I turned around to see Johnny pulling her away as her finger pointing was on 10. She was heavy in church and loved God. However, I think The Good Lord gave her a pass for this instance of cussing. The girls didn't know what to do or say. It was clear they were still shaken up

133

by everything. It was clear that I was pissed off and had got taken out of my element. I heard the click, letting me know the car was unlocked. I got in and buckled my seatbelt, and the rest of the family followed suit. I took some deep breaths and tried to regather myself. Everyone was quiet. There was no Ella versus Kyla roast battle. No one knew what to say or do.

"Mac. Are you alright?"

I turned to Johnny. I smiled.

"I'm good man. It's just I realized that no matter how good I do, how well I act, how great I conduct myself. To the world, you know what I am."

"Naw. You're not that to me, the wife, or the kids. You're family. That's how it's been for almost 15 years, and that's how it's going to be. I can't tell you what it's like being in your shoes because I will never be in them. I'll never know what it's like to walk down the street, see a cop car and fear for my life. What I do know, is that this family loves you. And, if we have to go down with you, then that's what we will do. Besides, Brenda would've thrown that old bitty into the falls had I not grabbed her."

I laughed, as did Brenda.

"Mac, we love you," Brenda said.

"I love y'all too," tearing up.

"We love you too Uncle Mac," the girls said in unison.

"I love y'all too."

"Uncle Mac."

"Yes Tyler."

"I swear I will never upset you and treat Ella like a queen."

"Hey man. You're a good kid. If my niece likes you, I like you."

I meant that shit. I couldn't cut any jokes right now.

"Uncle Mac."

"Yes Ella."

"Kyla's still a turd."

And just like that, shit went back to normal. We went back to weaving our way through the park for the next hour or so, seeing all kinds of shit. Animals that I could recognize, and even some that made me say you got it playa. We made it to the Old Faithful Yellowstone Visitor center.

"Sign says she blows at 3:15, so we made it right on time."

"This it Johnny?"

"Yep. Old Faithful. She shoots out pretty high too."

I had saw this shit on Nat Geo plenty of times in my life, but never up close and personal. We parked the truck and went out towards the hundreds who had already gathered in the distance. I saw the yellow rope, but I was betting money that someone would try to jump it and get a closer shot. Unfortunately, for my entertainment, no one jumped the rope, but entertainment was sure to come. As the clock ticked down the minutes to when mother earth would open her mouth and spew her anger, I observed everyone around me. More than 50% of these people were Asian. I wonder did they get hit with is this your child question when standing next to a Caucasian little girl. I knew the answer, but my curiosity persisted. I scanned the audience to see if any of my kind were in existence. There in the distance, towards the middle of the crowd, I saw another brother. His leather coat looked like a member's only jacket. His skull cap, parading the Greek letters for Omega Psi Phi around its side, was highly visible, due to the bright purple hue. Yet, on his side, was a white woman. Now, I don't have a problem of loving who you love. Yet once again, I started to wonder if he was pressed with the same question I was pressed with when someone noticed me with two, young, white adolescent females. I wonder was this white woman perceived to be in danger. Did Barbecue Betty pick up her phone and report that a white woman was in the clutches of a tall, Black man who stood about 6'3? I wonder had he seen me and think that if shit goes down, would the only other brother I see help me? It was a question to ponder.

"There she goes," Johnny said.

I immediately switched my focus back to Old Faithful. Phones were everywhere now, recording her goodness. She was releasing a few belches out of her system. Then, suddenly, she screamed, and two hundred feet in the air, she spit. Oh man, did she spit. It was some of the simplest, but coolest shit that you could ever witness. I watched in amazement how the earth marveled. It lasted about two minutes before her mouth closed and no longer spewed life out. As quickly as it started, it was over.

"Cool huh Mac?," Brenda asked.

"Yea it was. Gone be cooler when I hit this bathroom."

"Well go in the center," she said laughing. "Don't wait for us."

I wasn't waiting for them. I was just trying to walk calmly so that this shit wouldn't rush out. You know how it went. The quicker you approached the bathroom, the quicker the shit wanted to rush out. I walked with my steady pace through the doors of this monstrosity. It was huge and packed. I was praying to God not to let this bathroom be filled all the way up.

"I'll see you guys in a minute."

"JUST CALL US!!!," I heard Brenda shout, because I was power walking away from them.

Time was ticking and doo doo was knocking at the door like 12 serving a high-risk warrant. I got in the bathroom and held my stomach, all while having a terrible smirk come across my face. This was that bullshit. Every stall was taken. I mean, every muthafuckin stall. As bad as I had to take a shit, I was equally upset that every urinal was taken. I had enough petty in me to drop some turds off in one of those if need be. As I started to do a bop dance to not embarrass myself totally, I saw the most magical site. A door opened. The handicapped stall door for that matter. Man, homey couldn't have made it out any quicker. The minute both his feet exited the stall, I went in for the kill like a lion hunting a gazelle. As bad as I had to go, I wasn't no nasty ass brother. I did my dance while grabbing long ass pieces of tissue paper and placing them on the seats. I don't care how bad you gotta shit. You never in your life put your bare ass cheeks on any toilet. That shit right there was a no no. Finally, after laying down the paper right, after getting this belt loosened and dropping my jeans, I sat my Black ass down. The sound that followed was like when death met steak burritos and spoiled buttermilk.

"OH GOD JESUS CHRIST MAN!!!"

The white guy in the stall next to me said that shit in one complete sentence with no breaks. I didn't give a fuck. This shit was leaving my body. It felt like a demon that had possessed me for 40 days and nights was finally escaping. Another God-awful sound erupted from my asshole.

"MY GOODNESS PAL. WHAT DID YOU EAT???!!!"

That was the other guy in the stall on the opposite side. When people taking a shit were complaining about your shit, you knew that your shit was bad. I laughed internally because I truly gave no fucks at all. Hell, had I been at the crib, I know by now that I would've been ass naked, either watching the mini tv in the bathroom, or playing a game on my phone. I wiped my ass with this generous two-ply paper, flushed, pulled my pants up and headed towards the sinks. I saw someone else come out of their stall and walk towards the bathroom door.

"A NASTY MUTHAFUCKA!!! WASH YO FUCKING HANDS!!!"

He stopped by the door, before grabbing the handle and looking back.

"Are you talking to me?"

"YES MUTHAFUCKA!!! WASH YO MUTHAFUCK-ING HANDS!!! GONE WIPE YO ASS AND TRY TO LEAVE THIS BITCH WITH SHITTY FINGERS!!!"

I could tell the cats in here weren't used to people in here calling someone out. As I shook my hands out and reached for the paper towels, he slowly walked back to an open sink and began to wash his hands. I wiped my hands as I walked past him in disgust. He didn't look up at me. I couldn't stand that shit. Wash your damn hands. It only takes 20 seconds tops. Add soap, add water, germs are gone. I swear man, some folks just ain't have no kind of home training. I walked back out into the madness of the center. Fighting through the crowds, I finally made it into the restaurant section to see Brenda, the girls and Tyler eating ice cream. Their stomachs must have been strong to handle all of the dairy they had consumed. Johnny was in line ordering his own stuff.

"Sup y'all."

"Uncle Mac. Kyla said you were dropping turds the size of a mountain out your butthole."

"Stop lying. I didn't."

"You did too."

I looked over at Brenda and she was just shaking her head. Even she had enough of those two demons to the point that she didn't want to say anything. She continued eating her ice cream and let them argue. Johnny came back over with a sandwich in his hand and we were on our way back out the building. We jumped back in the truck and drove over to the sulfur pits. I guess for some odd reason, it was cool to smell rotten eggs and a shit like smell, all while observing nature. We got out the car and everything seemed normal. However, the minute we made it over to the first pond of water, the smell hit you.

"My god," I said.

"Yea, the sulfur is just pure. Like, terrible pure," Brenda said.

"Wasn't the healing waters full of sulfur to?"

"It had sulfur in it, but a whole lot of other earth minerals as well. So, the smell isn't as bad. Plus, you were relaxing, so it doesn't even bother you."

"Remember I told you Mac that this is one big volcano?," Johnny said. "Well, we are right in the heart of her here."

Damn, I was literally in her mouth. So, if her ass wanted to catch her period at this very moment, my Black ass would be grass. Instant Top Ramen noodle type grass. I shrugged it off as quickly as I thought about it, because I was damned if I do and damned if I don't. We walked around, all up through the hills of the sulfur pits. I spotted a chipmunk chasing after another chipmunk. I didn't know if it was chasing off a rival or trying to get some ass. I was just surprised to see a chipmunk chilling in this part of the park. Coming around one bend, the smoke off a larger body of water got thicker than Texas toast. Fuck, this shit stank. The walk continued until we got back around to the parking lot. I turned to see Ella and her boyfriend walking hand in hand. Had it not been for today's earlier incident and what he said afterwards, I may have snuck up on him and pushed him into one of the pits. Back in the car, we saw that it was after four. It was a long day here in Yellowstone. We had enjoyed it, but it was time to get the hell up out of here.

"You girls want pizza?"

"Yea," they both said in unison.

"Mom, can I choose my own pizza. Kyla always gets the bad pizza." "What do you mean I get the bad pizza?"

"Your topping choices suck."

"WATCH YOUR MOUTH ELLA!!!"

I swear Brenda's voice sometimes struck fear into me. Traffic suddenly slowed down, as we saw flashing lights up ahead. I was trying to see if I could see what it was up ahead. I couldn't. None of us could. After another 20 seconds, the whole car mouths dropped, and gasps were let out. To the left, there was a terrible roll over. An SUV, just sitting on its side. Judging from how the emergency personnel were responding, someone was in bad shape. Just as quick as we peeped it, we kept going. After another mile of travel, traffic slowed down again. This time, there were also cars parked on the side of the road. Now, all the action was on the passenger side. I lowered my window and did the birdman hand rub. What was I about to see? I was hoping it was some wolves munching on some white folks. I didn't wish death on anyone, but I just knew some white folks had fucked with something. As we slowed down, Ella saw it before me.

"Look mom. A bear with her cubs."

I couldn't get a good view through all the trees, but once we passed an open patch, it was clear as day. A mother bear with her two cubs. It was an amazing sight to see, seeing that I had only seen something like this on National Geographic.

"Look, it's a bear," some random woman said.

I wanted to tell her no shit sherlock. The fuck did she think I thought it was? A mountain lion? As amazing as it was to see, traffic went back to normal and we continued rolling. Now, I counted my adventures. A mother bear and her cubs. Old faithful. Hiking through sulfur pits to the top of a low sitting mountain. Me vs. multiple types of white people. I had done many things here. Yet, the best part about the whole trip was just being here period. What didn't break me, made me stronger. It was the Black people way. If you don't believe me, just check the history books. Not His-story books.

"Sheesh, look at this traffic."

Johnny said that, and I took my attention off my phone, looking up to what was ahead. Again, traffic had stalled. This line, however, was longer than the wait for Jay Electronica to drop a solo album.

"Can you see anything John?"

"No Brenda. Not at all."

This was literally the road out of the park and we were stuck again. Five, 10, then 15 minutes passed, and no one had moved an inch.

"Well, who's still hungry?" Brenda asked.

Johnny shut the truck off and we all got out, heading to the back where the cooler was. We pulled out the sandwiches, chips, drinks, all that. I swear we were all going to be fat by the end of this day. Obviously, others behind us, and even some up ahead got the memo as well. This shit had turned into one huge roadside picnic. There was some snow on the ground. Not much, but just enough to where kids were making snow angels and tossing snowballs. The girls, well, they started to turn their beef back on. The scurried down food and hurried over to the snow piles, making snowballs, and launching them at each other. I loved them both. I really did. However, I was wishing one of their bad asses would throw a snowball at me. I'm in my 30's, with a strong arm, and have hood negro tendencies. In the hood, when we threw snowballs, we were aiming for the chest or higher. We didn't play it safe. So, the minute one snowball was thrown at me, I already told myself that I was taking one of their heads off. It never happened. The girls were happy, they were bonding, and I was happy. Time passed as I started snapping pictures with my phone. I knew I was roaming, and all I could do was pray to God that I had unlimited roaming with Sprint. I couldn't honestly remember if I did. Either my bill was gonna be normal, or higher than giraffe cooch when I got home. Honestly, I'd take that hit. It's not every day that someone goes to Yellowstone. After literally an hour, traffic started to move. I snatched up two more sandwiches and took 'em back to the passenger seat. Brenda made these like my Granny use to make back in the day. Had the white bread that stuck to the roof of your mouth, that you used your tongue to get. It took about three billion tries, but eventually, you got it. As traffic flowed, and we got about a quarter mile down the road, we saw the reason why traffic had stalled. Two vehicles had fell into a marsh. Wait, scratch that. Two idiots drove themselves into a marsh. One car was already out and on a tow truck. The other was being pulled out while passing.

"I bet they veered off trying to look at a bison or something," Johnny said.

"Yea you probably right."

"Mac, what's the wildest animal you seen growing up in the city?" "Roaches. They set up shop at my Grandma house and had their own nightclub called kitchen shenanigans."

"Uncle Mac, roaches aren't wild animals," Ella said.

"In the projects they are baby."

"What's projects Uncle Mac?," Kyla asked.

This became interesting. Here I was, trying to explain hood life to two white girls who never had that experience, and were never gonna worry about that experience. For a split second, I thought about giving them some sugarcoated example to make them understand. But, I couldn't do that. It wasn't in me to lie on some real shit. If you are gonna give someone a glimpse into your world, then give them the clearest picture possible. They were 12 and 14 respectively, so in my mind, they could handle it.

"Basically, low income housing baby. It's where the people who don't have a lot of money stay."

"Is it a bad area?"

"Great people. Bad environment. But, the thing about it is that people make the best out of their environment."

"Did you stay in those?"

"Nah. Uncle stayed in a house with his parents. My Grandmother stayed there. It was fun when I went."

I wasn't ashamed to be from the hood. Some people might have beat around the bush. Not me. The hood gave me too many valuable life lessons to be ashamed of it. We rolled out onto open highway, which was finally a relief. We were out of that monstrosity of a park and headed towards Jackson Hole. After about 20 minutes of fast driving, we pulled off to the side of the road.

"Oh my God. You can see the tops of the mountain now."

Brenda was ecstatic. I knew what she was referring too. Earlier, there was cloud cover over the top of the mountains. Now, with the sun almost beginning its descent, everything was crystal clear. We all were out of the car, looking in amazement. This shit was truly and quite possibly the most beautiful sight I had ever seen since leaving Seychelles, East Africa.

"Johnny. I gotta get a pic man."

"Yea I'll take it for you."

As I walked over to the wall of stone, which was about four feet high, I looked over. Beneath it was a long fall. Trees, cliffs, you name it, it was down there. Now, the Black in me said keep your feet planted on solid ground, get your picture and roll back to the car. However, there was an itch of Caucasian madness that I wanted to scratch. I always talked about how crazy white people are. Well, I was with a group of them that weren't crazy, but shit, they were still white.

"Hold on man. I'm gonna get up on the wall."

"Alright. Be careful."

Now here's the trip part about that back and forth. Johnny said that like he was a brother. Translated simply, he said, aight muthafucka. You fall, and that's ya ass."

I said my statement like dude, this is going to be some gnarly shit. It was like we traded bodies for a good minute. I climbed up to the top of the wall and slowly turned myself to the front. This is when the nigga kicked back in. Johnny lifted my cell phone. I had raised my sleeves, exposing the many tattoos on my forearms. I looked calm, but I said to myself, muthafucka take this damn picture already. It seemed like an eternity up there.

"Okay Mac. Got it."

I jumped down. I didn't care if I sprained an ankle, tore up a knee or broke both of my damn legs. That spirit of Caucas was gone. Loosed, as they say in the Black church. As I walked back to the truck, I heard a voice in my head. It was like God speaking to me.

"Nigga, don't you ever do that shit again. Check ya skin color nigga." "Did you just call me a nigga and curse God?"

"Nigga, I'll call you what I want and say what I want. Don't ever question me."

Point, God. He was right. I'm glad that He hadn't gathered the angels around the cloud and said, watch this. I'm about to bring his ass home. We got back on the road. 15 minutes after leaving, the sun had completely disappeared, and it was dark. I'm not talking about normal dark. I'm talking that out in the middle of nowhere dark. If Black had a darker shade, this was it. Johnny cut on his brights as we passed by Jackson Hole Airport. It was a small joint, but this was where the upper echelon of society flew in to play at in Wyoming. You wouldn't think of Wyoming as a one stop shop to get it in. From what Brenda told me driving up here, it was a Hollywood playground. People like Harrison Ford and Kanye West had land, and homes out here. I mean, who could forget Kanye recording a whole album out here? The homes in the mountains were lit up and it was beautiful as ever. The little snow left gave this place an aura that I truly couldn't explain. The freeway eventually came to an end and we headed towards the main strip of town. Now, the lights were coming alive. I could see why they called this place the Hollywood of Wyoming. No, there were no skyscrapers. Matter fact, the largest building in the state of Wyoming is only 12 stories. There were no bright neon lights with flashing casino signs. There was none of that. However, there were lights and lots of them. You could see the main strip was made of restaurants, hotels, mom and pop joints, a few regular stores and everything you expected in a small, country town. Only this town let it be known. Let me put it like this. This strip was their Times Square. We cut through the street, looking for parking. There was nothing available. We got to the light at the intersection and made a right. After going down two or three blocks, nothing. I did however see a basketball court, encased in a cage, with some young boys shooting, showing me that even out here in the sticks, they hooped. The girls, you can tell they weren't having it. I looked back, and the looks on their faces said I'm hungry. Tyler, he was so nonchalant that I didn't know if he was hungry, or truly gave a fuck about anything that was going on. I also was seeing if he had his hands were on Ella. Sure enough, his arm was wrapped around her as she lay her head on his shoulder. I was trying not to be like this, Lord knows. I just couldn't kick that overprotective uncle instinct. We circled back. Finally, after what seemed like 40 days and 40 nights, we found a parking spot, right next to the Jackson Hole Welcome Center. I got out the car and stretched. Even the Jackson Hole air was different than the rest of the state. It was kind of, I say, city like. I felt like I was in LA or San Diego, even though I was nowhere close, nor was this place. Jackson couldn't hold a candle to the flame California cities were. They didn't have too. They were simply happy being a lit match. We walked into the visitor's center. Lord knows that I had to take a piss. As I headed towards the bathroom, I stopped. The words that graced the wall of this place were impossible to ignore.

THE LONGER I STAYED, THE MORE I LIKED JACKSON HOLE. HOMER RICHARDS, 65 YEAR RESIDENT.

I got a good chuckle out of that one. Most saw it as is appreciation for the city. I immediately thought about the episode of Martin where he caught Luis, his landlord, up in Mrs. Jackson's apartment, but Mr. Jackson wasn't home. Luis told Martin that he would like for Mr. Jackson to stay out of this. Martin replied with, well maybe you should stay out of Mrs. Jackson. I stood there and let out a loud ass laugh. I couldn't hold it in anymore.

"What's funny Uncle Mac?," Ella asked.

"I'll explain it to you when you're grown baby."

I turned and laughed all the way to the bathroom. After pissing the entire water supply of the country of Russia, I came back out to join the family. We walked out and onto the main strip. We knew pizza was what we wanted, but the smell of some barbecue quickly got our attention. We walked into the barbecue joint, and it looked like they were closing.

"I'll go find out."

As Johnny walked to the back where one of the employees were, my eyes locked on the television screen that sat in the front of the joint. Kawhi was shooting two free throws as the Raptors were leading 98-94. The first one, good.

"Well, they're closing for the night. Pizza it is."

As the family walked out, I slowly backpedaled to see him hit the second free throw. This was it. We the North was finally going to the NBA Finals. The bad thing is that Drake wasn't gonna shut the hell up about it. As I began walking back down the street, I glanced through the window one last time. Sure enough, there he was, on camera, jumping up and down. If we thought his music was something serious already, we hadn't heard shit yet. I can only imagine if they win it all. We strolled over two buildings down into the pizza place. The first thing I noticed was the sister sitting on the bench. She was giving me that look. You could tell that she hadn't seen no quality Blackness around these parts in a while. Hey, I was with fam, and I had no time for entertaining a woman. She looked good, I'll give her that, but I also had a woman. My lady was cool, but crazy. If she got that chill up her spine when she thought something was out of the ordinary, she'd mess around and blow up the earth. If you don't believe me, then let me explain. I can't remember the movie, but it was one that we both had wanted to see. After a few weeks of being released, she was feeling sick when we were supposed to go. She told me that I could go see it if I wanted to. Me being the man that I am, I went to see it. When I came out, I simply typed on Facebook that the horror movie was worth it. Oh, did she blow the fuck up. I got cussed out through Instagram, Facebook, on the phone, through text, e-mail, all of that. All I needed was a pigeon to carry me a note saying fuck you, and all the methods would've been complete. So, me even entertaining a woman while away, that was a no no. We all got seated and I sat wall side of the booth next to Ella and her boyfriend. It was wise of him to sit on the outside. If he leaned in for a kiss at any moment, he could make a clear escape when I reached over her to grab his throat and snatch it out of his asshole. We ordered four different types of pizza, because everyone had different taste buds. The pulled pork joint that Ella ordered, that made her my favorite niece by far. I had never in my life tasted swine on that level. This Wyoming food was something different. You could absolutely tell that nothing was artificial in any of their food.

148

This was what America was hiding from us. Everything nowadays was pumped up full of alternative everything, and people were just ingesting death into their bodies. America did anything for a buck. Maybe that's why places like this were so desolate because most of the population here didn't rely on mass hordes of name brand. Sure, they had name brand things, but a lot of people here farmed. They ate local produce. We continued to smash our food. The nondairy cheese and antelope sausage joint. The wood fired veggie joint with tomatoes was so good that I would slap a child if they reached on my plate. The last one, well, let's just say that pineapple does go on pizza. We sat in here, acting like one big family. It was one thing that me and Johnny were friends, whose relationship stood the test of time and distance. It was another for me to be accepted by his daughters and wife. We took pictures, we laughed, we joked. We literally sat in here for about an hour and a half goofing off. By the time we were finished, all four pizzas were completely gone. Six people, and all our stomachs proved to be bottomless pits. I'd say the kiddos ate about 65% of the pizza. Kids, I tell you. By now, it was 11, and it was time to hit the road. The itis would soon overtake everyone. As we headed out of Jackson Hole, I soaked in the laughter occurring in the truck. A few songs were sang which showed my age, cause I ain't know what the hell these kids listened too. Then, as soon as it started, it secured. We were now on open road, and as earlier, it was pitch black. Only this time, it was space black. Like, floating in space type black. Everyone was snoring a half hour in.

"You can go to sleep if you want to Mac," Johnny told me.

"Naw man. This shit looks like something you see out of some night vision goggles. I'll be damned if I go to sleep and wake up playing basketball with Jesus."

All the surroundings looked eerily gray.

"Yea, well at least if we do die, you could play sports on the clouds. I'm white and don't have an athletic bone in my body."

"Come on man. I know plenty of white boys that can hoop."

"Yea, well you aren't looking at one. Ask me to shoot and it better be a gun."

I laughed my ass off. We continued making small conversation on this dark, winding road. Then, came the treacherous part. The same mountain we climbed to get to Yellowstone, we had to climb back to head towards Riverton. Immediately, I noticed that on the way back, there was nothing keeping us from going over the side of the mountain. How the hell didn't I notice this on the way up? Probably because I was so much in awe of this state's beauty. I was scared shitless, but I had to be the tough guy. Suddenly, I looked up. We both let out a moan as we both saw a large set of glowing eyes. My heart started to go erratic inside of my chest.

"Bruh. Was that a damn elk?."

"Yea man. Haven't seen one that close in a long time."

The elk appeared on my side of the vehicle, standing on the edge of the road. The little edge that did exist. Naw, fuck this. I was wide awake now. I hadn't flown through the Rocky Mountains and all of its torturing turbulence just to die at the hands of Bambi. Nope, I wasn't going to sleep. I was gonna be extra attentive until we got off the mountain and back onto somewhat stable ground, heading back into Dubois. After around an hour and a half on the road, that stable ground had arrived. We were now back at the gas station with the giant jackalope. Ella, after acting like she was dying, got out to pump the gas. We were all outside stretching, tired, prepping to make the last hour and some change trek back into Riverton. I felt good for a hot minute. I was a Black dude at a gas station, at almost one in the morning, with other white people, and I wasn't considered a threat. Let this scene would've occurred somewhere in Indiana, and police may have been called, and blasted me immediately for existing while Black. The truck got filled and we continued on. Not even five minutes in, we had to stop. Like no shit, there was a deer crossing the road, and he looked dead ass drunk. He was literally stumbling and stopped walking for a good 10 seconds. He looked up into the bright headlights as if he were saying, fuck my dude, cut them shits off. He lowered his head back down and continued stumbling off the road. I don't know where the party was out here for the forest creatures, but he looked like that Hennessey and Jameson was too much for him. Hell, he reminded me of myself back in the day when I did drink to get fucked up. I'm glad I was in my 30s now, responsible, and not 25. Everyone went back to sleep as we continued our journey. Johnny cranked the gas this time, seeing how we didn't have to worry about mountains anymore. We were on straight flatland. We made it back into Riverton's city limits in a little bit over an hour. By this time, everyone was back up. Our beds were close, but we still had to go drop off Ella's boyfriend at his parents' farm. When we arrived, I saw the darkness outside and contemplated burying him. But it was too late, I was too tired, and he actually conducted himself well the entire day. I simply told the young man good night and we took off. That wasn't before I watched Ella hug him. I was waiting for the goodnight kiss, but it didn't happen. He may have looked like Shaggy, but he wasn't dumb like Scooby. He wanted to live. We then made the seven-minute ride back to the house. As soon as I got in, I headed downstairs and took off everything, changing into my sweats and a T shirt. Right when I started pulling the covers back, I saw Ratatouille and Daisy both at the door, staring at me like the evil twins in the movie The Shining.

"Not tonight y'all. I'm tired."

They just kept looking at me. Then, as soon as they appeared, they went back out. I got up and shut the door completely. Night three was down. Yellowstone and Jackson Hole had opened my eyes to a lot. Now, it was time to close them. Hopefully, until tomorrow afternoon. Knowing my Black ass though. I would be up in five hours. Goodnight world.

— 5 —

JESUS FEAST

The hours of sleep were refreshing. I got six hours to be exact, but it felt like more of an eternity. I thought today would be an ordinary day. You know, lounging around, watching television, sitting on Facebook for half of the day. However, I remembered we were going to church today. Brenda's father was a pastor, and church in this family was like fun in the military. Mandatory. I got up and did my usual. Brush my teeth, washed my ass and cooled down under the fan, as so many of us obsessed with fans do. I sat back on the bed, wondering how unique this experience would be. I say that because anyone Black knows that the church is the building. Chuuch, spelled exactly like that, is what we have. I had seen Catholic mass on television before. Ain't no way in hell I could survive that. It was too quiet, too calm, too serene. When you went to a Black church, it was damn near like going to a Kobe Bryant led Lakers game. The atmosphere at least. A sporting event didn't have shit on the Black church. Matter fact, lemme drop 10 facts about the Black church so that some of you can better understand.

1. You gone see a bunch of middle to elderly aged women sitting up front with what appears to be fruit baskets on their heads. Don't trip. These are not fruit baskets. They are complex hats. Wild looking hats, but hats none the less.

2. Announcements are the worst time for any visitors of the church. Black churches ask you to stand and give your name, where you're from, where's your home church, ask who your mama is, what's your social security number, birthday, do you got any felonies, warrants, pending court cases. Are you behind on your child support? Okay, some of those things I'm lying about, but you get my drift. You are going to have to tell some of your business.

3. The choir could be a good mix of men and women. It could be a youth choir. It could be old people's choir. It could be nothing but big sisters who are sweating chicken grease while they sing. And yes, you can expect someone to bust out a solo at some time during the song.

4. You will see a lot of dancing. This is called catching The Holy Ghost. If you wanna know where Chicago footwork, Memphis jookin, or any other dance originated at, just pay attention in the Black church.

5. It's gone be a helluva lot of offerings. You can't avoid multiple offerings in the Black church. Don't be surprised if you see the building fund. Don't ask me, but it seems like no Black church has ever been fully paid for, even after 75 years of existence.

6. There is always a hype man. This is usually an assistant choir director, or a deacon. They gotta get you turnt up before the first song is sung. Yes, this actually happens. Just roll with it.

7. It is possible that you can be in there all darn day. Once Black churches get in the groove, it's hard to stop. Being in church from 9 a.m. to 6 p.m. is nothing unusual in our community.

8. You will at some point be asked to look at your neighbor and say neighbor, followed by some phrase. This may be repeated several times during the service.

9. When pastor lays hands on you, you may have to fight. Some of those cats don't know their own strength. Either they will grip your skull extra tight, or they'll smack your forehead like you owe them money.

10. You will feel as if God is in the building.

That truly was the experience in the Black church. I knew this was gonna be awkward and the total opposite, but I had to remember the focus. We were there to worship, and whether it's a big building, a cabin in the woods, or a shack made out of straw, the purpose remained the same. I went in the fridge and grabbed some leftover potatoes. With a quick heat up and some pure tomato ketchup, not that high fructose corn syrup shit, I was good to go. Kyla was ready and Ella was dragging as usual. I was happy to see that everyone was dressed casually. I swear I used to hate as a kid that I had to dress up for church. What was the damn purpose? It was come as you are for a reason. The older I got, people would use the dumb phrase, if you can get dressed for the club, you can get dressed for

God. Yea, naw. Clubs had a dress code for a reason. It prevented ruckus from happening. Church was church. I'm quite sure God don't give a damn if one person was in pajamas and the other person was in overalls. If they are there for the appropriate reasons, let them do their thing. It was one of those things that distanced a lot of people from the church. Me personally, this was gonna be my first time going to church in a long time. I stopped going when religion became a priority over relationship. God is within us, and I didn't need a building to learn about Him. Nor did I need scrutiny or anything else negative that came with the church. I don't knock it, but it wasn't my cup of tea anymore.

"Ella are you ready?," Brenda said.

"Yes mom," she responded, as she came down the hall dragging her feet. "Niece, I'm gonna pray you stop having a morning attitude."

"I'm gonna pray God can start every day at noon, because mornings are terrible."

"Both of you need hands laid on you."

I laughed when Brenda said that. We all went outside to the car, still waiting for Johnny, who was in the bathroom doing #2. The sun was shining very bright this morning. I took it as a sign of things to come.

"Alright guys. I am good to go," Johnny came out saying emphatically, still adjusting his belt.

"Dad, did you spray?," Kyla asked.

"Of course, crazy child of mine."

"Dad, taking a dump isn't anything to brag on," Ella said.

"Didn't Moses tell Pharaoh to let his people go?

"Yea, and?"

"Well dad just let his people go."

"Ewww. Gross dad."

We loaded into the car and headed to Tyler's house to pick him up. Once that excursion was over and done with, it was back on the road out of Riverton, headed towards Shoshoni. We hit Shoshoni and made a turn thru the town, heading down the same highway we took to get to Thermopolis. After 20 minutes of driving, I saw a small building off to my right with a trailer. I was telling myself in my head that I knew good and damn well that this wasn't the church. This shit wasn't adding up. I was out in the middle of nowhere, with a small building and a trailer in the back. Yup, I was convinced this was now some Get Out shit. Well God, if I had to fight for my brain, I was ready. We turned off the road and shit got even weirder. Getting closer, I saw that it was a log cabin. I mean, like a no shit log cabin. At this point, no matter how friendly the fam had been, I was ready for whatever. We parked on the dirt and got out. I looked around. The air was crisp as ever, but a calm wasn't over me. It was eerily quiet. There wasn't any wind at all. It was like God said, you on ya own playa. Damn, when the OG say that, you know shit is serious, especially at one of His houses. I waited for the family to head up the steps, because I wasn't walking up in any building where I didn't know anyone. I analyzed every aspect of this building. First thing that was obvious, it was made from logs. The roof angled off at 45 degrees on three levels, encased in emerald green colored material. Sitting atop of the church, was the usual cross. Just like the cabin, that too, was made from logs. I walked up the steps and looked to my right. Now, I was terrified. I saw a no shit bell hanging on the right side. In the movie, the teacup set the victim back straight. Here, the bell gave me that feeling. I had an itch to run over and kick that shit into neighboring Montana. I took a deep breath and cracked my knuckles here at the top of the steps. If I had too, I was gonna lay hands on people in the name of the Lord. The minute I walked in; I saw a very small church. Very few pews, one cross, but the two tables full of goodies had my mind gone in a good way. Before I could dig in, I was introduced to a few people, including Brenda's dad. I never tried to make conversation so short in my life. The grub was calling me. They had a bowl of Swedish fish, crackers, watermelon fresh from the field, M&Ms and some smoked trout. Yes, I said that shit right. Smoked, muthafuckin trout. This was interesting. I never had seen no shit like this in my life. I was used to the high fat, deep fried foods of the Black church. Whether it was morning time with some grease filled bacon, or the post church meal with fried chicken, it was bad for our health. You only started to realize these things when you got older. I poured up a handful of Swedish fish, grabbed four slices of watermelon and took a piece of this trout. I took a bite of the fish and almost cursed. This fish was good. Wait, take that back. This shit was hitting on a whole other level. I grabbed three more pieces and put it on the plate. After another 10 minutes of conversation and being introduced to random people, we took our seats in the pews. I remember every detail. It was close to 15 of us in here. However, that wasn't the biggest thing. There wasn't any choir, no huge organ or piano to be played. Yet, that wasn't the biggest takeaway. For me, it was that people could have plates in their laps during service. That was some boss shit. At Black churches, you ate downstairs, or in some separate room. We were eating when service popped off. Johnny got up to kick things off. He read one verse from the Old Testament and one from the New Testament. Then, two more gentlemen joined him, and we broke out in song. It reminded me of music class in 5th and 6th grade. We just sang in unison, looking at words from a book. In Black churches, the organ player would kick it off with a tune, the hype man deacon would start giving the intro to the hymn and the choir would start blowing. I mean side to side, bouncing ass rhythm to go along with the singing. The church would turn into the club. Not here. It was read along and stay in tune. Once that was over, we sat down, and another gentleman got up. He said a few words and an offering occurred. Like the Black church, a plate was passed around. Unlike Black churches, only one plate was passed. Whether you put a dollar in, or 10 dollars, no one cared. There wasn't any double backing, no we need at least 20 people with 100 dollars, 10 people with 50 dollars, everyone else with five dollars, none of that. I looked at my watch to observe the time. It was 11:31. We started right at 11, and time was moving along simply fine. Brenda's father got up in front. He was in jeans, a button up shirt and some tennis shoes. He wasn't in a white robe, with a cross around his neck, looking like the Klan. He wasn't in a multicolored robe, telling the church to say Amen four or five times, like the Black church pastor. He was in the norm. This was about to be good.

"I'm sorry I'm starting late, but I promise we will be done by 12."

Wait a damn minute. My whole world stopped in that moment. Did this man really say he apologized for starting late? Starting at 11:31 was late? Ahh man, I could rock with this all day every day. Pastors in the Black church don't even start preaching until at least 12-12:15. As I listened to his simple and easy to understand sermon, I was elbowed. I looked over at Ella. See passed me a trout skin cracker sandwich.

"I don't eat the skin," she whispered.

Man, my niece was the whitest Black girl I knew. This was the stuff our folks did. Sneaking you candy when you weren't supposed to have any. My niece was here sneaking me cracker sandwiches instead. She kept doing it to for the next 10 minutes, and I kept chugging them down. In my head, I was Cedric the Entertainer from Kings of Comedy with trout skin cracker sandwiches instead of sunflower seeds. Instead of being a cold ass wedding, this was a cold ass church service. Even some of the cracker got stuck at the top of my mouth like the white bread of those sandwiches Brenda made for the Yellowstone trip. At 12:01, we were done. That was it. Church was over. I had to pinch myself to make sure that I wasn't dreaming. We were literally done with church. I got up, still munching on trout sandwiches. I turned into a n-i-g-g-a and took the rest of the Swedish fish that were left. It was a good amount but fuck it. These people had a whole hour to consume that goodness. I guess fish was the word of the day. I went from Swedish fish to Trout, all in the span of an hour. I walked outside, with another full plate. I don't know what everyone else was talking about and didn't care. I walked around to one side of the church, away from the trailer that I noticed when we first pulled up. There was a farmhouse. It looked beat up and old, with an old rustic car and some other tools inside. Behind there, was an even smaller farmhouse, that looked to be occupied. I came back around and walked up the dirt road, back towards the highway. I looked down one way. Not a soul in sight. I looked down the other way. Same thing. It was symbolic of how these last four days had gone. Mentally, at least. It was quiet in my head. Nothing disturbed me. Not my nephew getting locked up, not my dad dying, my brother's dad dying, not shit. I had reclaimed my mental. It was nuts that coming to Wyoming did that. Damn, I was ready for some more fish. I turned back and walked towards the church.

"You ready Mac?," Brenda asked.

"They got some more of that trout?"

"Naw. It's all gone. But trust me. When we go on that lake today, we're gonna get some more."

"Lake?"

"Yea. We're gonna go fishing on my dad's boat today."

Pause, timeout, flag on the play. The last time I had went on a fishing trip was when I was 12. Now, at that age, not one of us, meaning the cats I was rolling with knew what in the good hell we were doing. All I know is that when the fishing rods got put down, and we started walking towards the lake, one of the homeys bumped me in. It was the scariest moment of my life. I couldn't swim. I just knew that in that moment, I was gonna die. However, somehow, someway, God gave me the power of doggy paddling and staying afloat. I grabbed the edge of the land and pulled myself up. I was hot as shit at my boy, but even madder at myself for going near the edge of the water. From that point on in my life, I never went anywhere close to water unless the maximum depth was five feet.

"Cool. Let's do it," I said so reluctantly.

We headed back to the house with the girls talking instead of biting each other's heads off. The ride back saw us stop in Shoshoni at the gas station yet again. I had to get some more of those pork skins. By now, I had probably consumed the entire pork supply in the state of Wyoming. Leaving there, we rolled to the crib. As always, even though I was fresh and not funky, I jumped my Black tail in the shower. A new adventure called for some new ass washing tendencies. Seeing how it was a nice day out, I simply threw on my shorts and a track jacket. Actually, I took the shit back to the late 90's. I put my jeans on over my shorts. Yes, I knew this shit was out of style. No, I wasn't trying to bring that era back. When it was time to get on that boat, I could simply slip the jeans off in the car and be relaxed while on the boat. The turnaround was quick. Everyone was excited. I was just secretly praying to God to not let me fall off the boat. We made the trip out into the country. It wasn't the huge farm like her brother's house. This was even better. Homey had the house, two boats on the lawn, cars, an outhouse, and the gem of gems.

"AHH HELL NAH!!! I KNOW HE DON'T!!!"

I knew the fam was probably looking at me like I was bat shit crazy. I ran towards this gem, slowing down once in front of it. All I started to think about was being at my Grandmother's house and crossing the street to play with my friends at a park we nicknamed the Baby Park. We used to swing back and forth, getting high as we could, then jump off. As I began to swing, I thought about doing that just to relive my childhood again. However, with the way my old ass knees were set up, I told myself that I didn't need a third knee surgery. Naw. Fuck that. I slowed my momentum and just enjoyed it for a bit, rocking back and forth in the wind. After enough was enough, I got off. Brenda's father was getting the boats ready, while Ella and Kyla were throwing rocks in the branches of the high trees. I didn't know how this entertained them, but when I joined in, I immediately got sucked in. The crisp air of this 70-degree day, combined with the great sunshine that illuminated through the branches, had me feeling some type of way. We continued until it was time to split into two trucks and head on out. Here we were again, on the road back towards Shoshoni. I swear I had been on this highway so much since I been here that I was ready to adopt it for my damn self. We got to Shoshoni and turned back on the highway that took us to the church. We cruised along until I saw a sight that I recognized. The huge lake that we passed on the way to Thermopolis, we turned off to it. The hair on my skin started to stand. Lowkey, I feared water. How I conquered that fear for all these years, especially living in California, I honestly couldn't tell you. I just managed to make it work. You know, sort of like a bad sports relationship tandem that just so happens to win titles together. We parked, and I immediately got out, circling around, looking at the amazing red cliffs that surrounded us. Immediately, I started to think about my dad. I just knew he was sitting on top of one of these few clouds saying, ya Black ass better wear a damn life vest. Trust me pops, I was gonna have one on. I was born at night, not last night. You know, the same night you told mama that you had to go back to work, because you had to feed my big ass. Yea, that night. I know you remember. I dropped my pants and threw them in the truck. It was still nice out, so these shorts were the go-to. I walked over as her dad was backing the boat into the water. Man, I was about to have a real fishing trip. This shit was about to be one for the ages. One by one, we all walked out on the bridge, and the old man assisted us getting on.

"Everyone good?," her father asked.

With thumbs ups and cheers, we rolled out onto the water. We started off slow, just relaxed. I was sitting inside the boat, leaned back against the edge. I wasn't taking any chances. I did however see Ella and her boo thing over in the corner of the boat talking. Too many witnesses, I thought. I couldn't push the young man over and feed him to the fish my damn self. I wanted to still enjoy life, and not spend the rest of it in a jail cell. Look, I know y'all probably tired of me sounding like this, but I was overprotective of my nieces, and that was non-negotiable. If I had it my way, none of them would ever grow up. However, I knew that life had to happen and that I couldn't stop it.

"Hold on guys."

That's all I heard out the blue as pops cranked the boat up. He had some digital machine that pinpointed where all the fish were at.

"C'mon on up Mac."

It was Johnny on the other side of the boat. I got up and made my way through everyone.

"How many times you fish in life?"

"Man, like once or twice. I ain't never caught nothing."

"Well, we're in a good spot, I think. Just throw the rod and when you feel something tug, reel it in."

I did exactly what he told me. For the first 20 or so minutes, nothing. Then, pops moved over to another spot on the lake. I repeated the same process. As I sat there, overanxious for something to snatch my reel, I was lowkey getting upset. Here I was in the middle of a beautiful lake, in a beautiful state, and I wasn't catching a damn thing. Finally, I felt the line snatch. Fuck the bullshit. Whatever this was, it wasn't getting away. I started to reel. My reeling skills were about as good as a white folks doing the cupid shuffle. However, it was getting the job done. You would've thought I was playing tug of war with the incredible hulk. In my world, everything was black around me. Fire boomed from underneath, and to my sides. My muscle fibers were ripping and tearing from the battle that was ensuing. In reality, I was reeling in a hapless fish.

"Oh Mac got one."

When Brenda said that, on cue, I saw the first struggle he gave me above the water.

"Nah muthafucka. You going in some grease. Get ya bitch ass over here."

I was so into it, that I didn't even realize that I said that shit out loud. Finally, I had him. Johnny grabbed a net, snatched the fish out of the air, expeditiously took him off the hook and threw him in the bucket. Life accomplishment #46312. Hook a trout in Wyoming waters and deep fry his ass later. Yea, I was on one. We had fun for the next three hours, and two more fish would become my victims. By the time we were headed back to shore, which was about eight o'clock, the cooler was full of walleye and trout. Oh, tonight would indeed be a feast. As the boat docked next to the bridge we used to walk out, I got out, helping the others carry off equipment. This was my last full day in this foreign land. I was in America, but it felt like another world. In total, I maybe had saw 30 of my kind. I stayed with a white family. I walked into a gun store and didn't get any weird stares. I ate antelope. I soaked my body in Native American healing waters. I went to a town of 3,000 which was most famous for a young man murdering his entire family in the 90's. I saw swastikas that made me wanna burn that same town down, even after learning the true meaning later. I cussed an old, racist bitch out in the middle of nature. A Raven banged on me. In Jackson Hole, I felt free. I thought I was in a Hallmark movie. My Blackness was skin deep. My Caucasian gene was nonexistent, because Melanin dominated, and I wouldn't have it any other way. However, I learned what it was like to be a Black speck in an all-white world. Sometimes, like literally, sometimes, it wasn't all that bad. When it gets to the point where I can say **ALL THE TIME**, then and only then will I let my guard down. However, until the day I die, I know that my skin warrants a death sentence upon the majority of this earth. Out here, I was free. Once I leave, my face would once again flash on the wanted posters of white America's eyes, because most of white America couldn't see what Johnny and Brenda saw. They saw color. It was obvious. You can't avoid my color. You have no choice but to see my Blackness. Whether you wanted to incline about it was on you. There was a way to do that. Not with slick ass remarks. Not with can you teach me how to dance, because I hear Black people can dance so well. I didn't wanna hear what team do you play for? How many yards did you run for in your pro career? How many points do you average a game? Can you show me Iverson's crossover? That's the last thing that a Black man wanted to hear. We wanted to be normal. We wanted to be free. However, we couldn't. We had a stigma on this world that was both negative and positive. Truthfully, they were both negatives, with one disguised in a positive manner. You could watch a Lebron James and be awed as his greatness. A Kobe Bryant. A Michael Jordan. You could see little white kids running up to them, wanting to play the game the way they played. Adults, paying big time bucks to see these men elevate to a status that their unathletic asses could only dream of. However, amid all that greatness. Amid all those riches. None of them would ever trade places with them for a day. That's how beneficial it was to be white. Notice, I didn't say good. I said beneficial. There were poor white people. There were white people who lacked basic comprehension of some things. However, no matter the problems that came with their individual lives, they always had one thing going for them. Their white skin. This country was built on the back of racism. Even for a white man or woman who wasn't racist, they still had a privilege that no amount of money that a Black person obtained could buy. I remember my second night here when Johnny's daughter Ella started crying and telling me a story about when some kids at her school did some racist shit. They had dressed up as Klan members, thinking it was something funny to do. She asked me did I hate her. In uncle fashion, I told her never. I could never hate her. However, I also told her that she now sees the world for what it is. She's been exposed to different cultures because of her parents. Those other kids, they only believe in their culture. I may be the cool uncle to her friends, but its only because I'm Black. In their eyes, I'm a big, Black bully who can beat up anyone. That wasn't the stigma I wanted. But it was as the old saying goes. Everyone loves Black culture but doesn't love Black people. In essence. Everyone wants to be a nigga, until it's time to be a nigga. Ella, for her young age, realized this. Yet the one thing I wasn't ready for, was a question she asked after that conversation about her racist school mates that same night.

"Uncle Mac."

"Yea."

"Since I know a lot of white people are racist behind closed doors, will I have to suffer for their ignorance as well, even though I'm not?"

I paused. Shit had taken me back. Then, after a deep breath and a quick-thinking session, I answered the only way I could.

"Yup. All I can tell you is this Ella. When you get older, and you start interacting around more Black, Brown, whatever other race besides yours. You make sure you go to war for your people who don't have a privilege, the same way your mom and dad go to war for me."

"I love you Uncle Mac."

167

"I love you too sweetheart."

We got back to her father's house and the women of the home were going to work. Brenda, her mother in law, the other women who I couldn't even remember their names now, they were all prepping and cooking the fish. The house was smelling good. Beer battered walleye and trout, frying up in a huge pot of peanut oil. There I was, sitting in the kitchen, eating probably the greatest tasting salad that I had ever had in my life. This was what you called garden fresh. It literally was from the garden. I mingled with the adults, and the kids lollygagged in the somewhat lower part of the house, that I glanced over to on occasion, peeping out slick willie. Finally, the food was brought over. We joined hands for a group prayer, and it was time to feast away. Brenda's mother in law threw four pieces of fish on my plate. Two trout, two walleye. I knew the difference. I had never had walleye in my life, so it was time to sink my taste buds into something different. I broke it with my fork. It was tender, like slicing through hot butter. I blew on it. This wasn't like back in the day where I was willing to risk burning the roof of my mouth for some goodness. Don't ask me where I got it from. It's just some shit that Black folks do. Hell, they even drained off their fish proper. Granny used to use slices of white bread to soak up the grease. Hey, that was the ghetto fab life some of us were exposed too. I put the walleye in my mouth. Immediately, my taste buds started Memphis jookin. My God, this shit was yoga flame, like Dhalsim from Street Fighter.

"Is it good Joe?," her dad asked.

"Indeed, it is sir."

With a head nod from him, I went back into killing my plate. Everything from the fish, to every side dish was devoured in record timing. Of course, I was polite in asking for seconds. They calmly told me to help myself to as much as I wanted. Yea, that was all that I needed to hear. I graciously took me three more pieces of deep-fried goodness, added some more of that succulent pasta and had my way. By the time it hit 11:30, I was full as shit. I couldn't even move anymore. Everything inside of my body was happy.

"You alright Mac?," Johnny asked.

"Yea," I told him, rubbing my belly.

The family burst out into laughter with the way I said it. Yea, this was indeed something great that even words couldn't describe. You had to literally be here to experience it. I was leaving tomorrow evening, and I truly didn't wanna think about that shit. There were trips. Then, there were life changing events. This was one of them. As I made the slow bop to the car with the family, after saying all my goodbyes, two pieces of walleye in a container, in my hand, I stopped dead in my tracks and looked at the sky. The stars were brighter than their usual. At least that's how it appeared to be. I tried to count them, but it was humanly impossible. This was what my Bama folks meant when they said country life was the best life. You had a deeper appreciation for everything. All was well with my spirit. I think I finally let my dad rest when I realized he was indeed one of those stars. I indeed let the trials of having a locked-up nephew go. Was everything his fault? Not at all. There was a huge helping hand in the circumstances that he found himself in. However, at the end of the day, the choices he made were on him. I'd be waiting when he got home from behind the walls. Uncles may protect their nieces, but we revel in our nephews. Those were the men who were going to be the next generation of protectors and name carriers. Yea, it seems funny having all the girl and sex talks with them. We knew what was real though. I think the best thing I could teach all of them was how to survive and carry yourself as a Black man. We are born with two strikes, and a third is always lurking around the corner. Game had to pass on game. That was my only concern. We dropped off Tyler and got back to the house after midnight. Ella was now officially 15. I told her consistently throughout this trip that when it hit midnight, I was gonna bust her upside her skull with a pillow. As I lounged in my shorts and tee shirt, totally oblivious to that now, the room door burst open. I was bombarded with pillow shot after pillow shot. Once I stopped rolling round on the bed, I saw it was both of those turds. They sat back laughing once I sat up.

"Oh, really Kyla? You gone roll with her like that?"

They laughed and jetted out the room. Naw, it was payback time. It was no way in hell that those two turds were gonna get away with this. I gave it some time. I waited about five minutes, making them think that I forgot. I grabbed both pillows, covered in those hideous Green Bay Packers pillowcases. I tiptoed up the stairs and went through the dining room. I stood outside their door and put my ear to it. They were up, still laughing. I flung the door open and both of those turds had gotten comfortable in their beds, thinking that I was just gonna let that shit slide. They started screaming as I started to go to work on them. I went back and forth, from top bunk to bottom bunk. This was one of the most hilarious things that I had ever done. I hightailed it out the room, laughing hysterically. I heard Brenda through her closed door cracking up like there was no tomorrow. Uncle two, nieces one. I may have been old, but these knees were still good, seeing how I moved fast without a tweak or a crack. It was certainly different from my morning wakeups. As I got back to the basement, I sat on the edge of the bed, chilling, thinking about the past four days again. Out of the corner of my eye, I saw the cats roll up in my room. They both hopped up on the bed. Daisy just stared at me. Ratatouille, she chilled on the corner of the bed. They left after about three minutes or so, and I shut the door behind them. I cut off the lights and proceeded to get under the covers. Immediately, I got back up and cut the fan on. I couldn't sleep without a fan on. I was good now. I slipped back under the covers and closed my eyes so I could drift off into dreamworld. Then, a huge bubble of gas in my stomach erupted out my ass.

"OH SHIT!!!"

I lifted the covers and fanned them. After a good minute of clearing that sewage smell out from under the covers, I slipped back underneath them. Five minutes later, I felt it coming on again. I let number two release. This time, I just threw the covers off me. This was going to be a long ass night. I couldn't leave these covers off the whole night, because I was gonna freeze my ass off. Oh well. Time to suck it up. I pulled those covers back up over me. Goodnight world.

"DAMN!!!"

I let out another one. Boy oh boy. That fish did some work to my gut.

— 6 —

BLACK VANILLA

I had once read a book called A BLACK MAN HAS NINE LIVES. Not to give away the story, but it involved a young high school kid that played football. In the end, he and his friends shunned all the big-name schools and ended up taking full rides to the University of Wyoming. They did this all so they could honor the legacy of the Black 14, a group of Black players who were blackballed at the University in 1969, because they protested the Church of Jesus Christ and Latter Day saints for not allowing Black men to enter into its priesthood. Going anywhere, as a Black man, I was prepared for everything. Life sometimes shows you everything. All at the same damn time.

"Happy birthday niece."

"Thanks uncle."

I gave my baby a hug and a kiss to the top of her natural blonde hair.

"What time does your plane leave?"

"It leaves at three girls, so we have to leave here by noon."

The looks on their faces said it all after Brenda told them that.

It was something that I wasn't ready for. I could tell the love was genuine. While they were probably thinking that I influenced them, they for damn sure had one on me.

"Y'all wanna go get some ice cream?"

"Uncle Mac, it's 10 in the morning."

"Oh my goodness Ella. It's your birthday for crying out loud. Just say yes."

"I was turd. I just never ate ice cream at 10 in the morning."

"Well turd, I want some."

"Both you turds come on," I said.

I looked over at Brenda sitting in the living room. All she could do was laugh. As crazy as this was, I lowkey enjoyed this shit. I wouldn't hear these two bickering for a long time after this. We walked out the door and the beauty of the day encased us. In Wyoming, you had to enjoy this. The weather was bipolar. It could be 70 one minute and below 40 the next. We headed down the block, which was ironically quiet this Memorial Day. Back home, the barbecuing would've started at nine, maybe eight. Niggas would've been in the front or back yard playing dominoes, spades, shooting dice, or probably even lifting some weights. Hell, it was a stolen Black holiday anyway, so we had reason to commemorate it. If you don't believe me, look it up. I finally saw my first person on this gorgeous morning. The girls waved and yelled hi to whoever this lady was. Me, I followed suit raising my hand. She acknowledged me. It felt good to know that a Black man could walk two white children to Dairy Queen and not be shot down in cold blood. I answered a million questions on the way there. Kyla was a walking, breathing questionnaire. What does that tattoo mean uncle? When are you moving up here? Can we come and stay in California with

174

you? You won't kill my boyfriend when I get older will you? The shit was so funny and refreshing man. Most people would be tired of a child talking their ear off. Me, nah. This was family. This was one half of my babies. The nutty duo. The turd monsters. It didn't bother me at all. Plus, this wasn't talking. I once had a co-worker who brought his son to work. He was five then, and this kid asked me everything under then sun from who was the girl on my Facebook feed, to what's that shit lying on my desk. Lil Ja was a teenager himself now, and he transitioned all that questioning to the football field, where he was developing into a great football player, and even better young man. My homey other son, Josh. Well, that was a different story all together. When he brought his thug, toddler ass to work, he didn't like no one near his daddy. I said what's up to him. He walked his one year old behind up on me with balled up fists, with a mad look on his face. The kid was insane as all to be damned. I had never been run up on by a toddler and instantly thought of fighting him seriously. Now, this kid was 10, and well on his way to becoming a future football star like his older brother. I watched him at camp tackle someone once, without pads. Josh didn't give a damn. He was gonna be that type of football player to lay someone out and look over at the paramedics as if to say, are y'all gone get this muthafucka off the field so I can crush someone else's skull? Kids were indeed amazing. We walked into Dairy Queen without a care in the world. I was surprised Wyoming had a Dairy Queen to be honest.

"What y'all want?"

"Just a chocolate ice cream," Kyla said.

I looked over at Ella, but the way her face looked concerned me.

"Why are you staring at my uncle like that?"

I looked up towards the young lady at the register. Immediately, I could tell that her facial expression shifted.

"Hi sir. What would you like?"

The cracks in her voice told me the only thing I needed to know. The big, Black man was scary. Here we go with this shit.

"Ella you know what you want?"

Ella was staring a hole through this girl. If it was someone you didn't fuck with, it was me.

"Chocolate ice cream cone. Because vanilla can be pure trash at times."

She said that shit with conviction and never took her eyes off that girl. "Umm yea," as I wrapped my arms around Ella. "Three large chocolate ice cream cones. Please."

I threw on the please at the end. I didn't do it because I wanted to ease her fears. I did it because I was raised with manners. I paid the money and waited. Kyla was completely oblivious to what was going on. Ella and her 15-year-old brain picked up the animosity quickly. I saw Kyla wandering around, simply waiting for an ice cream cone. Ella was wrapped in my right arm, hugging me, not taking her eyes off that girl. She was pissed, but I couldn't let her see me the same way. I knew how to handle this. I was 35. She was 15. She wanted to lash out. My lesson in restraint was telling her to chill.

"Here you are sir."

She didn't even wanna look at Ella.

"Thank you," I said, ensuring to make eye contact. "And you have a great day."

Two things I was taught. When you say thank you, or make a toast, always look someone in the eyes. It is a secure feeling you are giving them. The girls and I walked off, with me catching Ella turning her head and sticking her tongue out at the girl. I simply laughed and shook it off.

"Uncle Mac. Why was she acting like that?"

"Long story niece. Long story. I'll explain it to you later."

Kyla ain't give a shit bout our convo. She was skipping along about a good four paces ahead of us. One niece was ecstatic. The other had become my protector, walking with me side by side, as if I were the child, and she were the adult. Halfway to the house, which was nothing but another two minutes of walking, we heard the sirens.

"Yall move on over to the sidewalk."

We all drifted towards the right side of the street. We heard them getting closer and closer. From the sounds of it, I could tell they were shooting down the main road through town. It was lowkey exciting to hear that shit out here, considering that you wouldn't think that shit went down in Wyoming. I know Brenda told me that sometimes the Native Americans on the reservation bang on each other, but nah, I really couldn't see that happening. I don't know man. Maybe because where I'm from, when you hear the term banging, you see guns blazing, bodies dropping, mama's crying, all that. But hey, as I knew, you could get banged on anywhere. As we continued to walk, literally 30 seconds from the front steps, I turned my head to see the police rounding the corner. There were two squad cars.

"Man, I know on my mama these niggas ain't coming for me."

The girls both looked at me, stopping dead in their tracks. I knew that I didn't say that shit out loud for them to hear, but my mind was in another place. I remained calm and walked with my babies.

One car then literally skidded right in front of us to a complete stop. I didn't even pay attention to what the other car did at that point.

"GET BEHIND ME YALL!!!"

Kyla ran behind me and Ella clutched me tight.

"What's happening Uncle Mac?," Ella said.

"I love you. Just remember that if they kill me."

"PUT YOUR HANDS UP NOW!!!"

From what I saw, four cops and four guns were now aimed at me, in broad daylight, in a quiet town, in the middle of nowhere. The ice cream that was dropped spilled all over my forces, which right now was better than my blood being spilled over my nieces.

"DON'T MOVE!!!," one cop yelled again.

Two seconds later, I felt a sharp pain in the back of my neck, as an officer from the other car mashed me down to the ground. His knee was in the middle of my spine. He snatched my arms backwards, strapping me in cuffs. I could feel the barrel of the gun literally hovering over me. The heat of its breath was screaming in my ear to release a yawn of epic proportion. I heard only one of my nieces yelling and crying. I think this is what amazed me the most. My lifeline was on the verge of going flat, yet all I was concerned with were two teenage white girls, even though I was being oppressed by the same skin tone. They snatched me up and sat me on the curb. Rather tossed me to it, and then sat me back straight. Guns were still aimed at me.

"HEY!!!," I heard a yell from across the street.

With a quick cut of my eyes, I saw Brenda and Johnny running out of the house.

"MA'AM STAY BACK!!!"

"THAT'S MY KIDS UNCLE!!! WHAT ARE YOU DO-ING???!!!"

I literally leaned over, because my head was hurting now from that smack to the back of my neck before they threw me down to the ground. I don't even wanna imagine where I would be if he had taken my head full force into the concrete.

"EXCUSE ME!!!"

"THATS MY KIDS UNCLE!!! MY HUSBAND'S BEST FRIEND!!!"

Johnny was holding her back as best he could. Brenda was livid and so was I. Pain just masked my anger right now, as I started to develop the biggest headache in the world.

"Ma'am we got a call about a possible abduction that occurred in a Dairy Queen. A Black man snatching two girls. And this description is him."

I didn't know where my nieces were at this point. I didn't care. I just wanted them safe. From what I saw, the whole block was out now. Memorial Day fireworks hadn't shot off officially, but there were enough here to last until the Fourth of July. Now, there were numerous white people yelling at these white devils in blue uniforms. Here it was in the 2010's, looking like the 1810's. Only this time, it wasn't a field of cotton and master whipping me with a belt. It was a new form of slavery. It was to exterminate anything with Melanin at any and every cost. This was a scene that none of them wanted. Not the police, and not a small town such as this. By now, more cop cars had shown up. I was stood up. Townspeople were going the hell off on their asses. I saw police looking dumbfounded, sad, depressed, in a complete state of shock. Crazy how when you own kind rebuke your irrational, fucked up methods of power, suddenly its we must do better. It's no fun when the rabbit has the gun. Had this been an angry mob of my people, we already know what would've gone down. Tear gas, riot police, numerous arrests, maybe a call for the National Guard or some other form of over the top ass punishment. For days I was a Black Caucasian. Now, the Caucasian part was dropped. I was back to a nigger that wasn't greeted and treated as if I were a part of their family. I was once again the enemy. My hall pass had run out. The Chief of Police for Riverton pulled up. Great, just what the fuck I needed. The Imperial Grand Wizard. Other cops were directed to take control of the crowd.

"Dan. Get his hands out those cuffs and get back to the station. I will deal with you all later."

Dan didn't say a word as he followed his master's orders. I was looking this Chief dead in his face as my cuffs were released. To my surprise, no gun was pulled on me, no threatening motions were enacted. Nothing. He took a deep breath, never taking his eyes off me. I popped my knuckles out of anger, not for fighting. The look in our eyes said something different. Ironically, I wasn't in fear at this point. I was just lost.

"Sailors belong on ships."

I turned my face up.

"What?"

"Sailors belong on ships."

After a few deep breaths, I responded.

"Ships belong on sea."

"Haze, grey and underway."

"The only way to be."

"Yea you and Johnny did talk a lot like he said, I see.

"Yea well. He was the Navy guy, and he would say it so damn much that I memorized it."

"I know. You know you would think that living in America, a nation founded on immigration, you could go anywhere, relax, interact with all kinds of people, and just enjoy life. Yet, you have to deal with something I could never imagine. That's being Black. The sad thing in all of this is that Johnny came to me days before you got here. Told me he has a friend named Mac coming to visit, and that there is always a chance that a few assholes may not take kind to him because of his skin color. Now the fact that I promised him you would be okay, and now, I have to see this, makes me appalled to wear this badge. Hell, it makes me appalled to be white. I can't apologize because an apology will do nothing for you. I can fire those guys, terminate them. Yet still, it won't do anything for you. Because at the end of the day, you have a trial that I could never even imagine facing. You're hated because of the way you look. So, as a man, a veteran, all of that. All I'm gonna ask you is this. Do you wanna hit me? For all the shit faced, racist fuck inbred Anglo Saxon ass people who roam this country, thinking it belongs to them and them only. Your choice, Mac."

In the midst of my rage, my anger, the blood boiling inside of me, I pictured punching the dog shit out of him for every Sean Bell, Mike Brown, Tamir Rice, Trayvon Martin, Philando Castile and every other Black man that had been gunned down by police. I looked over to see my nieces on the porch, holding their mom, crying their eyes out. I looked back at the Chief, rage burning inside of me.

"No. If I hit you, I'm dead. I know this setup shit. And you can't fucking fool me."

He chuckled.

"DAN!!!"

To my surprise, he will still around after Chief told him to bounce. He came jogging over, as the rest of the force was trying to keep the crowd at bay.

"Yes sir."

BOP!!! He punched Dan and he dropped faster than the temperature in this muthafucka come December. The block got quiet. Shock rang across everyone's faces. The shit even made me raise my eyebrows.

"GET UP!!!"

Dan struggled to get to his feet. Woozy, holding his face, Chief turned to me.

"You want your shot? Mac?"

I looked at Dan, then back to Chief.

"I gotta plane to catch Chief."

He nodded his head.

"Just like a stand-up man. Go high when pieces of shit go low. We'll be in touch Mac."

I walked off towards the house, knowing all eyes were on me. I stopped right in front of the steps, where Johnny was. We had the look in our eyes as if this were 2004 again, crossing paths for the first time. Johnny wasn't the fighting type. He wasn't the confrontational type. He wasn't anything like me. That's what I loved about him though.

"It's not your fault," I told him.

I walked up to see Brenda and the girls crying. I looked at all three of them.

"Mac, I'm sorry," Brenda told me, with tears streaming down her face.

I shook my head. I looked at my nieces.

"Kyla. Ella. Don't kill that girl behind the counter."

With that, I walked in the house. Immediately, however, I turned back around.

"Ella."

"Yea Uncle Mac," she answered, still crying.

"I really mean that. Don't kill her. You've got some of me in you. I don't need you in jail."

That got a chuckle out of all three of them. I walked back in and began to pack my bags. As I tried to forget everything that had just happened and get the last of my things in before I had to take off, there was a knock at the door.

"Sup Brenda."

She came in, shut the door, and sat on the edge of the bed.

"You seem upbeat for everything that just happened."

"Yea well, it could be worse. I could be dead. You know. Another Black man on the news. Gunned down by law enforcement for no reason."

She got quiet for a minute, as I stuffed this Wyoming shirt in to complete my packing. It was 11:30 on the dot and we were bouncing in 30 minutes.

"What was it like Mac?"

I looked up at her.

"What was what like?"

"Growing up. I'm trying to understand. That's the only way we get ahead in this world is to understand each other. Was there always a hatred for police like this?"

I sat down on the bed. I never questioned how genuine she was because it was obviously there in the way she asked and her tone.

"I mean. For us. When you grow up in the inner city, the hood, whatever people wanna call it, the police are just someone who you naturally don't fuck with. I mean, we had a few cool ones. Like one of my partners, his dad was a cop. He kept us on the straight and narrow. But we could relate to him, and he to us, because he was raised in the same parts. He stayed in the same neighborhood he came up in. So, knowing that, we looked at him differently. He didn't approach us out of fear and hate. He approached us out of love. If we were doing something wrong, he fixed us. Hell, if we thought about doing something wrong, he got it out of our heads before we had the chance to do it. In general, a lot of those paid to protect and serve were just there to serve us misery. I dunno. It's like a hereditary trait that's passed down for generations. You know, with the police. Our grandparents were hosed, beaten and bitten by dogs. Our parents were profiled, and when they see ghetto Black kids, excuse my French. They see niggas. That's probably the best way I can put it. I mean, this may sound nuts. But, when we left the Dairy Queen, and I heard the sirens, I knew some shit was gonna go down. I saw the movements in that place. Like the girl went to the back for a hot minute when the ice cream machine was right there in the front. I already knew some fishy mess was going down. But, I ain't wanna alarm the girls, so I just rolled along. Once they rounded the corner, I just told myself here we go. Either this was gonna go smooth and civilized, or I was about to be on CNN. Those were my God honest thoughts. It's not your fault."

Even more tears started to stream down Brenda's face now.

"I just somehow in a small way feel responsible for it."

I chuckled a little bit.

"Don't. I know you know how I feel about white people in general. That's not to say I don't care about you, Johnny, or the girls. Individually, you've shown me that there are those who do care about others' plights. Things that they go through because of their skin tone. I know you ain't know, but I saw you kind of stare down that elderly lady in Thermopolis when she was staring at me at the pool. I guess she thought the water was dirty or some shit because I was in it. I see things. I observe a lot. I may not say it, but I do. My guard is always up around white people. It's just how I am. So, don't feel bad. Just keep being you. I'm gonna keep being me. I'm not gonna let one fucked up person's views of what they think Black is destroy my world. I do however appreciate you talking with me. Shows me a lot."

"Yea. It's hard to see someone you care for go through unnecessary things. I mean, I know we were connected by John. And, I love you as family. But the girls, they are crazy about you. You don't know how every night they asked me is Uncle Mac coming next year. Can he stay here? Can we move him up here with us forever? It's one thing for adults to feel a certain type of way. But kids tell the truth. Like, the rugged truth."

"You mean like Ella and her why did you feed my chickens truth?"

We both laughed.

"Thanks Brenda."

"Thank you Mac."

We got up and hugged. Imagine that. A Black man and a white woman. Hugging. No ill will, no hatred, none of that. Just family. I just wished I could change history. Seems like every interaction with a white woman in the past resulted in a lynching for one of us. Whether it be Emmett Till who was lied on and died as a 14 year old. Or, the white woman who ran out of an elevator screaming because she didn't want the other whites to know she was involved with a Black guy. What did that turn into you ask? The bombing of Black Wall Street. And by the way. Don't think for one second that my people were not fighting back. As many of ours that died that day, trust. It was a whole bunch of racist ass white folks getting clapped on in the name of The Lord. Had it not been for those military planes, and later Interstate 244, Greenwood would still be thriving today like it did back in the 1910s.

"Girls are you ready?," Brenda asked.

Those two came out of the damn room arguing.

"Oh my goodness. What are y'all arguing about now?," I asked.

"Kyla says she's your favorite. I said no. How can you be his favorite with braces?"

"Uncle Mac had braces before?"

"Yea well he fed my chickens?"

"Well he doesn't like your boyfriend, so I win by default."

"Girls."

"YES!!!," they both said in unison.

"Both of y'all crazies are my favorites. Ella, you're about as independent as they come. Kyla, you are funny. That British accent you did passing those folks when we saw the bears was classic. I love both of y'all."

"See Ella. He loves me more. He remembered a specific event with me." "I mugged the racist girl at Dairy Queen for him."

I simply looked up at Brenda. She couldn't contain her laughter. I looked over at Johnny. He just sat at the chair in the dining room, drinking a glass of orange juice. He always dealt with three women in this house. He more than likely learned to shut the fuck up and let them have it. Me, on the other hand, it was what it was. Lord, please let me have boys. If I had girls, and they were anything like these two, I would be bald. Not George Jefferson, some hair left bald. I'm talking Tommy from Martin bald, with no job, just shaking my ass for cash on occasion. We got back on the road heading to Casper. Not even 15 minutes in, the snow started to fall.

"Oh my goodness. Can this weather make up its mind?"

"That's Wyoming Mac," Brenda said.

As we hit Shoshoni, a cop car pulled up behind us, cutting their lights on. I just leaned my head back on the seat. Great, I thought. Here we go with another episode of Bad Boys. What's this shit going to be about? Oddly, the cop didn't pull up behind us. Instead, they pulled up alongside. Brenda let the window down, and it was the Chief of Police from Riverton.

"I stayed quite a distance behind you Brenda so you wouldn't be alarmed. I had to make sure one of our family members got to the airport safely. How do you feel Mac?"

I smiled and nodded my head at him.

"Good sir. Thank you."

"I'm Chuck. The only people I want calling me sir are the knuckleheads in the high school."

I chuckled as he signaled for us to pull off.

"Wow, a police escort. That's odd to say the least."

"Told you Mac. Not everyone is a douche."

"Kyla is."

"Shut up Ella."

"Will you two cut it out already?," Brenda said.

187

"She's mad she looks like dad and not pretty like me and you mom." "Wait hold on," Johnny said.

"Are you calling your old dad ugly Kyla?"

"No dad."

"Well if Ella's ugly, then I'm ugly."

"Yup dad. She said you ugly. Don't worry. We're pretty. She's not."

"So are you calling me ugly?," Brenda asked Ella.

"Umm, no mom."

I was in the front seat cracking the fuck up. This shit was literally a late 90's Chris Rock stand up session. These two needed their own show. The continuation of this road trip to the airport saw nothing but great joy as the laughs continued. By the time we reached Casper Airport, it had stopped snowing. However, the mouth of the sky had opened and was regurgitating Niagara Falls. We sat in the parking lot, trying to wait it out. My flight didn't leave for over an hour, so I was still good to go.

"Well, Mac. Did you have fun? I mean, besides the crazy mess."

"Yea man. I needed those Native American waters in my life. Crazy man. I feel like there isn't an impurity in my body right now."

"Speaking of waters guys. This rain just got light. Let's go in before it turns into a monsoon again."

Brenda was right. It was time to go in before the angels started to cry once more. The girls, they wanted to stay inside. We all got out. I gave both my little minions hugs and kisses on the cheek.

"Y'all be good to each other you hear," I said with my arms wrapped around both.

"Only if Kyla agrees to not be a turd."

"You're a turd."

"THATS IT. IM GONE!!!"

I let those knuckleheads loose and got my bags out the trunk. We walked through the drizzle into this baby airport.

"Yo, before I go. I need to take a pic by this bison."

"I got you," Brenda said.

I posted up on the well painted statue of the bison, casting a genuine smile. After a good four shots, that was it. I hugged Brenda, then Johnny. Me and Johnny's embrace was a bit longer than usual. We both did a good job holding our tears back, even though we both knew that the emotion was there. We broke apart.

"You take care of yourself Mac."

Looking at each other, you could tell we were holding back tears like a muthafucka. I don't know if it was because we didn't wanna show each other that we would miss each other, or whether it was us trying to uphold our macho egos as much as possible.

"Question."

"Yea Mac."

"How many Black people did you grow up with?"

"Huh?"

"How many Black people did you grow up with?"

After a few seconds, it registered with him.

"I didn't care Mac. I see color, but I see a man's character more."

As if it was 2005 again, and our first major conversation was going on. Those words resonated with me now as they did back then. I turned around, not looking back. Much like many of my relationships with family members, Wyoming was behind me. All I needed to do now was fly to Denver, then head back home to California. An hour passed, and that rain had turned into snow. Now, my on-time flight was now delayed. Another hour passed,

189

and we were still delayed. Fucking great. Fuck me, right? I texted Brenda, consistently letting her know what was up. A 3:45 flight was now 5:00. My joint in Denver was taking off at 7:15. There wasn't any way I was gonna make it there and make it through that big ass airport to connect to my next flight. Then, something happened that quelled my anger for a hot minute. One of the airport workers came out with a huge box of snacks. I mean, not that airline peanuts and cheese crackers shit. Naw. They had Doritos, Twizzlers, Welch's Fruit Snacks, some sandwiches, Gatorade's, and a bunch of other fruit drinks. It didn't make up for a late flight, but it damn sure settled me down. Now, I knew what it was like to be a woman, because Lord knows a woman without food was a human version of a category 5 hurricane. Finally, around 5:30, they said we were good to go. This was gonna be some shit. I was unplugging my charger when my phone buzzed. I looked to see that I had an email notification. I opened my GMAIL account to see the words DEEP GREENWOOD. Instantly, I thought it was spam, but something told me to just open it. Upon doing so, my life changed forever.

Mr. Baker, known in the spoken word realm as Blaxploitation. We are hosting a theater piece on Black Wall Street in Tulsa, Oklahoma, this upcoming weekend. We are sorry this is on short notice, but would it be possible for you to fly down and bless us with your presence, art, and overall aura. Please contact me within the next 24 hours, so that I can solidify your spot. Thank you.-Mia

At this point, I could've walked back to Cali. That's how happy I was. In on Monday night and back out Friday morning. Yea, work was just gonna have to take a back seat. If the boss was mad, then he could kiss my ass. Spoken word was my first love, and it was time for a reunion with her. This was a once in a lifetime opportunity that a nigga refused to miss. That universal energy from feeding a Raven had come back around. My suffering here was rewarded with the opportunity to be great in another place. I boarded the plane with a bit more swag than usual. The flight was 40 minutes, but by time we got to Denver, I knew my connecting flight would be booking. Oh well. Couldn't shit piss me off at this moment. Not even a missed flight. We took off shortly before 6:00 p.m. The snowy green hills and mountains were a sight to see indeed, but beauty took a back seat. I was anxious. Finally, after what seemed like an eternity in the air, we finally landed. 6:44 p.m. was the exact time that I exited the plane. My joint left at 7:15. Funny, when things go normal at an airport, you can find any screen easily to see what gate your flight is at. This time, fuck no. I was at the small terminal for the short flights. I ain't have time to be searching for any screens. I asked the flight attendant behind the desk what gate I would have to go to. When she told me, I knew it was time to turn into the world's fastest man. Then, right before I stared to run, I said fuck it. I'm gone miss this shit anyway. I might as well take my time and prepare to hunker down for the night. I walked normally. Seeing how it was almost in the same spot that I landed, I knew it would be at least a 20-minute walk, to include the train that I had to catch to the other terminal. I ain't slow bop it, but I damn sure didn't rush. When I finally arrived at the gate, at literally 7:26, it didn't look like a flight that took off. I knew that the next upcoming flight couldn't have filled up the gate already. If it did, these were some on time people. I looked at the sign by the flight attendants. Delayed to 8:45 p.m. Man, I could've danced like James Brown at this point. Shit, if I was late, all y'all niggas was gonna be late as well. I high fived God in my head. He gave me about 10 bags of fruit snacks and made everyone else late right along with me. Not all heroes wear capes. Some of them sit on top of clouds saying, I got you. I guess that's what you call Melanin looking out for Melanin. Time progressed and it was time to head back to Cali. It was a packed flight as well. And I'll be damned if I ain't check my ticket ahead of time. I had a middle seat, second row from the back. Fuck it, I thought. This shit could be worse. I got on and awaited my fate to see who I would be squeezed in between. After a while, I let out a sigh of relief. I had two women I was in between. One, a Latina baby. The other, a sister, who was clearly mixed. Her eyes were green, and you could tell they were natural, and not any contacts. Man, talk about the mile-high club. We took off, and just like when we flew into Denver, the turbulence hit as soon as we got over the Rocky Mountains. Yea, fuck this shit. If I could find a flight out there next time that didn't go over these joints, I was damn sure taking it.

— 7 —

G.A.P.

The next three days were literally a blur. I was too excited to even
think about anything else. I was about to travel to where the shit
went down at. The show was Saturday night, and a nigga had an
arsenal of spoken word in the mental armory. It was Thursday night.
I was all packed up. I had checked the bank account about four or
five times. If nothing else, I was going to go down there and pour
as much money as I could into Black business without going broke.
I owed it to myself, the current residents, and the ancestors. I read
up all night on the Tulsa Race Massacre. I had read up on this shit
a million times before. Now, however, I was delving deeper than I
ever had before. Of course, I only read anything about this through
Black news sources. I'd be damned if I was gonna read this shit
through any site or publication that was whitewashed and white
owned. Matter fact, I truthfully ain't wanna see anyone white at this
point. That harassment by the Klan in blue suits was still fresh in my
mind. My flight was at six in the morning, but the intellectual gas
tank was open. My whole focal point was to be as full as possible.
Truthfully, that was a tactic of mines to erase bullshit later. I don't
know if y'all watched Married with Children, but I most certainly

did. I had nothing but love for Al Bundy. Matter fact, the older I got, the more I started to understand that nigga. The more I watched episodes over and over, I saw little gems being thrown out. There was an episode where Kelly, his dumb blonde daughter was going to be on a game show. Al literally bombarded her with facts, and whatever he taught her, that was it. She couldn't learn anything different from the night prior until the end of the show. If she learned one new thing, she would forget a fact that she learned. Well, all was well until the host made casual conversation with her and she learned something new. Al was scared shitless. However, she continued answering everything, all the way through the bonus round. In the final round, and a chance for $10,000 I believe, the simplest question was asked. Who set the city record by scoring four touchdowns in the city championship game? Al rejoiced with his now classic line, *Excuse me Peg, while I kiss the sky.* Kelly, shall I say with all pun intended, looked dumbfounded. She couldn't answer the question to save her life, even though her dad was the correct answer. He had told the story one million times, so you just knew that was something she would remember off top. But it just wouldn't be on that day. I became full of Black internet write ups. I wanted to unlearn everything by Sunday, with face to face knowledge sessions. Three in the morning came around and I arose. I got a good five hours, and I could get even more on the plane. I wasn't about to park my shit at the airport and get hit with $35 a day in parking fees. Naw. Fuck that shit. I did what any smart person would do. I parked my shit in a residential that I was comfortable with and signaled for an uber. Truthfully, I parked over by my old apartments from years ago, because I knew my car wouldn't get fucked with over here. Plus, me and the landlord were tight, and he remembered the make, model, and license plate of my shit. If anything went down, he would give me a ring. He ain't trip, as long as I stayed on the street and didn't bombard some current resident's spot. Trust me, its niggas that do, and they come back to a hot ass $450 impound fee, plus whatever the cost is by day. I waited patiently for my uber driver. They would be here quick, seeing that from the tracker they were only three minutes out. I stayed in my whip. Yes, this was a cool area, but this was also California. You could never be too cautious in this state. Niggas was known for the jack move, and I'll be damned if I became a victim. My uber showed up. I waited until he got out or rolled the window down. I don't touch other people's cars without permission. He rolled the window down. It was a middle-aged Arabian guy.

"Mac."

"Yes."

He got out and popped the trunk.

"Here here. I take your bag."

"Thank you."

I got in and we were on our way to the Southwest terminal, aka the Black folks getaway station. Wanna get away was their motto. The next commercial should have a Black person saying, nigga yea, right after they asked the question. You could never sleep on them or those $49 specials they hit you with every now and then. We made it to the airport in a good amount of time. Small talk was made, but nothing too serious, seeing how it was three something in the morning and everyone was still half sleep during this hour. This was the only time you could drive in L.A. and not get caught in a traffic jam. I made it to the airport, walked in, checked my bag, got my ticket, and proceeded over to the security gates. They had just opened. No need for Pre TSA right now, cause this bitch was bone dry. I made it through quick with no hassles. The only problem was that my Black ass would have to wait until five o'clock to get some grub in me. Nothing opened before then. Shit, I wasn't even a bagel guy. However, that Einstein Brothers logo was looking like the sexiest thing alive right now. As soon as the clock struck five, it was gonna be me and her. In the meantime, I sat down, plugged my phone in one of the jacks, with a special device that didn't allow for hackers to steal your info. I threw my headphones in and flipped in between classic hip hop hits and classic comedy sketches.

"I AINT SCARED OF YOU MUTHAFUCKAS!!!"

Boy oh boy. The great Bernie Mac man. If it was anything that would wake me up, it was him. I laughed my ass off at this Def Comedy Jam skit. Even though I had seen it a million times, the shit never got old. I circulated between him, Chris Rock and Eddie Griffin, who by far is the funniest muthafucka alive. I damn near lost track of time, because when I finally checked the time on my phone, it was 4:59. I looked up and it was already three people in line for those Einstein bagel sandwiches. I wrapped my phone charger up and got up to join them. I was mad cause I couldn't be first one in line. This was how bad my hunger was. I got me two-egg white, turkey and cheese joints, with an orange juice. Not that concentrate, watered down shit either. I'm talking about the fresh squeezed, actual factual juice that was some fucking juice. It took them a good six minutes to complete my order, but man was it hitting. I had eaten breakfast sandwiches before, but when your dumb ass doesn't even snack before you leave, it becomes a little bit more satisfying. Now, sitting back down, waiting for boarding call, the area became full, as now everyone and they mama was here. I had to go to Phoenix first, layover for two hours, then head to Tulsa, which would be a two hour and some change flight. I kept bobbin my head to my listening pleasures until they called for A boarding group. I swear man. Southwest Airlines check in was a race against time. Once that 24 hours hit, I was already locked and loaded on my phone, tapping the check in button. I got lucky. A24 on this flight. A38 on the next flight. I boarded, and quickly obtained me a window seat towards the back of the plane. Fuck that middle seat shit. The aisle was no better. I swear people would run into you with a whole aisle to move around. As the plane boarded, I paid attention to everyone getting on this joint. I asked God to please not let any one of these folks sit next to me. So far, so good. Eventually, one brother sat in the aisle seat, in my row. Ok, cool. I was gravy with that. Now, the question became was someone going to plop their ass in between us. Once I saw that cabin door close and no more people entering, I gave God a solid. Me and this unknown salt and pepper bearded ass negro was chilling, with no interruption in between us. He could get an arm rest if he wanted to, as could I. I was straight now. The only thing left to do was my usual whenever I took a flight. I bowed my head, said a prayer for God to cover the plane and I was good to go. Once we took off, even though it would just be a little over an hour, I took my Black ass to sleep. I wasn't that much of a heavy sleeper unless I was dead tired, and that was usually after a slaughter session at the gym. I got a good nap in. They announced the descent into Phoenix and my eyes were open. We landed smoothly and I walked off just as relaxed as I did when I walked on. I peeped the screen to see where my connecting flight was. It was all good as well. My connecting joint was a 30 second walk from where I landed. This wasn't Denver on repeat.

I see the ancestors of Tulsa were already looking out for a brother. Once again, I was hungrier than Dennis Rodman when he saw a ball come off the rim. There was a joint I saw called Barrio Cafe. Mexican food was my weakness and it was time to indulge. Actually, it was too early for that shit, so I decided on traditional breakfast. However, it didn't look like the other restaurant served breakfast food, so I said fuck it. I was hoping to just have some pancakes and eggs. As I was seated, and the waitress gave me the menu, I saw they did have breakfast grub. Cool, I thought. I continued to scan the menu. Then, I saw it. A pork burrito. I had to pause. I only ate one burrito outside of Cali and that was in Florida. I couldn't lie. I was impressed down there, and it should have been no surprise seeing how big their Latino population was. Phoenix was in the same boat, but I was always skeptical. Eating any Mexican food outside of Southern California, particularly San Diego, which had the best in the nation, always made me feel like I was cheating on my main chick with a woman of lower quality. Fuck it. A brother had to see if they could compete with the king of Mexican food. I ordered the burrito that came with some eggs. When it came, I had three joints that were cooked to a perfect over medium, and a wet burrito that was laid out on a plate, smothered in some kind of sauce that I had no clue what it was. This was quite different than what I was used to. I was used to picking up my burritos. Sitting them vertical on the plate because they were so stuffed full of goodness. I would from that point inhale that muthafucka, bite by bite. Don't let that shit be Gods burrito, which was a bacon wrapped carne asada joint. It had no chance in hell of survival. I had never eaten a burrito with a fork and a knife, let alone a wet one. I felt a little embarrassed to be eating this joint like this. Oh well, here goes nothing. I sliced into it and immediately, there was a juicy overflow of whatever sauce and luscious pork. I scooped up a forkful and took my first bite. I dropped the utensils on the plate and looked over to see this white lady smiling and laughing. I can't lie. She was kind of cute. However, the only white meat I messed with was the pig. I couldn't get down with the swirl thing. Wasn't gonna be any way that she was gonna have me stuck in a basement, wrists strapped to a chair and have me falling into the sunken place. My taste buds were now Crip walking. My lips had swelled up, absorbing the goodness with ever chew. I was in food heaven. As fast as I started, I ended.

"Is it good?"

That was the waitress when she came back to refill my water.

"Oh, this shit fire."

"You must got a flight to catch."

"Not for another two hours."

She laughed. Yes, girl. I ate this shit fast. I can't lie. She was cute as shit too. I sat there and let the pork marinate in my belly for a little bit. I eventually paid my bill and went over to the gate to sit down and patiently wait for the plane to get here. I had the itis, and I felt myself falling asleep. I got up, took my phone over to one of the charging stations without stools and stayed on my feet. The last thing I wanted to do was to fall asleep and miss my flight. Airport people were rude as shit and uncaring. It was every person for themselves. I could be the last person at the gate sleep. Even the flight attendants behind the counter wouldn't wake me up. Nah, that risk wasn't to be taken. Time went by slowly. That was a good thing. It gave me time to think about my mental state and how I wanted to prepare it. My hotel was down in the Greenwood District. I did my best to find a Black owned hotel in Tulsa, but it was to no avail. This whole opportunity had me mentally telling myself that nothing outside of Black people were getting my money, or anything else. This included manners. Everyone would get rendered the proper courtesies. My Black people would get that times 50. The time came and we boarded. We were a little late in taking off, but 25 minutes to fix an issue was way better than leaving without it fixed and falling out of the sky. I couldn't sleep. I did everything I could to occupy my time. I opened one of the airline magazines. I completed the two crossword puzzles and the sudoku. I also read about half of the magazine. To my dismay, that only took up an hour of the flight. My skin started to tingle. The hairs stood on end, as if they were contracting some energy from a realm that existed outside of my own. I understood if we were making our descent into the city. However, we were nowhere near it. I looked out the window. There was nothing but brown land. I didn't know what state we were over, but it wasn't Oklahoma. I sat there, leaning my head back, closing my eyes. I tried to envision the stage and an empty arena. I looked up the capacity of the building where the event would take place before I left home. Maxed out, it fit 1,000 people theater style. I didn't know how many tickets were sold, but I know with the history of that place, it wouldn't disappoint. I battled the physical realm and my imaginary bliss for the next hour.

"Ladies and gentlemen, flight attendants will be making one last walk through the aisles to collect any trash. We are starting our descent into the Tulsa area."

My heart. That inward pen that had written so many stories over my 30+ years of existence, was now spewing ink out at an alarming rate. It was a heart attack without having one. The city came into view. I looked to see if I could find anything that would tell me the ancestors were welcoming. I couldn't. Their energy was present, but they wanted me to wait to feel it. That was fine and dandy. They earned that right to tell me their story when they got good and damn ready too. I hadn't done anything in life worthy of any shortcuts or hook ups from them. No amount of soup kitchens, community events or mentoring kids could amount to the sacrifice those people made. As I saw the plane turn and drop steady, I closed my eyes once again. I saw fire, bullets, heard screams and saw Black men defending their neighborhood to the death. This wasn't in my imagination. This was playing out in front of me. I was in another dimension right now. I couldn't touch anyone. I called out, telling my people to move right, left, duck, shoot, run, whatever I could to help them. Then, I saw the planes. The planes were coming in deep. Oh shit, I thought. We had nothing for this. This was it. It was over. Black Wall Street was no more. I opened my eyes to feel us rolling on the runway. I was here. Ironically, now, I didn't feel anything. The energy wasn't there. The hairs were lying flat on my arms as they always did. My tattoos didn't seem to pop off my skin. Egypt was literally ink again. Tulsa had a fair-sized airport. It was nothing like Casper. You had to walk through this joint to get where you needed to be. I got to baggage claim and awaited my next trial. My bag. There was only one time that my bag didn't arrive where it was supposed to be. Lo and behold, that one time was when I flew Spirit Airlines. Never again in my fucking life would I fly them. The name was right. Spirit, because they ghosted the shit out of you when it came to customer service. I spotted my bag coming around the carousel. The blue bandana tied around the handle stuck out like a sore thumb. I took my bag and went into my Lyft app. Immediately, a ride was available, not even a minute out. A middle-aged white lady in a Nissan rolled up. I flagged her down after recognizing the license plate. The first challenge was being in the car with a white woman as a Black male. I didn't know how bad Oklahoma was with racism, but I was on my Ps and Qs.

"Hello, how are you?"

"Fine."

I gave no ma'am behind that fine. Again, my anger was still quelled in the bowels of my stomach on how my trip to Wyoming ended. My people would get complete manners. These others would get part time mannerisms like reserves who play part time military on the weekends. It was a quick eight-minute drive to Archer Street. Little talk was made. Truthfully, no attempt to talk was made on my end. She started the convo. I obliged with short answers. I didn't release my angry tone. I did, however, keep my Blackness very mellow. Finally, we made a turn off a bridge downtown. I was here. Archer. I didn't see the hotel. I only saw Archer, cause a building didn't mean a damn thing to me right now. "Thank you."

She popped the trunk and handed me my bag.

"Have a good day."

"Same," I replied.

As she took off, I stood in front of the doors of the hotel, doing a full 360. I was pissed and in awe at the same time. I was here, but I wasn't here. Gentrification was defined by Oxford as the process of renovating and improving a house or district so that it conforms to middle-class taste. In simpler terms. It was where white people take over Black people shit after they have made the current conditions unlivable by raising rent, or purposely implementing drugs, or other detrimental products into a neighborhood, so they can increase mass arrest, thus increasing mass migration of Black people to prison, which leads to the redevelopment of land for white benefit. That's what the fuck gentrification really means. I walked in.

"Welcome home."

Thank God. It was a sister at the desk.

"Afternoon sister. Reservation for Baker."

She searched through the computer.

"Found it. Here's everything you need for your stay sir."

She handed me pamphlets, showed me where everything was on this mini map and handed me my room keys. 226 was the number. I took off to the elevator. It was already open as there were a good four or five people heading up to their respective dwellings for the day. I myself, was alone with a Middle Eastern couple in exiting to the second floor. I followed the sign to the left and found my room. I pressed my key against the digital lock and entered my home for the next two and a half days. First thing first, I had to turn this heat down. I knew there was a little bit of a breeze outside, but it damn sure wasn't a Chicago winter. After turning the temperature down from hell to normal, I sat down on the plush couch in the room, relaxing, still in awe that I was here. It was just barely three o'clock in the afternoon. The Greenwood Cultural Center, where the event was located at, closed at five. Wanda J's, the soul food spot, closed at seven. I figured a good 15 minutes of relaxation was enough rest before I got up and started this excursion of my trip through Black Wall Street. I was good and relaxed in five. I couldn't wait anymore. I didn't come here to sit down. I had all night to sleep. I was here. It was time to go see my folks. I walked out the hotel and hit an immediate right. I stopped about 100 feet from the door as I noticed a bronze plaque embedded in the concrete. It was the name of a business that existed in 1921. Underneath the engraved 1921, it read not rebuilt. Six steps ahead of that, there was another one. This one was rebuilt. These continued until I got to the end of the block. I hit a left on Elgin and then another right at the stop sign. Now, I was walking pass a huge baseball field. This was for the minor league team they had here in Tulsa. Yes, I researched all this shit before I got here. Now that I was here, I wish I had a cocktail bomb so I could set this bitch on fire. My blood began to singe the inner layer of fat beneath my skin. I got more and more upset with each pace. With every seat I noticed and every blade of grass I saw, I wanted to really do damage. This is what you did America. You did this. You and your white privileged crooks stole from the original Black and Brown inhabitants. This is not your land. I swear I wish I could put you all on a boat and send you back to Europe, so we could finally enjoy peace and tranquility. I mustered up the biggest hawk of mucus from my lungs and spit as I passed the last bit of bricks of shit creek field as I called it. It may have been called Trust Field, but trust and white people didn't go together in my eyes. I walked, almost wanting to cry. The energy was here. The souls of hundreds of dead Melanin warriors had once again reared up inside of me. Right now, you could have sent me on the hunt for the biggest and baddest terrorists in the world, and I would've come back with several Caucasian heads in white sheets on my platter. I wanted to scream. Then, I stopped. I stared. I looked back, and it was much like my past. I let it go. I was now at the cross section of Greenwood and Archer. I was tall at 6'1, but even with a jump, I would be barley able to touch the sign. Plus, the way my knees were set up, I didn't want to tear another ACL. I slow bopped it up the block towards the center. It was an amazing sight to see all these

Black owned businesses on both sides of the street. I didn't know if I was in Tulsa or if I had won a first-class trip to Wakanda. I crossed a brother getting out of his car.

"What's going on King?," I said to him.

"Aight now strong brother," he replied.

Now that was the shit I was talking about. There was no mean mugging, what set you from, none of that dumb, ignorant shit that we had become accustomed too. It was genuine love coming from a genuine place. I made my way towards the end of the block and headed under the overpass. Underneath here were painted the words WELCOME TO GREENWOOD, in all caps. Oh man, refreshed and rejuvenated were the exact words I had right now. I passed underneath. The cars above me were screams in voices that only God could transfer to human ears. Some were saying welcome. Others were saying don't get to happy. I didn't know why, because right now, not a muthafuckin thing could kill my vibe. As I got to the other side and almost to the center, I stopped. There, painted on the wall, on the other side of the freeway, was a huge Black Wall Street mural. Dope was an understatement. This art spoke life to me. The painting came alive. All the letters were huge and outlined in white. The B had embedded in it The Dreamland Theater, painted in lime green. The L contained the cross in red, with the words Mount Vernon AME Church, which was a staple in this community. The A contained three jazz men holding guitars and a base. One had on a purple suit. The other two, in gold and white. I knew it was before his time, but I had no choice but to think about the great Kobe Bryant in this moment. The C contained a Black family, with the Greenwood and Archer street signs. The K got me hella emotional, as buildings with flames rose up and out of the top of the letter, ending at the barrier on the freeway. The W contained an old school whip. The next A contained another jazz man. The first L was half yellow, with a maroon and white eagle coming out of it. The next L was literally outstanding. That word flowed out from the letter in gold, while three green letters inside spelled GAP. If you are thinking it, yes. This was a tribute to the Charlie Wilson and the hometown GAP Band. GAP stood for Greenwood, Archer and Pine. The top half of the S was decorated in gold and maroon piano keys, while the bottom was painted purple with dancing figures, with the word JUNETEENTH written across it. Lastly, the T was maroon inside, with a huge hornet inside. I didn't know what the hornet stood for, but I knew I would find out with enough time. I now turned my attention to the center. I walked the minute and a half walk to the door as if I was being escorted to my death sentence by lethal injection. Except this time, I would be injected with the blood of those who allowed me to be here. I took a deep breath as I got within reach of the handles on the double doors. I let myself in. Within a few steps, I made it through the second pair of doors. I didn't see anyone. I did a quick glance in the office to my right and left. In the office to the left, I saw a Mexican woman on a computer, but she was completely oblivious to me. I wandered through the halls, observing each picture and story attached to it. This was history on another level. It was our story, told by us. It wasn't in some trumped-up textbook written by caucasian hands who'd rather tell his stories than Black stories. I came back towards the middle of the hall. I looked to my right. There was another set of double doors. Through the rectangular windows, I could tell that this was where the magic would happen tomorrow night. I turned and walked towards the doors. In my head, the Stone Cold Steve Austin music had hit. I got a little cocky and arrogant. I was 6'1, but I was 7'2 when my ego kicked in. I flung open the doors. All I saw were chairs. Chairs were lined up from one wall to another. The crazy shit was that the walls would be retracted back. This place could easily sit 1,000 like it said on the website. From what I saw from the set up, it was already 350-400 chairs put out. That amount of people would be nuts. Just imagine a full fucking house with 800 to maybe 2,000 eyes on you. The juices were flowing to say the least. I walked out and left the center. My swag was on 250, and the only thing that was left to do was to eat. Wanda J's was the next stop. I walked into the small, quaint joint. It smelled like you were walking into Big Mama's house. There was a small statured woman who welcomed me in.

"Eating in or takin' out?"

"Naw I'm finna sit down."

"Whatever seat you want."

I walked it over to the window. I felt an obligation to stand watch while eating. In case someone tried to come in and take this, they would have to meet me at the door. Either I would die protecting what was mines, or we'd both die, and God would tell me thanks for delivering another one to me. Folks failed to forget skin of bronze and hair of sheep's wool was only one kind of people on earth. Funny how everyone hated niggas, but they worshipped the Head Nigga in Charge every Sunday. Judgment day was going to be funny as shit when they realized heaven was Wakanda and hell is the trailer park. I ordered a sweet tea and she brought it over. I took the first sip. I quickly realized it would be my first and last tea while down here. This shit was literally diabetes in a white cup. I then looked on the window seal to see an amazing sight. There, in green and yellow bliss, was a flyer of tomorrow night's event, with my name on the flyer. Deep Greenwood, featuring Mac Baker Jr., a.k.a. Blaxploitation. Savage was an understatement. My catfish dinner with fries came. Man, I hadn't eaten catfish in years. Them shits were literally the bottom feeders of the sea. Growing up, you couldn't tell me that it wasn't the steak of the sea. I ate healthy at this current time in my life. Every now and then, I had to let it go for some deep-fried goodness. I cut it with the plastic fork. Yes niggas. Plastic fork. One bite and I started dancing inside. This shit was good. The fries were popping too with a little bit of salt. It was simple, satisfying and it put money in Black people pockets. I ate up and saw that it was now a few minutes after five. I went up to the register, paid by card, left a hefty tip, and told them to enjoy their night. I walked back to the hotel. This time, the gentrification didn't pester my soul as it did when I first walked over here. Maybe it was the food. Maybe it was me knowing that the Black experience wins everyday over the bullshit experience. I don't know what it was but either way, I felt like I was on cloud nine. I made it back to my room and immediately got into my stand-up shower. One thing I will say about Oklahoma, is that this water came in two temperatures. Hot, and what the fuck. It was like cold didn't exist at all. I literally played hopscotch in the shower. I wanted to be clean, but I didn't want to boil the sin out of my body. The Zest body wash I had was hitting. I never went anywhere without my own shit, especially if I was staying in a hotel. That little bottle shit they provide you with would be empty by the time a nigga got to scrubbing his whole lower half. And, I don't care what the hell some of y'all were talking on Facebook many moons ago. You wash your legs in the shower. You wash your whole ass. I can't remember if it was a challenge but let me hear someone say I don't wash my legs when I take a shower. My foot was going to wash so deep in their ass that they'd be shitting out the check mark on my Nikes for a month. I got back in the room and just let my nuts naturally air dry. A nigga was chilling. Fuck it. My Black ass was just gonna sit naked for the next hour. I got up and grabbed one of the unused towels from the bathroom and laid it across the recliner. I kicked my feet up and chilled like a muthafucka. A water would be good right now, but that in room shit was a set up. Drink a water, four dollars. Eat a snack, two fifty. Yea damn that. I scrolled through the channels. It was a lot of good shit on, and they had 400 channels worth of entertainment. John Wick 3, Casino Royale, US. All my favorites were on. Then, I came across it on the guide. I flipped the channel. Now, I found myself yelling at the TV.

"THE FUCK YOU DOING!!!"

Man, I got so pissed. When a man ain't being a man, and letting his woman make a terrible decision for him, this is how I react. Then, of all things, he wasn't even fighting back on how small she made something feel, even though it was big enough to sustain them both. Men, we had to do better. Watching Home and Garden channel as a 30 something year old can raise your blood pressure. This was indeed life. Hours passed and I continued to watch every episode where couples were looking for their future homes. Each episode gave me a smile, but lots more anxiety. I looked up at the clock. It was 9:30 on the dot. I had gotten hungry again. I threw on my jeans, a hoodie and headed out. When I got downstairs, the Black lady was still behind the desk.

"What's a good eating joint round here late night? Particularly for us." "Oh sure. They got this joint called Sisserou's."

"How far is it?"

209

"Not that far. Just like two blocks that way," she said, pointing into downtown, the opposite way of the cultural center.

Now, there were two concerns with these directions. One, she gave a point. Now niggas are known for this. They always point like you can just follow their finger to its mysterious location. Like a bat signal was just gone appear in the air saying, walk here nigga. The second red flag was that she said it was a few blocks. Now were these white people blocks, or nigga blocks. Lemme give y'all a clear-cut picture for my non Melanated people who are following this. When white people come to pick you up, and they say that they are five minutes away, they are just that. Five minutes away. When niggas say they are five minutes away, it means a good 20. Even crazier is the phrase I'm around the corner. When niggas say they around the corner that means they aren't pulling up for another 10 minutes.

"Aight, thanks."

I walked out the hotel and put google to work. I typed in the name of the joint. Just like I thought. That it's not that far, was the Black edition. This shit was 20 minutes on foot. It wasn't that bad, but this what I meant when I talked about Black people's down the street. I should be able to see down the street. This shit was down in Tulsa's DM. Way down in that muthafucka. I walked the quiet Tulsa blocks into the heart of downtown. From the looks of things, I must have been in the arts district. This was like North Park in San Diego, or like River North in Chicago. I became a tourist. It was comforting to be in a downtown that wasn't overcrowded or filled with blaring music coming from random buildings. Finally, after what seemed like an eternity, I made it to the restaurant. Then, there was a dilemma. Next to the joint, was a Mexican restaurant called Mexicali Border Cafe. Here's where my allegiance was tested.

This was Oklahoma, but I loved Mexican food. This was Oklahoma, but again, I fucking loved Mexican food. Yea, fuck that. Arizona, Florida, cool. This wasn't the place to pop a cherry. Nah, I was straight. I walked into Sisserou's and immediately got a sense of the Caribbean vibe. I stood in the doorway for a good four to five seconds. Man, this place was packed and lit up to the T. I walked towards the server at the podium, asking for a takeout menu. She handed me one, and I went and sat down at a booth near the bar. Immediately, my eyes started watering out of sheer joy. I got up and went straight to the bartender.

"Yea lemme get that snapper with them jerk shrimps."

I said it just like that too. The white lady laughed taking my order. I could tell she had dealt with enough Black folks to know that this was a viable order. We said shrimps, even though we knew that shit didn't come with the letter S at the end. I went and sat down, scrolling through my Facebook feed to observe the madness for the day. Of course, the ratchet was still ratchet. The overly woke were still fucking annoying, especially them niggas who thought they were high and mighty cause they had a Swahili name or some shit that normal folks couldn't pronounce. Salesmen were salesmen. All in all, it was a typical day on the book. After 15 minutes, my order was complete and ready to go. I grabbed that bag and it was smelling so damn good. I began the trek back to the hotel. As always, going back seemed quicker than going there. Once I made it back to room 226, I sat down near the TV and just indulged. This snapper was yoga flame. The jerk shrimps were brackin, crackin, hittin, slappin, whatever your region of the earth called it. I savored every bite from the fish to the fried plantains. Once over, I brushed my teeth and cranked that heat up, because it was a little nippy outside. I got

211

down to my shorts and put my Black ass under those covers. Day one in Tulsa, which was more like half a day, was done. I smiled but didn't close my eyes. I looked around the room. It felt like eyes were on me. It wasn't a feeling of negative energy. I didn't see any ghosts or encounter any paranormal activity. However, I knew, something was here. I plopped my head on the pillow, looking dead at the ceiling.

"Ancestors. Please speak through me tomorrow night. Live through me because that's what I'm here for."

I pulled the covers over my head, closing my eyes, trying to ensure that I got a good night's rest. Truthfully, I know I wouldn't sleep well because of the sheer excitement that I had. Sleep would be broken. My mind would be 7-11 tonight. It would be open for 24 hours. Even knowing this, I tried to shut my mind off. Stop all the images of me screaming on a stage. I tried and I tried. My eyes stayed closed, but my senses were wide awake. Then, that gas bubble grew in my stomach and I released the most lethal gas known to man. I tried to lay in one spot, hoping that the smell wouldn't creep up. Shit, that wasn't happening at all. Once that smell started to singe my nostrils, those covers came up so damn fast. That snapper. That catfish. That shrimp. That diabetes in a Styrofoam cup that they call sweet tea. The fried plantains. It all contributed to this very moment. Truthfully, it had never stank so damn good in my life. I was here. Black Wall Street. Tonight, I rest. Tomorrow, I raise the dead.

— 8 —

THE TALKING DEAD

I arose at seven o'clock on the dot. The play director had texted me last night telling me to be at the center at nine. I spent the first 20 minutes lying in bed, scrolling through Facebook, much like 95% of the world did when they awoke. That just showed you how much we were programmed as a society, me included. Had my lady been here, the phone wouldn't have been an issue. I would've opened her app and downloaded a new update inside of her first thing. She wasn't, however, so this was my entertainment. Finally, I got up and went to brush my teeth. AIM was the toothpaste of choice for me today. It cost $0.99 and it was mint flavored. Cost efficient and it made my breath smell fabulous. You couldn't beat that. I tossed on a shirt and walked out the room, heading towards the elevator. I got down to the first floor. To my surprise, I only saw one other person down there in the breakfast area. I grabbed a paper plate and got the usual breakfast food. Sausages, bacon, scrambled eggs, a biscuit, another biscuit, and I poured gravy over everything except the eggs. Then, as I went to sit down, I saw it. An automatic pancake maker. I never saw one of these. Naw, they couldn't have invented something like this. So, just to see if this was what they said it was, I pressed the button. It said the pancake would be ready in a minute. I grabbed a plate and put it under where it was going to be dispensed. I swear it seemed like this was taking 40 days and 40 nights to come out. If I had to wait this long, this had better be a Jesus pancake. I better had taken one bite and instantly be cleansed of all sin with 30 days added on to my life. It dumped out, like the machine was taking a robotic shit. It was a perfect six inches in diameter. I pressed that hoe two more times for two more pancakes. I dropped some syrup on them and took it to the table. That first cut with the fork was amazing. I didn't know machine made pancakes could be this fluffy. I took the first bite and man oh man. That shit was fire. I scraped both plates. I even got the few crumbs of the biscuits left in the gravy. Now, I was ready to rehearse. I went back upstairs to grab my hoodie and I was on my way to the Greenwood Cultural Center. As soon as I stepped outside, I instantly got upset again. The pain of seeing the bronze plaques in the concrete, the baseball field, and the all-out destruction of what I deemed The Black Atlantis, it made my heart sink to the bowels of my stomach. My ear drums rang from screams of the deceased who were shot and burned. I put my hands to my ears to drown out the noise, but I was forced to swim in rivers of Black blood. I was a madman walking in the body of a Black male who appeared to be normal. Maybe my all black attire would constitute to my lifeless body in another city. Here, it was symbolic of my skin and my heart towards the people who did this. They slaughtered my cousins, aunties and uncles that were here before I was a sperm cell in my daddy's nut sack. It was already bad enough that I didn't know where I originated from. Worse than that was me carrying around the last name of a slave owner who deemed my ancestral queens fit to fuck, and nothing more. They were simply a chocolate nursery where he could implant his white mark of the beast. They say Jesus is coming back. I beg to differ. He wasn't. He was going to work through all His people. The nappy headed sheep flock who had to suffer through 400 fucking years of oppression. The worse part was that those folks expected us to let it go because we could play basketball on national television. I honestly believed that's what it meant when they said He was coming back. God lived in us. The uprising was approaching, and they knew it. Every law passed, every measure taken to deprive us of a quality life, it was all to deter us from a hellish uprising which saw us use the whips and put them in the chains. Maybe they wouldn't pick cotton because their pale skin wouldn't be able to handle that sun. Maybe we'd have them run greenhouses or some shit. I don't know. I just knew whenever hell opened its doors, heaven would smile. I made it to center right dead smack at nine o'clock. I walked through the doors and immediately towards the performance area. Upon going through the double doors, I saw not a soul in sight. I walked up to the stage, thinking that they may be running on CPT time. I sat there, with the dim light emitting from the hallway, leaving just enough for me to see the chairs. Suddenly, all the lights came on. That woke me up real quick.

"CAN I HELP YOU???!!!"

"I'M JUST WAITING ON THE CREW FOR THE SHOW!!!"

He began walking up towards the stage.

"Yea I don't know about that one. I've been here for years and know everything from who coming in at what time, to the roach I stomped out in the bathroom back in 2017. Ain't nobody scheduled to be here. Who told you to be here this early?"

"The play director."

"Well you might wanna call 'em back. Only people here this early are me and maybe one office worker."

I texted the director, telling her I was here. About a minute later, she hit me back.

"Oh my bad. I meant to say we were leaving at 9. See you at 12. We just left OKC."

Well ain't this bout a bitch. I got up early for no damn reason.

"Man. You right OG. She just texted me 12."

"See. I been around for a while. I know these things," he said laughing.

"How long you been working here?"

"Gone come over here and take a seat."

I jumped off the stage and joined him in the first row of seats.

"Man, I remember when this place was the spot. Little Las Vegas is what they called it. See that's what history don't tell you. They tell you Black Wall Street got burned to the ground. But they never tell you how it got burned, and the future that came of it. Have you seen the big church when you walked over here?"

"Yea."

"Yea well, it didn't look like that back in the day of course, because it's been rebuilt. But, when the white folks came over to go to war, they forgot our people were self-sufficient. Black men were armed up here. Oh, they didn't take no shit. Even shot one of them at the courthouse the morning of the riots. One by one, those devils in pale skin fell. Oh boy. They were getting their Euro stealing asses whooped. Now, we had lost some ourselves, defending against the ones that rushed in. But we had killed way more of them. They underestimated our smarts, thinking we would build everything, and not have an armory stash to defend ourselves. They had no choice but to call the military in. That's the only way they killed us. We had guns. Didn't have military planes. No sir."

"You were around for all that?"

"Hell nah. But my mama and grandparents were. See after that, they still didn't want us. They left us to rot in this same spot. But they forgot we had something they don't possess. You know what that's?"

"No sir."

"It's will to live. See white folks don't have a will like we do. We've had the richest empires on earth and the poorest circumstances all in the same manner. What you can never measure is someone's will to fight. Yup, they rebuilt this place to twice its glory. More banks, more schools, more grocery stores, more tailor shops. The whiskey and the juke joints. Aww man, it was some hot mamas in there."

That's when you know you're dealing with an old school brother when he says hot mamas.

"I was just a simple kid back then in the 50's. This place used to light up something serious. Yup. Little Las Vegas is what we called it. And you know what. The white folks got mad again. They thought they had broken us down, but we came back stronger than ever. The community was educated. We financed US. We protected our women and children. Men were men. We partied, we drank, we worshipped. Aww we did everything 100 times as much as my grandma and them did. Then guess what they did? They put the freeway through the heart of this neighborhood. See they couldn't

217

burn it and bomb it anymore. They did that. Times had changed. Now, they had to be discreet in how they showed their hate and disdain for us. They proclaimed that they needed another road to help ease traffic in the city. In simple terms, and I'm sorry cause I hate this word. They wanted a way to decrease the population of niggas and take as much of this land back as possible."

He paused for a minute, wiping his eyes.

"You need me to go get a tissue sir?"

"Nah. I ain't scared to cry. Crying shows emotion, not weakness. Don't you ever forget that. But we fought. We fought tooth and nail. They tried to buy our homes from under us. It didn't happen. They tried snake tactics of we'll give you this if you let us get this property. We gave them crackers the biggest fuck you I could ever remember. In the end, let's just say that they had to physically get us out of here. Whether it was with forceful backup or trumped up charges to put us in prison, we didn't go down without a fight. Nope. We weren't built like that. So, when you walk back to the hotel and come back here with your peoples, I want you to appreciate what's left. We got a few blocks right now and we still fighting. Soon, it's going to turn into one more block and one more block. And eventually, they gone say damn. How in the good hell are they still making it? Easy. Cause we Black folks. That's the only answer anyone needs to know."

The phrase sitting in silence was a severe understatement. HIS-story had wanted me to find him and whoop his ass for a good while. I'm not talking about you stole my lunch money ass whooping either. I mean that you killed my grandmother, I've been hunting you for 20 years and now I have found your bitch ass type of ass whooping. My eyes stared at this man as if he were my grandfather. My fists clinched as I was ready to hit any person, he ordered me too. My mouth, it wanted to ask him so much more, but he would ask me something I deemed the most important.

"Will you be here tonight?"

"Of course."

"Our history gone be on display. You gone back and rest up somewhat. You in the play right?"

"I'm opening it with poetry."

"Just do me one favor then young man. Speak for the dead. Rather let them speak through you. Night of the living dead isn't a movie. It's your job. Let the world hear their voices, through you. I'll see you tonight." He got up, tapped me on the shoulder and walked back towards the doors, out of the performance area. I sat there for the next 10 minutes in dead silence. I had learned more in the last 15 minutes or so than I had learned in 12 years of a bullshit ass education system. I started to cry, hoping that the tears that hit the floor would soak through the tiles and quench the thirst of distant relatives who hadn't drank in nearly 100 years. I picked myself up by my bootstraps for the first time in life and it was meaningful, and not some bullshit racist ass AmeriKKKa had told us as a comforting statement to soothe their shitty ego. I aggressively burst through the side door and began my trek back to the hotel. The streets were clear, which was probably good, because I needed to punch something or someone.

"FUCK YOU!!!"

I screamed at the baseball field as I power walked next to it. My lungs were clear, but I hawked up as much spit as I could to disgrace this fuckery disguised as a family friendly environment. My rage was to the point of no return. As I entered back into the hotel, I put on the act of acts. Straightening up my face, as if I hadn't been crying for the past 10 minutes. I made it to the elevator without a witness to my pain. I hit room 226 and literally plopped down on the side of the bed. It was 10:21. Ironically, in this moment, Corinthians 10:21 popped in my head.

Ye cannot drink the cup of the Lord, and the cup of devils: ye cannot be partakers of the Lord's table, and of the table of devils.

I learned that white people did this on a daily and had mastered it. IN GOD WE TRUST was printed on their money because money was their God. The evil they did with it showed that there were indeed two sides of the table in this country. Their wine was a potion I had no taste for. Sadly, some of mines were so desperate to bleach their skin from the inside out, that they stayed drunk on a constant. How they were able to maintain that dark tan all these years was something that boggled my mind. I slowly exhaled my anger with each breath as I sat in this quiet room, recollecting my thoughts until it was time to head out again. Those breaths lasted over an hour, as I saw the clock had hit 11:40. I got up and proceeded back to the route I had taken multiple times already. I didn't let the sights bug me out this time. The ancestors had talked to me. They told me to block out all negativity and focus on the task at hand. I was the most important person in Tulsa tonight. The actors, whose depiction was meaningful as well, still didn't have the job to make the audience feel the power of the dead. The audience was expecting a play. They weren't expecting to see God tonight. The theater cast was either gonna regret having to follow my act or get motivated by it. The audience was either going to repent for their sins or commit some of their own once they left the venue. I made it under the overpass to see a huge van pulled up at the side door.

They were here. It was time to indeed make magic happen. I went through the main doors, taking the long way into the performance area. This time, Razor Ramon's theme song came on inside of my head. They were about to say hello to the bad guy. If I really wanted to be disrespectful, I would've put a toothpick in my mouth and threw it in the face of the first person I saw. However, we were all Black. That shit might turn into a shootout quick. I went in and saw a group of people over by the stage. I kept walking and before I could even open my mouth, one spoke.

"Mac."

"Yea. Mia right?"

"Yup. Nice to meet you."

We embraced with a friendly hug.

"You need some help with this stuff?"

"Yea cool. Its appreciated," she said, nearly out of breath from carrying things inside.

I went out to the van to help them bring in additional props and everything else that was needed for tonight. In straight negro fashion, we were all either in shorts and t-shirts, or pajamas. Oh yea, I could tell this was gonna be turnt up tonight. One thing about us is when we are relaxed beforehand, it was only in preparation to put on an epic performance. We set everything up, and I even found myself helping the brother who had to fix the lights. D was the moniker that he chose to go by. He was from the Westside of Chicago. K-Town to be exact. We chopped it up for over an hour as we had to sturdy this incredible hulk sized ladder to adjust the lights in the overhead. You would think that people would upgrade and have the shit that you could adjust with the press of a button. Naw. We had to do this shit manually. As we completed other additional taskings, including mic checks, it was time for the crew to shift gears and run through a dry rehearsal. I sat towards the back as instructed by Mia to make sure the actors could be heard. All was well from the last row of 20 something. With a thumbs up from me, they began their run. Scene one went as planned, outside of a few kinks, which was expected. When scene two popped off, my gangster was tested at an astronomical level. It started off with three white males at a table, being highly disrespectful about the Black residents of the city. Even though everything was going along fine, I was forgetting that it was a stage act. I took a few deep breaths, readjusted myself and continued to observe. Then, that first nigger dropped. Now, it wasn't the word that got me. It was the passion that homeboy said it with. I readjusted myself again. I slapped my right ear two or three times to make sure my shit was working properly. A few seconds later, another one of them dropped an even more vicious N bomb.

"NIGGER!!!"

I had now sat up in my chair, folding my hands and leaning forward. I tried to snap out of it, but I couldn't. That nigger was so emphatic. In that moment, I was taken back to 1921, a whole 98 years prior. I locked in. Even when they had a break to correct some things with Mia, I didn't take my eyes off any of those white boys. I forgot that this was a play. This was another caucasian invasion where they tried to sneak in their realistic feelings and cover it up as simple acting. Snap out of it Mac, I told myself. You're here for reasons bigger than yourself. They aren't those people. Yes, you see their color. Seeing color is inevitable. You must trust your sister in arms. She wouldn't have them here if she felt they were a threat, or if she felt they had ulterior motives. I relaxed and let out another deep breath. I ended up doing that for the next four hours, as this rehearsal, combined with all the setup, was draining. This gave me a whole new respect for actors and playwrights alike. You had to be on point. Truthfully, it shouldn't have taken this for me to garner their respect. Being a performer myself, I know more than anyone that when the lights come on, its fucking game time. The feeling of seeing a crowd who paid their hard-earned money, especially in these uncertain times to see you, that shit spoke volumes. The settings, the atmosphere, all of that played a part. And you, yes you, had one shot at perfection. If you fuck up, you should be so good at what you do that no one notices it. Afterwards, you could kick yourself in the ass when you are back in the dressing room. The audience, however, should see flawlessness regardless. That's where I was at. I didn't want to fuck up. I damn sure didn't want to fuck up someone else's shit, especially when they invited me into their world too enhance it. Nah, that shit wasn't flying with me. Time lingered on. I was now restless. As four o'clock hit, I couldn't wait any longer. I still had to eat, walk back to the hotel, and wash my ass. I didn't care what the occasion was. Mac Baker Jr. rule #1 is to have a good, clean ass. If the world was ending, God would probably catch me in the shower.

"Hey Mac. It's God. I'm here to take my peoples."

"Well God, hand me a towel. I'm going up just like this. Put me in one of those heavenly robes."

That's probably the conversation that I would have with Him, or Her, depending who you asked.

"Hey Mia. What time do you need me back, cause I still gotta go back to the hotel and clean up?"

"Oh, we're nearly done. One more scene and we out ourselves. But, be back at six. Sharp."

That's all I needed to hear. I jetted up out that joint. First thing

223

first, was Wanda J's Soul Food. Invest in my people because that was the primary goal. I ordered the wing dinner this time. Matter fact, I got two of those joints. I couldn't do three wings. I need a full six as if I was visiting Chicago and hitting J&J's on Cicero, leaving Midway Airport. It was a little more packed than yesterday, so my grub was taking somewhat longer than I expected. I kept looking at my phone, which was now at 15%. It was now 4:45 p.m. I didn't want to rush my folks, but they needed to hurry the hell up. Hell, Mia, and the crew had walked in now, and I left a full 20-30 minutes before them. At five, finally, I got my shit. I jetted out and power walked it to the hotel.

"Welcome home," the sister behind the desk greeted me.

"Waddupdoe."

I had to hit her with some Midwest, Detroit slang as I kept it moving to the elevator. If it was one thing I hated, it was being late. A brother wasn't gonna be that. I made it to my room, saying my prayers on the way to the bathroom to cut on the shower water. I then made it to the chair by the TV. No programming for me. I was locked in on the show in front of me. Greasy goodness, starring me, this nigga, smashing. This wasn't me anymore, as fried foods and unhealthy shit wasn't the norm. However, I had to put that shit to bed, especially since I was starving. I opened the boxes up and operation food smash was in session. I knew the wings would be a good size, but these were country sized portions. Cornbread, cabbage, macaroni, and the pinto beans were beyond enough for a few people. Yet, this was just for me. I ate like a madman. Years of hanging round fast paced, always in a rush L.A. folks had prepared me for this. In 15 minutes, everything in that Styrofoam container was wiped clean. The chicken bones were so clean that I could put them on display in a museum. 5:24 was now the time. I tossed my clothes like Bruce Almighty when he was about to break the back of Grace and headed towards the shower. Of course, I wasn't in their barefoot. I had my shower slippers on. Rule #824. Always have shower slippers when visiting other places. You don't know who the fuck been walking on these floors, or what's been on 'em. I scrubbed like a madman. The shower was no more than seven minutes, but it was a thorough one. I ensured to hit my pits and my ass twice as nice. Scrub negro scrub is what I told myself, as I let Zest body wash do its thing. I got out and dried off with rage, and fury. I opened the door to let the steam corral out. I peeped the clock. 5:35. I was making good timing. I sat my naked ass on this freshly made up bed for a good two minutes, collecting myself. Once I felt good, I threw on the fresh boxers that gave my nuts room. I had to make sure my nuts were breathing, because ain't nothing worse than having some too tight ass draws on and walking round with your balls in a bind. Men, we owed it to our balls to let them breathe as much as possible. I then went to the closet. I pulled out my crispy creased jeans. Say what you want, but this shit wasn't a trend to me. I took pride in how I looked. So, if other niggas didn't crease their jeans, then that was them. I always liked to look presentable. Sure, I had cats in the past roast me because they said the shit was out of style. Hey, that just goes to show you where their current mindset is as an adult. I learned a long time ago that some people live in grades nine through 12, because everything from 18 and up has been a sheer disappointment. Luckily, I lived a fruitful life, doing what I loved to do and getting paid for it. Others did what they could do, just to get by. I tossed on my Black Juneteenth shirt, followed by the gem of gems. An Egyptian brother had a store just south of L.A.

and made me a custom hoodie. It was a black joint, with the word KING in gold lettering. Underneath the gold letters of KING, was a golden circle, with the letter K in gold, and a gold crown above it. On both sides of the circle, a thick red line extended, which was surrounded by two thick green lines, and rounded off on the end in gold. On my left sleeve, the word KING ran down it in gold, with a gold crown atop. To say that my Blackness was on display was an understatement. I threw on my all black Oregon State fitted, which had an African design pattern on the bill, and the color scheme went with my hoodie perfectly. As I saw the clock hit 5:42, I stepped back into the bathroom one last time. I looked in the mirror at myself. I kept telling myself I got this. I closed my eyes, trying to bring my nerves down. When I opened them up, my dad was staring right back at me. There was no expression on his face. He mimicked the look on my face. I stood there in a trance. Me looking at him, him looking at me.

"Sup Pops."

"Tear some shit up tonight Mud."

Mud. I still to this day don't know how in the good hell he came up with that nickname for me, but it was his norm. I closed my eyes again. Upon opening them, I saw myself. It was time to show my ass. I took off out the door. As I made my way back through the streets, busting that left on Greenwood, I saw cars lined up for days. People were making their way to the center. My face wasn't on any of the advertisements, so they didn't know who I was. To them, I was just another audience member. My heart started to race furiously. The amount of bodies heading there were turning me on in a poetic way. If my lady was here, I'd try to smash her in a back-dressing room. That's how much my juices were flowing right now. I made it to the center at no shit six o'clock. I walked in and headed straight to the performance area. I looked to see all the cast members in a side area through some separate doors. I joined them in the back. Everyone was relaxed and chill, which I dug, because it put me in that same mind frame. I made no small talk with anyone. I found an exit door in the back, which led to the parking lot outside. I stepped out and began to recite my pieces. A car pulled up on the hill above the center. It was just some more folks from earlier who were involved in the show. They came down, I gave my hellos and I continued doing what I was doing. Around 6:30, after reciting my shit three trillion times and saying a prayer to God, I walked back in.

"Mac."

"Yes Mia."

"Look you can start right at seven. Last night they was on CPT time in OKC. They packed out already. Do ya thang. Oh, do you wanna host this?"

Timeout, offsides, flag on the play. Ten yards. Automatic first down. "Host."

"Yea. You come out, do ya thang and say some words about the play. Do ya thang again and bring us out."

"Oh, so that's what that additional email was for earlier huh?"

"Yea. You got the energy. I know you gone set the tone. Again, do ya thang."

She tapped me on the shoulder and headed back to her dressing area. I didn't believe that nonsense of everyone was out there. These were my people we were talking about. I walked out the door into the darkness of the side of the performance area where no lights were cut on. I peeked behind the retractable wall. She wasn't bullshittin. It was a packed house. Not a thousand, but a couple hundred to be fair. I turned and walked back towards the back of the performance area, where D was controlling the lights.

"Hey bro. Let's do one more test of the lights."

"Cool."

I went over to the light switches as he directed me. I told him every area that lit up so he could properly label the switches. It was 6:54 when we completed it. As I prepped to head back towards the front, he grabbed me.

"Hey. What you think if you come from the back? The piece you got is dope. They'll never see it coming."

I looked at him, then looked at the crowd. Men, for y'all in long term relationships. You remember when your woman first got naked in front of you, and it was one of the sexiest sights ever? Well, that was the feeling that I now had. This place was naked in my eyes and I was about to fuck the dog shit out of her ass.

"Man, I'm game fam."

"Aight bruh. 7:02 Do ya thang. Give 'em a two-minute delay before we tear it up."

We dapped up. This was my moment and I wasn't about to fuck this up for anyone. I looked at my phone which now read, 6:59. I asked God not to let me fuck this up. It probably wasn't the right combination of words to say to the Lord before a performance. He probably wrote this down in the book, under the title, *Kids say the darndest things section.* Man, I owed Him for this one. The lights dimmed. I was on the other side of the retractable wall, looking up. I looked over at D and he gave me the thumbs up with a head nod. Right before I spoke, I heard God's inner voice.

"Fuck shit up."

"Wait God. Did you just tell me to fuck shit up?"

228

"Don't question the OG nigga. Now, do ya shit."

"Say no more fam."

"LADIES AND GENTLEMEN!!! WOULD YOU PLEASE RISE AND REMOVE YOUR HATS, AS WE HONOR AMERICA, WITH THE SINGING OF OUR NATIONAL ANTHEM!!!"

I peeked around the wall. Slowly, but surely, they all stood up one by one. Most of them had a confused look on their face and didn't know what the fuck was going on. That's when I knew I had 'em. I counted down from five and made my grand entrance.

AmeriKKKa's Anthem

Oh say can you see, that our women and children are being driven away from the father and husband authority figures so they can possibly create more niggas and bitches, so by the dawn of the early light, our lights have become dim and that's one more Black soul residing in darkness permanently, what so proudly those guns are held, as the twilights from the barrel illuminate the funeral homes, whose broad stripes and bright stars are earned through perilous fights with our own kind, bangin over blocks that we have no ownership over, because your projects were a project to project us to prison, o're the ramparts they watch, planting the flag over the walls they kept us in throughout segregation, cause we were merely their colored entertainment, and integration while it seemed nice, made me realize that I can't go to no city in America and find a lil Africa anywhere, and the rockets' red glare, the bombs bursting in air, ask Philly how they felt about those bombs in 1985, ask Tulsa how those rockets caused a red glare over

229

their city as it burned from white mobs, that gave proof through the night, that your flag which stands for oppression, injustice, medical cost that won't allow cancer patients to get treated, shootings of unarmed black men, deportation of Mexicans who owned this fucking country before you ever stepped foot in it, was still there, O say does that star spangled banner yet wave, blowing in the wind of the dying breath of those who served this country, yet look like me, and are still labeled dusty ass niggas in uniforms, so you think by giving me a medal that takes away how society will see me, you think by giving me a medal that I won't be racial profiled, fuck nah and fuck you, o'er the land and of the free, what's free, we pay for medical, dental, I don't know who the fuck FICA is but she sounds like my bitter ex-wife, and the home of the brave, you right, cause it takes bravery every day for a Black man to step out of his front door, this is your beloved anthem, you play it before every professional contest, your NBA finals, your World Series, your Super Bowls, see America is truly a one hit wonder that constantly gets played over and over, so the shit is beat into my head, so even when I don't wanna hear this song, it has become like a severe case of PTSD, and I tried, I really tried to wrap myself in the red, white and blue, but in turn they wrapped me in poverty, racism and cointelpro, so as those stars spangled, my ancestors dangled from trees, so please, forgive me for not placing my hand over my heart anymore, because America, has left me heartless

"WHAT'S GOING ON TULSA!!!???"

I said that, and you could still hear a mouse piss on cotton. I started clapping.

"WHAT'S GOING ON TULSA???!!!"

They all broke out in applause. That's exactly how I wanted this shit. They were stunned. They ain't know what the fuck they had just experienced.

"Y'all can take your seats. Gone head sit down."

They began to take their seats. I asked them did they feel that one. They erupted. I went into the demographics of the play. How there would be some language that may offend them. How they may get mad. How this shit was gonna stir up some heavy emotions. From scanning the room and seeing a good number of elders, I knew the shit was gonna have people in their feelings. This shit was about to happen. After I finished all that mumbo jumbo, I went ahead and went into my next piece entitled dance.

DANCE

I grew up in a city where our dance of style was called footworkin, twerking was called jukin and White Castles was the after spot after the club, that was East Chi, but now we die doing the same dances we grew up accustomed to seeing, I find myself doing the running man every time I see blue and red lights flashing, because when they pull me over, I know they gone notice the graffiti laced subway station on my arms, tell me to get out the car, both hands up, keep 'em where I can see 'em, both feet planted on the ground, and I don't know the name of this dance, but it seems like the nigga version of the macarena, turn yaself around like the Casper slide and keep both hands where I can see 'em, and as he pats me down looking for dope and swishers, hoping that he can pull out his baton and beat another nigga, I'm praying to God that he say I ain't breathing to hard, because nowadays, cops will shoot you and say he was reaching for oxygen, and when he can't find nothing, he'll cuff me for his safety and the questions will begin, is this your car, why are you in this neighborhood this time of day, your hat is blue, are you associated with the Crips, and I said sir, no disrespect, but many of your brothers have sent my brothers on steps towards the graveyard, that's the only Crip walk I know, yes this is my car, bought and paid for in the Lord's year of two zero one eight but your profiling me like this is 1958 in one of those southern states where I couldn't sit at a counter because those were whites only plates, and I'm in this neighborhood sir, simply because there is a nice jazz club and I simply want to dance, that's it, I just wanna dance, find a beautiful Black woman and take her hand, two step and stroll across the dance floor, and no, I don't have anything against white women, I'm pretty sure some have great dance skills, but I'm not trying to become the modern day version of Emmett Till, plus, I've seen GET OUT, and I'll be damned if I'm gone be a sex slave missing half my brain drinking tea all day, see I'm a law abiding citizen, I pay my taxes, I pledge allegiance even though allegiance hasn't been pledged to my people, I've got the degrees, I've got no felonies, my license checks out, my registration checks out, sir I'm not ready to check out simply for driving while black...then he gave me my license back, said enjoy your dancing boy, and as they drove off, I saw the blue and red lights dancing on top of his car, reminding me of the clubs I used to frequent to just dance, so I left my car there and walked, to get better acquainted with my feet, just so the next time I get pulled over for existing while Black, I can have my dance steps down packed, because FOX news, will always make it seem like it was my fault for dying, simply, for being Black

I rocked the audience again. The applause was unlike anything I had ever experienced. I introduced the theater piece, letting Mia and the actors do their thing. For the next two hours, my mind was intrigued. A range of emotions flooded my being. There were stories, and then there was Black Wall Street. The crazy shit is that many people still hadn't heard this story. The ones that did, they more than likely didn't hear the real version. As they ended, I came out once again, announcing each cast member one by one. It was indeed the most meaningful performance of my life. The question and answer session after the play I expected it to be like any other Q&A. However, that was quickly changed. A woman got on the mic. She didn't want to ask questions about the theater piece. She didn't give a damn about my poem. She was a granddaughter of one of the survivors. She gave praises to the cast. More so, she gave a story that her grandmother relayed to her. This woman had to be well into her 80's. She spoke with passion and conviction. I felt like I was trapped in 1921. She introduced the great grandchildren of some folks from that era. They grew up and got married, probably unaware that their great grandparents both existed at the same time until their adult years. By the time this woman was done talking, there wasn't a dry eye in the room. I was off to the side, in the back of everyone. Even I dropped a tear. It was one thing for us to tell it. It was another for someone who lived it. Once the Q&A session was over, people lingered around. I took pictures. I mean a lot of damn pictures. If I thought to myself that I have never arrived with spoken word, the love I was getting let me know different. I was questioned by young and old, but the icing on the cake came when it was almost time for me to bounce. A white lady approached me with her daughter. The good job vocabulary that spilled out of her mouth didn't mean shit to me. But, as she kept going, two words became entrenched into my head.

"I'm sorry."

"Why are you apologizing ma'am?"

"You see my daughter. She doesn't know how privileged she is."

The little girl looked at her confused, because she didn't know what in the good hell she was talking about.

"I know as an individual, I can't change what my lineage did. And, I'm not proud of it. At all. Some white people love to pretend to be white Israelites."

"I'm lost ma'am."

"Why. Your people are the true people. Oh sure, you have some white people who watched this play tonight and still won't change anything about their mindset. But they dance to your music. Eat your food because its seasoned well. Revel at the Black faces on television because the artform they excel at intrigues them. They love the culture, but they still don't love you."

The tears in her eyes and the shivering of her lip told me this was a different breed of white person. One we needed more of but were in hibernation day in and day out. I took a deep breath.

"Well, Ma'am. As they say. Everyone wants to be a nigga. Until it's time to be a nigga."

"Thank you," she said, as she extended her hand out, tears dropping from her face.

I had a stone-cold face, but it wasn't due to me being upset. I was stuck in a trance, completely thrown off by this. Growing up, I hated white people because of the experiences I encountered with them whenever I left the safe confines of the inner city. As I grew, my hatred didn't die. It just became tolerable. I once didn't see color, as they so fondly say in regard to us. It was the only way to keep me on my toes when dealing with them. I grew fond of some, but in the back of my head, there was always that chance. If anything, they should thank Johnny for breaking my barriers. The lady was long gone by now, and so was my mental state. I found Mia. I hugged her goodbye, thanking her for the opportunity. I did the same with every one of the cast members. When I greeted the white ones, they embraced me harder than anyone else. Their hugs and the shakes felt genuine. It was like they were telling me that their off-stage character does not reflect the performance. I dipped out the building, into the Tulsa night. I was on a high for several reasons. I made it under the overpass, and I stopped. A rush went through my body. I hadn't felt this way the whole night. I took a few deep breaths, trying to get myself back to normal. Two steps later, another rush felt like it left me. I looked up and a small mist looked like it was slowly floating away. I was convinced it was the spirits of those who lived and died here since 1906. They were telling me good job kid. You made us proud. That's all that I wanted to do. I continued down Greenwood Avenue until I hit the intersection with Archer. L on G was a quiet eating joint during the day. Right now, that thang was jumping. I said the hell with it. The least I could do was go in and look inside. I walked in that joint. The music was hitting. This bitch was packed. And it was redbone city in here. I swear that's all I was seeing in Tulsa. As cool as the sights were, the risk outweighed the reward. I already saw women looking at me, recognizing me as that nigga who shut it down a few hours ago. Nah, hell nah. I wasn't about to do this shit. I made my exit as quickly as I made my entrance. I laughed on the way out. This trip had given me some of everything I needed. History lessons, laughter, sadness, happiness, everything. I bopped back to the hotel, giving a middle finger to the baseball field as I passed that joint. I hit the next block and debated walking deep into downtown. Yea nah. Fuck that. I entered the hotel.

"Welcome home," the sister said.

"Home sweet muthafuckin home," I responded.

She laughed as I chucked a deuce her way, hitting the elevator. I walked down the hall, got to my room, and stopped. That energy hit me again. This felt like a peace and a calm. I knew at this moment that the ancestors were truly indeed proud of me. I see they walked me to my home for another 12 hours or so. I was complete. The mission was completed. 30+ years had led to three hours that changed my life forever. There was nothing more I had to say or do. I had indeed reached the pinnacle. The crazy shit is that I still had another half a day. If you think a man needed a whole day to do some shit, well you didn't know me then. I wasn't a normal man. I was a God because that's what Black people were. Gods. God was in us. You heard God when we spoke. It was a wrap. People were waiting for the Book of Revelation, failing to see that we were the revelation. Goodnight....

— 9 —

PLANTING SEEDS

"Bury me in the ocean with my ancestors that jumped from the
ships, because they knew death was better than bondage."
—Killmonger, Black Panther

I woke up this Sunday morning and stared into the darkness that
was my hotel room. It was 7:49 a.m. on the dot when I looked over
at the clock. Last night had indeed seemed like a blur. I looked
around some more, expecting to have that feeling that someone was
indeed watching me. Nothing. I waited patiently to feel the energy
that had entrenched me before I stepped foot on that stage, and
back in this room last night. Nothing. It was indeed over. The
madness, the anticipation, the buildup. Everything was gone. I had
done what I set out to do. I arose, sitting on the edge of my bed.
Thoughts of my daddy danced in my head. He never smiled until
last night. It was amazing what you could do when you were no
longer here. I didn't know where he was. Truthfully, I don't believe
in the existence of a physical hell that exists in the pits of mother
earth. Earth is hell. There was never any hell in our spiritual doctrine
during the days of Kemet. So, was this all created? I mean, The Bible

was written by man, which of whom is flawed. Energy never died. It only transferred. So how do we truly die? We don't. What is to become of us, or what lies in the next phase. I honestly couldn't tell you. When pops smiled, it made me wonder and had me thinking outside the box. I got up and stretched those good old exaggerated nigga stretches that only niggas could do. I shook out my limbs. I walked over to the window and snatched the curtains back. This was a horrible damn view to say the least. My shit looked out into the parking structure of another establishment. I scratched my balls without a care in the world. If anyone saw me, oh well. That's what men did. Nuts itch, we scratch. I shut the curtains and went into the bathroom, sliding in my flip flops because I was too damn lazy to pick my feet up. I cut on the light and again, scratched my nuts. As I grabbed my toothbrush, wetting it, adding toothpaste, then wetting it again, I stared in the mirror at myself. I closed my eyes, once again, hoping that last night would repeat itself. Upon opening them up, nothing miraculous occurred. It was just me and this AIM toothpaste, existing on these bristles. I gave my mouth a good brush. Got all the sides, top, bottom, and did a DJ UNK two step on my tongue. I had to make sure the taste buds were refreshed. I hadn't forgot about that automatic pancake maker downstairs. I was gone smash some more of those hoes before I got out of here. I rinsed my mouth out and proceeded back into the room. I threw on my shorts, my hoodie from last night and slow bopped it out the room. Mind you, I had my headphones in as well, with Da Baby's, "Bop" having an afterhours party in my ear drums. I was truly up now. I was out of the early morning trance and back to normal. The elevator even opened differently this time. It seemed like it said, *Welcome my nigga. You killed that shit last night.* I did a fist pound to the button labeled 1. The song was truly marinating my brain right now and I was grooving without a care in the world. As the doors opened, I didn't even realize how much I was into it. I was greeted by a white couple who was looking at me in the weirdest of ways. Fuck 'em, I thought. Don't be mad at me because my Melanin comes equipped with rhythm and soul, while your pale skin comes with offbeat sensations. I serenaded my way into the breakfast area. Oh, it was full as hell today. Everyone and they mama wanted to eat breakfast seeing how it was checkout day. Despite all the people, nobody, and I mean nobody was over here at the pancake machine. This was about to be like a kid taking candy from a baby. I grabbed a plate and hit the button. One golden flapjack of goodness came out. I pressed it again. The second golden circle joined the first. Then, three. Then, four. Fuck it. For good measure, I hit the button one more time. I had five of them hoes on the plate now. Nah. I ain't really like the number five. Six. There we go. Six was the perfect number. I watched the machine shit out flapjack number six. I then grabbed the syrup and drowned those babies in it. I rounded the corner and found a booth all to myself. The booth had that good, plush cushion too. Oh yea. This last day was indeed going well so far. I indulged in this golden goodness while looking at the muted news. As I observed the television, my mood changed when looking at the story, with the closed caption scrolling across the bottom. Police had raided the wrong house. They kicked in the door of an elderly Black man who had done nothing wrong. The house they intended to raid was two doors down. A white male, who was cooking up meth and distributing it out of his basement was the intended target. Now who in the good hell confuses the numbers 939 and 935? One was a damn five. The other was a damn nine. The elderly Black man went into cardiac arrest and died on the spot. I saw my people gathered outside at the scene, furiously speaking into the mic. It was a good thing this TV was on mute, because even closed captioned told lies. This had to be some days ago from what I was taking in. It was appalling. Just think how it is to be Black. Imagine if they told you to stay inside for your own safety for let's say, a virus that had started a pandemic. Now, imagine you following all the rules and regulations. Then boom, in spite of all that, the police kick in your door, scare you so damn bad that God says come on bruh, cause I don't want you here to deal with the brunt of this bullshit. Your home was no longer a home. Your protection was null and void. Oh sure, they arrested the right guy afterwards. That was after he had a chance to bust through his back door and make an escape. Luckily, Tulsa's SWAT team caught his ass running out and proceeded to chase him, along with having other units pursue the suspect. However, the damage was done. My pancakes were now a little less tasty and became dry instead of fluffy. Damn, I wonder what it would be like if I could just wear a white face for a day? Hell, maybe they had white privilege sales on the corner in some areas. Maybe, I could get a loan at the bank freely, whether home or business. Maybe, I could harass the police with 50 guns drawn at me, and none of them shoot me because I'm white. Maybe, just maybe I could live the life all minorities dream of, but only one group gets to experience without dribbling a basketball or selling out movie theaters. Maybe, I could murder in cold blood, but have the world tell me hey, he's white. Give him a second chance. We all deserve a second chance. Oh, the thought of a life like that would be amazing. However, my reality was this. I was Black. My skin was dark 24/7. Nothing would change this. I couldn't hide this. Nowhere. At no time ever. I needed to vent. I took one last bite of my pancakes and threw them away. I walked outside to catch some fresh air. It seemed that death lingered today. It was life last night. This morning, I was at the world's largest funeral, yet I was the only person in attendance. I began walking down towards the baseball stadium on the hotel side of the street. I stopped at every bronze plaque cemented in the ground. I analyzed, studied and paid homage to those we lost. They were only doing what Black folks were designed to do. That was to exist and exceed greatness.

East End Feed store, 318 E. Archer, Destroyed, 1921, Not Reopened

Dennis Barbershop, 318 E. Archer, Destroyed, 1921, Re-opened

Clark Tailoring, 314 E. Archer, Destroyed, 1921, Not Reopened

Harris Restaurant, 314 E. Archer, Destroyed, 1921, Not Reopened

Bunn's Shoeshine, 316 E. Archer, Destroyed, 1921, Not Reopened

I walked some more, all the way down to the corner of East Archer and Greenwood Ave. All the businesses were still closed, but for this history lesson in Black greatness, class was now in fucking session. I continued to touch plaques that lined the street, telling the story of what once was.

Economy Drugstore, 110 N. Greenwood Avenue, Destroyed, 1921, Reopened

Netherland C.L. Barber, 110 N. Greenwood Avenue, Destroyed, 1921, Rebuilt

Hughes Cafe, 116 N. Greenwood Avenue, Destroyed, 1921, Reopened

Attorney E.I. Saddker, 122. N. Greenwood Avenue, Destroyed, 1921, Reopened

Dixie Theater, 120 N. Greenwood Avenue, Destroyed, 1921

As I touched the last plaque in the ground, I dropped to my knees, screaming, crying, banging the palm of my right hand on the cold concrete of this chilly Sunday morning. How? Why? What did my people do to deserve this? I was on all fours, tears dripping into the concrete. I looked over through watery eyes to Interstate 244 that had been built right through the heartbeat of this neighborhood.

"FUCK YOU!!! FUCK YOU!!!"

I screamed continuously at passing cars that were oblivious to my cries. My middle finger assisted in expressing my feeling to the natives. If only it were a laser that could destroy instead of merely act as sign language when I didn't want to speak. I stayed in this position for the next 10 minutes, balling my eyes out. I knew the human body consisted of 75% water. What I didn't know is that one human could deplete that amount in the span of 10 minutes. I was drained. I was depleted. I could die right now because I truly felt like I had no life left inside of me. America had held me and my people in bondage since 1619. I now understood what Killmonger meant at the end of Black Panther. Biblically, suicide meant hell. I wasn't biblical at that moment. I sure as hell contemplated slitting my throat or running into oncoming traffic on a busy street. I'd

242

rather dance in eternal bliss with my African forefathers than to continue being a son to a father whose sole purpose in life was to torture me to the point where I would say fuck it, I accept what you give me. I arose, dusting myself off. I wiped my eyes with the back of my hands. I had become so entrenched in my anger that my palms started to bleed poems that only the concrete could decipher. I opened my eyes to see Black Wall Street. Like no shit, Black Wall Street. It was lit up. I looked down. There were no plaques in the ground. I looked up, and there were two Black men laughing, in suits, walking towards me. The music from another building across the street sent vibes through the morning air.

"Sir?," I said to one of the gentleman who were crossing in front of me. I received no answer. Was this real? Was this a dream? Yea, a nigga had to be dreaming. I looked again and nothing had changed at all. At the building on my right, two men were getting their shoes shined right here on the sidewalk. Their hats were of old school pimp quality. The two kids, who I would estimate at either seven or eight years old, started to buff more vigorously when the nickels got dropped into their money cans. I looked across the street. There was a woman, in one of those fancy fruit basket church hats, with her child, bags in hand. All around me, I saw Black people. They were dressed clean. I looked up at a sign which wasn't lit up yet, because it was still a good ways away from sunset. Nah, this couldn't be. I walked back down the block, knowing that someone was going to say something to me about my attire. I had literally taken a trip back into the past and I was looking like future shit. Everywhere I turned, it was live. Stores, libraries, a medical clinic, a fucking bank. I had to pause on that one. We had our own damn bank. I stopped back at the corner of Greenwood and Archer. An old man crossing guard told everyone to halt. A group of school children were walking with males in ties. Wait a damn minute. We had Black male educators. Nothing against the women, but a Black male educator was rare. A group of them was a once in a lifetime event. That shit was impressive. The old man signaled for everyone to cross. I crossed with the crowd. I was fucked up mentally. Either I had died and gone to heaven, or this was one dream that I damn sure didn't want to wake up from. Yea, that was it. I was still in the bed. I really didn't eat any pancakes. I didn't scratch my nuts in the window of my hotel room. Boy, this was some shit. I parlayed it out into the middle of the intersection. I look one way and it was Greenwood. I look down the other way and it was Archer. That baseball stadium was nonexistent. That area was lined with stores galore. People continued to cross me every which a way. Then, I felt a tug on my shirt. I looked down. It was a young kid. Little man had a Kangol on his head, titled to the right. A gray vest, which was accompanied by a burgundy tie. Man, he was fresher than a lot of adults that I knew.

"Excuse me sir. Can I carry those bags for you?"

I looked at my hands, to my side, even behind me.

"Umm. Sorry young king. But I don't have any bags."

The moment I said that, an eerie quiet came into the air. I was still looking at little man and he had his eyes locked on me. I glanced up and the whole town had stopped. They were all staring at me. I slowly did a 360. From every corner and the front of every establishment, even the crossing guard brother who was a mere four feet away from me, all eyes were on me. I wasn't talking about no 2Pac shit either. I observed again. Men, women, and children were all staring me down. This was some poltergeist shit. Either

I was in another dimension, or I was about to take one hell of an ass whooping. Little man tugged on my shirt again. I looked back down at him.

"Can I carry your bags sir?"

I looked back up. Nothing had changed. Everyone was still looking at me, still and dead silent. Yea let me wake my ass up. This shit wasn't real, but it would damn sure go down as the weirdest dream that I ever had. I closed my eyes. Tight. I counted backwards out loud from five.

"Five, four, three, two, one."

I opened them back up. The sight had now drastically changed. There was literal hell all around me. Gunshots. Stores on fire. I saw men directing women and children out of harm's way. Some were shot. A body fell in front of me. Black men were shooting back, defending their turf from a mob of white devils. I was confused. Nothing but black smoke, sirens, blood, and hell surrounded me. I looked down as I felt my hand being grabbed. Here was this kid again, calm as ever. I tried to take off with him, but my body couldn't move. I looked down at him again. Either this little dude had one hell of a grip, or someone put my ankles in the concrete when I wasn't looking. I tried to take off and run again but it was to no avail. I looked back down at the kid. He didn't budge as he looked me dead in my eyes. I calmed down all because of him, even amid chaos. I stood there with him, hand in hand. Nothing, or no one touched us. We watched in horror and amazement as an all-out race war was going down.

"GET THOSE NIGGERS!!!"

The voice of that phrase sounded like sheer evil mixed with hatred and bigotry. Two seconds later, a bullet ripped through his skull, leaving his brains on the ground. He fell right in front of us. I chuckled. He had been shot in the left side of his head. I guess he had to get his mind pushed right. Then, the most God-awful sound started to ring through my eardrums. I looked above my head. Hordes and hordes of planes were flying overhead. **BOOM!!!** I looked over to see some blocks down, that a loud explosion had occurred. **BOOM!!!** Another loud explosion. **BOOM!!!** Another one. Amid all this craziness, I couldn't cry, be fearful, move, any of that. I just had to watch in sheer terror. My hand was tugged. I looked down. The kid was looking up at me again.

"Yes man. What do you need? Let's get you out of here. You have to survive this. I've lived my life."

He smiled at me and then looked up. I raised my head to see a huge bomb headed right for us.

"NOOO!!!"

After that yell, I took a deep gasp of air. My eyes readjusted. I looked around in every direction. I was the only one out here. My Black ass was really in the middle of an intersection going plum crazy. I looked down. The kid was gone. I looked each way. The shops and the crowds were gone. I patted myself down. I checked my pockets. I had to make sure no one slipped any shrooms in my pockets or anything.

"HEY!!! HEY YOU!!!"

I looked over to see a middle-aged man standing in front of one of the buildings. Sweat pouring down my forehead, I wiped it off with my hoodie and proceeded to walk over to the brother.

"Are you okay young brother?"

"Yea. Kind of. Umm. Got emotional about some things."

He wagged his finger at me.

"You the poet from last night ain't you?"

'Yes sir," I said, still catching my breath.

"That was some clever stuff. You had me confused as ever. But, when you came in saying what you said, it hit me."

"Thank you, sir. Thank you."

"Come on in. Lemme show you my shop."

I walked in and was immediately amazed by all that I saw. This was better than FUBU, VOKAL, KARL KANI, or any other Black owned clothing company I supported back in the day.

"This all me. Me and my peoples. This Mrs. Bridgette. This Mrs. Cyndii."

"We don't do handshakes over here baby. We do hugs."

I laughed as I hugged Mrs. Bridgette. She inadvertently became another auntie to me in this moment. I hugged Mrs. Cyndii, whose vibe gave me that she is the lady down the block who will whoop your ass, then call your mama, so you can get your ass beat again when you come in the house. I looked at her as another mama.

"So here it is man. Look around. See if you like anything. We make everything in house. It's ours. They took our land, but we getting it back. Oh yea. We getting it back."

I was listening while walking, truly in awe at everything around me. Damn, I thought. I hit my pockets. Phew. I had my wallet. Hell, I thought that thing was back at the hotel. I saw everything from Black Wall Street snapbacks, beanies, hoodies, wristbands, to even dinner plates. This place had it all. I didn't hesitate to snatch gear off the walls. I grabbed the yellow and black, BLACK HISTORY 365 hoodie. The all black, hand stitched 1921 BLACK WALL STREET hoodie, with the whole history summarized on the back was my next cop. I then grabbed two BLACK WALL STREET wristbands and beanies. One was for me and the other one was for one of my partners. Lastly, I snatched up the black and gold bricks hoodie for an educator friend of mines. History wasn't written. It was told by the voices who experienced it. I couldn't personally tell it because I wasn't there, but I could damn sure flaunt its greatness at every moment I could. I took everything to the register. It was a $500 plus investment. Yes, I said fucking investment. This was more than buying clothes. This was investing in home. My home because the shit felt like home. Tulsa was no longer a tourist destination for me. I felt like I could sleep on the streets out here and be totally at peace. This is where I believed all Black spirits resided when they died. I saw the visions. I saw the joy. I saw the pain. More importantly, I saw the thriving. We existed in another realm. It was one of happiness. This place kept Black business alive. This place kept me alive. All hail Black Wall Street. The last thing I did before I got out of there was go on Facebook live. I had to put on for my people. I gave them a good five plus minutes of exposure. It was refreshing. They always talked about how Black people didn't want to see others shine. Well, here, that was a bold-faced lie. It was love. All love. I had never been called king before ever in my life when greeted by another Black man. It was to say the least, amazing. I hugged all three of them, and me and Mr. Cleo had one last task. Across the street, plastered on a brick wall, was a huge sign, with every business that existed in Black Wall Street back in its heyday. The picture said 1,000,000 words. What it didn't show was the 20 or so that gathered around me for the pictures. I felt that energy again, like the crowd was there. Hands were on my shoulders, telling me that my purpose was achieved and that I did an excellent job. With a dap, embrace and a "God got you," from Mr. Cleo, I was on my way back to the hotel. I arrived, packing my shit up. It was nearing noon and time to roll. I got my stuff together and took a deep breath before I left this room for the final time. I still had 30 minutes. I put my bag down and searched frantically for a notepad. I know they had one. They always put everything else in the damn room, so I know a pen and a note pad had to be in here. Finally, I found one. I snatched the curtain back so I could have ample lighting outside of the lamp. I began to write.

Role Reversal

Imagine role reversal, white people, let me enslave you for 200 plus years in fields, making you pick greens in 100 degree heat, but don't worry, for you house wiggers, you will only serve not cook, cause y'all don't season shit, or how about I cut on my red and blue's, pull you over for driving while Caucasian, ask for your license and registration, and as soon as you reach for the glove compartment, I yell GUN, and next you got 15 bullets from me, 15 from my partner, 30 more from the other two coppers, but again, my bad, we thought that piece of paper was a pistol, and I'll get a paid vacation, while under investigation, or how bout I walk into the store, and hear that country music playing loud, offensive to me, I slit your throat, or how bout I shackle you all up on a boat, introduce you to 400 different diseases and then hit you with a bible to be controlled, quoting scripture, skin of bronze, hair like sheep's wool, yea bitch, God is Black, or what if all the presidents in history were black, now you feel that oppression, racial discrimination ain't changed, and all we would yell to you is, BUT YOU HAVE A WHITE PRESIDENT, HOW CAN RACISM EXIST, BECAUSE I VOTED FOR THE WHITE GUY, what if we stole yo poor man's recipes and claimed it as a delicacy, what if you started to holla WHITE LIVES MATTER, and then I counteract with no, ALL LIVES MATTER, to make your movement sound irrelevant, what if when February came around it was white history month, you only had 28 days to show what your people have done, but with your child the only one in an all-Black school, a few of us gone put some peach makeup on our faces, and sing that old Caucasian spiritual, THE BRITISH ARE COMING, THE BRITISH ARE COMING, TWO ARMS, TWO ARMS, THE BRITISH ARE COMING, what if me and my people rallied up at the borders because hordes of people from Europe were coming, threatening to take our jobs and suck up our tax breaks to pay for their medical cost, our country can't be lost, we must fight to the death to protect the red, black and green, or what if we told you that you can't breathe, what if Black people started to bleach their skin, dye their hair blonde, you'd be happy to yell the phrase EVERYBODY WANNA BE A CAUCASIAN, UNTIL ITS TIME TO BE A CAUCASIAN, or most of all, what if my privilege allowed you to feel what the fuck I feel on a daily basis, hey white people, that shit don't sound so good, now does it.

I finished up my pieces and put 'em on the dresser. I changed out of my shorts and into my jeans, placed the sheets of paper in my pocket, left the room and headed downstairs for the lobby to check out. There was no other patrons at the desk, so I knew this would be quick.

"Can I have the shuttle to the airport in 20 minutes? I have to go down the street and handle something."

"Sure thing sir."

The clerk took my bag and placed it in safe keeping. I walked out the hotel and down the street, across from the baseball field, where they had broken ground on another building. There was a gate around the perimeter of the site, but the gate door was unlocked. I walked into the construction site. I pulled the notes out of my pocket. I sifted through them one last time, scanning my words. I bent down to dig a hole about a foot down with my hands. I placed the papers in there and piled dirt back on top. A little dust was on my jeans and my Curry's, but it was no biggie. I dusted off my hands. I was done. My final gift to my ancestors was in place.

"HEY YOU. STAY RIGHT THERE!!!"

Out of nowhere, this voice of a white man bellowed. Ahh shit, I thought. I was caught trespassing. He was unlocking another gate door on the adjacent side, which was stupid because if I wanted to run, I could just go out the same way I came in. He flung the gate door open and started power walking towards me. It was a damn Sunday. No one was out here working. Why the fuck was he here?

"WHAT ARE YOU!!!"

With those three words, he suddenly disappeared into the earth. I stood there, not knowing what the fuck just happened. I looked around. There were no cars up and down the street. Nobody was out walking. It was just me on this construction site, and I just watched a white man disappear into the darkness. I was nervous as fuck now. My mind told me to high tail it out of there and get back to the hotel. My spirit, however, told me to walk over where that man had disappeared. The spirits hadn't led me astray this entire time, so why would they now? I walked over towards the spot where the man had mysteriously vanished. I stopped about five feet before the spot to see a grate. I glanced ahead to see a hole. It had to be three feet by three feet, cut out like a rectangle. I eased my way over there, cautious because the dirt could be loose anywhere. I looked down into the hole. I didn't hear a sound. There was nothing but darkness, so this hole went down some feet. If I had to guess, it was probably 50 feet or so. I glanced back at the grate. I took my hoodie off. It looked heavy at first glance, but I just had a feeling that it was light. I wasn't a welder by any means, but judging from the shine of the metal, I would say that it was some lightweight shit. I grasped the grate with my hoodie, ensuring that I left no fingerprints on the surface at all. Carefully, I placed the grate perfectly over this opening in the earth. I stood over, looking at it. Then, I looked up. A cloud, as if ordered by God himself, moved away from the sun, and it was now gleaming in bliss. I hadn't seen the sun glow like this the whole time I was here. Well, I guess the ancestors got their revenge, even if it was one body. I smiled and walked out of the construction site, hoodie back on, headed to the hotel to catch my shuttle. Bury me in the ocean, with my ancestors that jumped from the ships, because they knew death was better than bondage. I chuckled thinking about that. I guess the oppressors got buried under the earth, so they could meet hell directly. I walked into the hotel. The van driver was waiting. The lady passed me my belongings and I was off for the airport. As we drove off, we ironically passed by the construction site. Now, all kinds of people were out walking. Cars were up and down the street. Unbeknown to them, there were now two seeds planted in the earth. One sprouted love. The other, was a festering disease that no longer was here to wreak havoc on my people. I smiled for the next eight minutes that it took to get to the airport. Once I arrived and made it through security, I indulged in some of Oklahoma's best barbecue. To have a one of a kind rib joint inside of an airport was something that I never experienced.

I smashed a three-meat plate of baby back ribs, brisket and pulled pork. Yes, I know. Two servings of swine. I was gangster like that. Time passed and before I knew it, boarding call had gone down. I would have one stop in Vegas before heading back to Southern California. To my delight, the flight wasn't full. Talk about a great end to a day. I said my prayer as always and just put my head back on the seat. As I began to get good and relaxed, I looked across to see another brother had occupied the row across from me. I had a whole row to myself. He had a whole row to himself. It seemed like life was good for a Black man for once.

"Sup King. Mac."

"Vinnie. Nice to see you as well."

"What book you got there in your hand?"

"Giovanni's Room by James Baldwin. Nothing better to stimulate my mental during this flight."

"Amen. That's a nice pendant around your neck. Mind me asking who that beautiful woman is?"

"That Queen is my mother. She passed when I was 14."

"Sorry to hear that King. My dad passed away last year when I was 33."

"Well remember. Jesus died at 33 as well, or so they say She died."

"Amen to that King. Amen."

ABOUT THE AUTHOR

Joe Rainer McClain Jr. is a seasoned author and spoken word artist. His written works have been obtained by multiple A-List celebrities to include, but not limited to Alfonso Riberio, Laurence Fishburne, Reggie Bush, Nick Cannon, and a host of others. In September of 2019, he competed in the Individual World Poetry Slam, placing 24th in the world. He has headlined multiple cities in spoken word performance to include, but not limited to Seattle, Las Vegas and Tulsa, Oklahoma.

Made in the USA
Middletown, DE
20 March 2021